"I've missed you so much."

Meg was playing a part—Niklas got that—but as her lips met his cheek, it did not matter that she was playing, for it was the first reprieve to his senses in months.

It was a kiss for others and his mind tried to keep it at that, except her breath still tasted of the outside. He drank it in, and the feel of her in his arms allowed temporary escape. It was Meg who pulled back.

Meg stood with her cheeks burning red, and there were tears of shame and hurt and anger in her eyes. Her lips pressed closed as the guard said something that made the other one laugh, and then a door opened and they walked into a small, simply furnished room. She couldn't stand for very much longer, so she sat on a chair for a moment, honestly shaken.

Not just at the sight of him, not just at the shock of seeing Niklas with his hair cropped almost as short as the dark stubble on his chin, dressed in rough prison denim, for he was still the most beautiful man she had seen.

"Why would you come here?" he demanded, and then she looked at him and he could see her green eyes flash with suppressed rage and heard the spit to her words when finally she answered him.

"You're *entitled* to me apparently."

Dear Reader,

We know how much you love Harlequin® Presents®, so this month we wanted to treat you to something extra special—a second classic story by the same author for free!

Once you have finished reading *Playing the Dutiful Wife,* just turn the page for another one night with consequences story from Carol Marinelli.

This month, indulge yourself with double the reading pleasure!

With love,

The Presents Editors

Carol Marinelli

PLAYING THE DUTIFUL WIFE

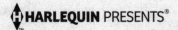

HARLEQUIN PRESENTS®

Recycling programs for this product may not exist in your area.

ISBN-13: 978-0-373-13127-3

PLAYING THE DUTIFUL WIFE

Copyright © 2013 by Harlequin Books S.A.

The publisher acknowledges the copyright holder of the individual works as follows:

PLAYING THE DUTIFUL WIFE
Copyright © 2013 by Carol Marinelli

EXPECTING HIS LOVE-CHILD
Copyright © 2007 by Carol Marinelli

HARLEQUIN®
www.Harlequin.com

Printed in U.S.A.

CONTENTS

All about the author...
Carol Marinelli

CAROL MARINELLI finds writing a bio rather like writing her New Years resolutions. Oh, she'd love to say that since she wrote the last one, she now goes to the gym regularly and doesn't stop for coffee and cake and a gossip afterwards, or that she's incredibly organized and writes for a few productive hours a day after tidying her immaculate house and a brisk walk with the dog.

The reality is, Carol spends an inordinate amount of time daydreaming about dark, brooding men and exotic places (research) which doesn't leave too much time for the gym, housework or anything that comes in between, and her most productive writing hours happen to be in the middle of the night, which leaves her in a constant state of bewildered exhaustion.

Originally from England, Carol now lives in Melbourne, Australia. She adores going back to the UK for a visit—actually, she adores going anywhere for a visit—and constantly (expensively) strives to overcome her fear of flying. She has three gorgeous children who are growing up so fast (too fast—they've just worked out that she lies about her age!) and keep her busy with a never-ending round of homework, sport and friends coming over.

A nurse and a writer, Carol writes for the Harlequin® Presents and Medical™ Romance lines and is passionate about both. She loves the fast-paced, busy setting of a modern hospital, but every now and then admits it's bliss to escape to the glamorous, alluring world of her Presents heroes and heroines. A bit like her real life, actually!

Other titles by Carol Marinelli available in ebook format.

Harlequin Presents®

3109—BEHOLDEN TO THE THRONE *(Empire of the Sands)*
3102—PLAYING THE ROYAL GAME *(The Santina Crown)*
3097—BANISHED TO THE HAREM *(Empire of the Sands)*

PLAYING THE DUTIFUL WIFE

CHAPTER ONE

'I'M GOING TO have to go,' Meg said to her mother. 'They've finished boarding, so I'd better turn off my phone.'

'You'll be fine for a while yet.' Ruth Hamilton persisted with their conversation. 'Did you finish up the work for the Evans purchase?'

'Yes.' Meg tried to keep the edge from her voice. She really wanted just to turn off the phone and relax. Meg hated flying. Well, not all of it—just the take-off part. All she wanted to do was close her eyes and listen to music, take some nice calming breaths before the plane prepared for its departure from Sydney Airport—except, as usual, her mother wanted to talk about work. 'Like I said,' Meg said calmly, because if she so much as gave a hint that she was irritated her mum would want to know more, 'everything is up-to-date.'

'Good,' Ruth said, but still she did not leave things there.

Meg coiled a length of her very straight red hair around and around one finger, as she always did when either tense or concentrating.

'You need to make sure that you sleep on the plane, Meg, because you'll be straight into it once you land. You wouldn't believe how many people are here. There are so many opportunities…'

Meg closed her eyes and held on to a sigh of frustration as her mum chatted on about the conference and then moved to travel details. Meg already knew that a car would meet her at Los Angeles airport and take her straight to the hotel where the conference was being held. And, yes, she knew she would have about half an hour to wash and get changed.

Meg's parents were prominent in Sydney's real estate market and were now looking to branch into overseas investments for some of their clients. They had left for Los Angeles on Friday to network, while Meg caught up with the paperwork backlog at the office before joining them.

Meg knew that she should be far more excited at the prospect of a trip to Los Angeles. Usually she loved visiting new places, and deep down Meg knew that really she had nothing to complain about—she was flying business class and would be staying in the sumptuous hotel where the conference was being held. She would play the part of successful professional, as would her parents.

Even though, in truth, the family business wasn't doing particularly well at the moment.

Her parents were always very eager to jump on the latest get-rich-quick scheme. Meg, who could always be relied on for sensible advice, had suggested that rather than all of them flying over maybe just one of them should go, or perhaps they should give it a miss entirely and concentrate on the properties they already had on their books.

Of course her parents hadn't wanted to hear that. This, they had insisted, was the next big thing.

Meg doubted it.

It wasn't that, though, which caused her disquiet.

Really, when she had suggested that only one of them go—given that she dealt with the legal side of things—Meg had rather hoped they might have considered sending only her.

A week away wasn't just a luxury she required—it was fast becoming a necessity. And it wasn't about the nice hotel—she'd stay in a tent if she had to, just for the break, just for a pause so that she could think properly. Meg felt as if she were suffocating—that wherever she turned her parents were there, simply not giving her room to think. It had been like that for as long as she could remember, and sometimes she felt as if her whole life had been planned out in advance by her parents.

In truth, it probably had.

Meg had little to complain about. She had her own nice flat in Bondi—but, given that she worked twelve-hour days, she never really got to enjoy it, and there was always something at work that needed her attention at weekends: a signature to chase up, a contract to read through. It just never seemed to end.

'We're actually going to look at a couple of properties this afternoon…' Her mum carried on talking as there was a flurry of activity in the aisle beside Meg.

'Well, don't go agreeing to anything until I get there,' Meg warned. 'I mean it, Mum.'

She glanced over and saw that two flight attendants were assisting a gentleman. His face was blocked from Meg's vision by the overhead lockers, but certainly from his physique this man didn't look as if he required assistance.

He was clearly tall and extremely fit-looking, and from what Meg could see he appeared more than capable of putting his own laptop into the overhead locker, yet the attendants danced around him, taking his jacket and offering their apologies as he went to take the seat beside Meg.

As his face came into view Meg, who was already struggling, completely lost her place in the conversation with her mother. The man was absolutely stunning, with very thick, beautifully cut black hair worn just a little too long, so that it flopped over his forehead. He had a very straight Roman nose and high cheekbones. Really, he had all the markings of a *very* good-looking man, but it was his mouth that held her attention—perfectly shaped, like a dark bruise of red in the black of his unshaven jaw, and even though it was a scowling mouth, it was quite simply beautiful.

He threw a brief nod in Meg's direction as he took the seat beside her.

Clearly somebody wasn't very happy!

As he sat down Meg caught his scent—a mixture

of expensive cologne and man—and, though she was trying to focus on what her mother was saying, Meg's mind kept wandering to the rather terse conversation that was taking place beside her as the flight attendants did their best to appease a man whom, it would seem, wasn't particularly easy to appease.

'No,' he said to the attendant. 'This will be sorted to my satisfaction as soon as we have taken off.'

He had a deep, low voice that was rich with an accent Meg couldn't quite place. Perhaps Spanish, she thought, but wasn't quite sure.

What she *was* sure of, though, was that he demanded too much of her attention.

Not consciously, of course—she just about carried on talking to her mother, her finger still twirling in her hair—but she could not stop listening to the conversation that was none of her business.

'Once again,' the flight attendant said to him, 'we apologise for any inconvenience, Mr Dos Santos.' Then she turned her attention to Meg, and although friendly and polite, the flight attendant was not quite so gushing as she had so recently been to Meg's fellow passenger. 'You need to turn off your phone, Ms Hamilton. We are about to prepare for take-off.'

'I really do have to go, Mum,' Meg said. 'I'll see you there.' With a sigh of relief she turned off her phone. 'The best part of flying,' she said as she did so—not necessarily to him.

'There is nothing good about flying' came his brusque response as the plane started to taxi towards the runway. Seeing her raised eyebrows, he tempered his words a little. 'At least not today.'

She gave him a small smile and offered a quick 'Sorry,' then looked ahead rather than out of the window. After all he could be in the middle of a family emergency and racing to get somewhere. There could be many reasons for his bad mood and it was none of her business after all.

She was actually quite surprised when he answered her, and when she turned she realised that he was still looking at her. 'Usually I do like flying—I do an awful lot of it—but today there are no seats in first class.'

Niklas Dos Santos watched as she blinked at his explanation. She had very green eyes that were staring right at him. He expected her to give a murmur of sympathy or a small tut tut as to the airline's inefficiency; those were the responses that he was used to, so he was somewhat taken aback at hers.

'Poor you!' She smiled. 'Having to slum it back here in business class.'

'As I said, I fly a lot, and as well as working while flying I need to sleep on the plane—something that is now going to be hard to do. Admittedly I only changed my plans this morning, but even so…' He didn't continue. Niklas thought that was the end of the conversation, that he had explained his dark mood well enough. He hoped that now they could sit in mutual silence, but before he could look away the woman in the seat next to him spoke again.

'Yes, it's *terribly* inconsiderate of them—not to keep

a spare seat for you just in case your plans happen to change.'

She smiled as she said it and he understood that she was joking—sort of. She was nothing like anyone he usually dealt with. Normally people revered him, or in the case of a good-looking woman—which she *possibly* was—they came on to him.

He was used to dark-haired, immaculately groomed women from his home town. Now and then he liked blondes—which she was, sort of. Her hair was a reddish blonde. But, unlike the women he usually went for, there was a complete lack of effort on her part. She was very neatly dressed, in three-quarter-length navy trousers and a cream blouse that was delicate and attractive. Yet the blouse was buttoned rather high and she wore absolutely no make-up. He glanced down to nails that were neat but neither painted nor manicured and, yes, he did check for a ring.

Had the engines not revved then she might have noticed that glance. Had she not looked away at that moment she might have been granted the pleasure of one of his very rare smiles. For she seemed refreshingly unimpressed by him, and Niklas had decided she was not a *possibly* good-looking woman in the least...

But she spoke too much.

He would set the tone now, Niklas decided. Just ignore her if she spoke again. He had a lot of work to get through during this flight and did not want to be interrupted every five minutes with one of her random thoughts.

Niklas was not the most talkative person—at least he did not waste words speaking about nothing—and he certainly wasn't interested in her assumptions. He just wanted to get to Los Angeles with as much work and sleep behind him as possible. He closed his eyes as the plane hurtled down the runway, yawned, and decided that he would doze till he could turn on his laptop.

And then he heard her breathing.

Loudly.

And it only got louder.

He gritted his teeth at her slight moan as the plane lifted off the runway and turned to shoot her an irritated look—but, given that her eyes were closed, instead he stared. She was actually fascinating to look at: her nose was snubbed, her lips were wide and her eyelashes were a reddish blonde too. But she was incredibly tense, and she was taking huge long breaths that made her possibly the most annoying woman in the world. He could not take it for the next twelve hours, and Niklas decided he would be speaking again to the flight attendant—someone would have to move out of first class.

Simply, this would not do.

Meg breathed in through her nose and then out through her mouth as she concentrated on using her stomach muscles to control her breathing as her 'fear of flying' exercises had told her to do. She twisted her hair over and over, and when that wasn't helping she gripped onto the handrests, worried by the terrible rattling noise above her as the plane continued its less than smooth climb. It really was an incredibly bumpy take-off, and she loathed this part more than anything—could not relax until the flight stewards stood up and the seatbelt signs went off.

As the plane tilted a little to the left Meg's eyes screwed more tightly closed. She moaned again and Niklas, who had been watching her strange actions the whole time, noted not just that her skin had turned white but that there was no colour in her lips.

The minute the signs went off he would speak with the flight attendant. He didn't care if it was a royal family they had tucked in first class; someone was going to have to make room for him! Knowing that he always got his way, and that soon he *would* be moving, Niklas decided that for a moment or two he could afford to be nice.

She was clearly terrified after all.

'You do know that this is the safest mode of transport, don't you?'

'Logically, yes,' she answered with her eyes still closed. 'It just doesn't feel very safe right now.'

'Well, it is,' he said.

'You said that you fly a lot?' She wanted him to tell her that he flew every single day, that the noise overhead was completely normal and nothing to worry about, preferably that he was in fact a pilot—then she might possibly believe that everything was okay.

'All the time,' came his relaxed response, and it soothed her.

'And that noise?'

'What noise?' He listened for a second or two. 'That's the wheels coming up.'

'No, that one.'

It all sounded completely normal to him, yet Niklas realised *she* probably wasn't quite normal, so he continued to speak to her. 'Today I am flying to Los Angeles, as are you, and in two days' time I will be heading to New York...'

'Then?' Meg asked, because his voice was certainly preferable to her thoughts right now.

'Then I will be flying home to Brazil, where I am hoping to take a couple of weeks off.'

'You're from Brazil?' Her eyes were open now, and as she turned to face him she met his properly for the first time. He had very black eyes that were, right now, simply heaven to look into. 'So you speak...?' Her mind was all scrambled; she could still hear that noise overhead...

'Portuguese,' he said and, as if he was there for her amusement—which for a moment or two longer he guessed he was—he smiled as he offered her a choice. 'Or I can speak French. Or Spanish too, if you prefer...'

'English is fine.'

There was no need to talk any more. He could see the colour coming back to her cheeks and saw her tongue run over pinkening lips. 'We're up,' Niklas said, and at the same time the bell pinged and the flight attendants stood. Meg's internal panic was thankfully over, and he watched as she let out a long breath.

'Sorry about that.' She gave him a rather embarrassed smile. 'I'm not usually that bad, but that really was bumpy.'

It hadn't been bumpy in the least, but he was not going to argue with her, nor get drawn into further conversation. And yet she offered her name.

'I'm Meg, by the way.'

He didn't really want to know her name.

'Meg Hamilton.'

'Niklas.' He gave up that detail reluctantly.

'I really am sorry about that. I'll be fine now. I don't have a problem with flying—it's just take-off that I absolutely loathe.'

'What about landing?'

'Oh, I'm fine with that.'

'Then you have never flown into São Paulo,' Niklas said.

'Is that where you are from?'

He nodded, and then pulled out the menu and started to read it—before remembering that he was going to be moving seats. He pushed his bell to summon the stewardess.

'Is it a busy airport, then?'

He looked over to where Meg sat as if he had forgotten that she was even there, let alone the conversation they had been having.

'Very.' He nodded, and then saw that the flight attendant was approaching with a bottle of champagne. Clearly she must have thought he had rung for a drink—after all, they knew his preferences—but as he opened his mouth to voice his complaint Niklas conceded that it might be a little rude to ask to be moved in front of Meg.

He would have this drink, Niklas decided, and then he would get up and go and have a quiet word with the attendant. Or an angry one if that did not work. He watched as his champagne was poured and then, perhaps aware that her eyes were trained on him, he turned, irritated.

'Did you want a drink as well?'

'Please.' She smiled.

'That is what your bell is for,' he retorted. She didn't seem to realise that he was being sarcastic, so he gave in and, rolling his eyes, ordered another glass. Meg was soon sipping on her beverage.

It tasted delicious, bubbly and icy-cold, and would hopefully halt her nervous chatter—except it didn't. It seemed that a mixture of nerves about flying and the fact that she had never been around someone so drop-dead gorgeous before resulted in her mouth simply not being able to stop.

'It seems wrong to be drinking at ten a.m.' She heard her own voice again and could happily have kicked herself—except then he would perhaps have her certified. Meg simply didn't know what was wrong with her.

Niklas didn't answer. His mind was already back to thinking about work, or rather thinking about all the things he needed to get finalised so that he could actually take some proper time off.

He *was* going to take some time off. He had not stopped for the last six months at the very least, and he was really looking forward to being back in Brazil, the country he loved, to the food he adored and the woman who adored him and who knew how it was…

He would take two or perhaps three weeks, and he was going to use every minute of them indulging in life's simple but expensively prepared pleasures— beautiful women and amazing food and then more of the same.

He let out a long breath as he thought about it—a long breath that sounded a lot like a sigh. A bored sigh, even—except how could that be? Niklas asked himself. He had everything a man could want and had worked hard to get it—worked hard to ensure he would never go back to where he had come from.

And he *had* ensured it, Niklas told himself; he could stop for a little while now. A decent stretch in Brazil would sort this restless feeling out. He thought of the flight home, of the plane landing in São Paulo, and as he did he surprised himself. His champagne was finished. He could get up now and have that word with the flight attendant. But instead Niklas turned and spoke with *her*.

With Meg.

CHAPTER TWO

'São Paulo is very densely populated.'

They were well over the water now, and she was gazing out at it, but she turned to the sound of his voice and Niklas tried to explain the land that he loved, the mile after mile after mile of never-ending city.

'It is something that is hard to explain unless you have seen it, but as the plane descends you fly over the city for very a long time. Congonhas Airport is located just a couple of miles from downtown…'

He told Meg about the short runway and the difficult approach and the physics of it as she looked at him slightly aghast.

'If the weather is bad I would imagine the captain and crew and most *paulistanos*…' He saw her frown and explained it a little differently. 'If you come from Sao Paulo or know about the airport then you are holding your breath just a little as the plane comes into land.' He smiled at her shocked expression. 'There have been many near-misses—accidents too…'

What a horrible thing to tell her! What a completely inappropriate thing for him to say at this moment! And she had thought him so nice—well, nice-looking at least. 'You're not helping at all!'

'But I am. I have flown in and out of Congonhas Airport more times than I can remember and I'm still here to tell the tale… You really have nothing to worry about.'

'Except that I'm scared of landing now too.'

'Don't waste time in fear,' Niklas said, and then stood to retrieve his computer. He did not usually indulge in idle chatter, and certainly not while flying, but she had been so visibly nervous during take-off, and it had been quite pleasant talking her around. Now she was sitting quietly, staring out of the window, and perhaps he did not have to think about moving seats after all.

The flight steward started to serve some appetizers, and Meg had an inkling that Mr Dos Santos was being treated with some tasty little selections from the first-class menu—because there were a few little treats that certainly weren't on the business class one—and, given that she was sitting next to him, by default Meg was offered them too.

'Wild Iranian caviar on buckwheat blinis, with sour cream and dill,' the flight attendant purred to him, but Niklas was too busy to notice the selection placed in front of him. Instead he was setting up a workstation, and Meg heard his hiss of frustration as he had to move his computer to the side. Clearly he was missing his first-class desk!

'There is no room—' He stopped himself, realising that he sounded like someone who complained all the time. He didn't usually—because he didn't have to. His PA, Carla, ensured that everything ran smoothly in his busy life. But Carla simply hadn't been able to work her magic today, and the fact was between here and LA Niklas had a lot to get done. 'I have a lot of work to do.' He didn't have to justify his dark mood, but he did. 'I have a meeting scheduled an hour after landing. I was hoping to use this time to prepare. It really is inconvenient.'

'You'll have to get your own plane!' Meg teased. 'Keep it on standby…'

'I did!' he said. Meg blinked. 'And for two months or so it was great. I really thought it was the best thing I had ever done. And then…' He shrugged and got back to his laptop, one hand crunching numbers, the other picking all the little pieces of dill off the top of the blinis before eating them.

'And then?' Meg asked, because this man really was intriguing. He was sort of aloof and then friendly, busy, yet calm, and very pedantic with his dill, Meg thought with a small smile as she watched him continue to pick the pieces off. When the food was to his satisfaction there was something very decadent about the way he ate, his eyes briefly closing as he savoured the delicious taste entering his mouth.

Everything he revealed about himself had Meg wanting to know more, and she was enthralled when he went on to tell her about the mistake of having his own plane.

'And then,' Niklas responded, while still tapping away on his computer, 'I got bored. Same pilot, same flight crew, same chef, same scent of soap in the bathroom. You understand?'

'Not really.'

'As annoying as your chatter may be…' he turned from his screen and gave her a very nice smile '…it is actually rather nice to meet you.'

'It's rather nice to meet you too.' Meg smiled back.

'And if I still had my own plane we would not have met.'

'Nor would we if you were lording it in first class.'

He thought for a moment. 'Correct.' He nodded. 'But now, if you will forgive me, I have to get on with some work.' He moved to do just that, but just before he did he explained further, just in case she had missed the point he was making. 'That is the reason I prefer to fly commercially—it is very easy to allow your world to become too small.'

Now, that part she *did* understand. 'Tell me about it.' Meg sighed.

His shoulders tensed. His fingers hesitated over the keyboard as he waited for her to start up again.

When she inevitably did, he would point out *again* that he was trying to work.

Niklas gritted his teeth and braced himself for her voice—was she going to talk all the way to Los Angeles?

Except she said nothing else.

When still she was quiet Niklas realised that he was actually *wanting* the sound of her voice to continue their conversation. It was at that point he gave up working for a while. He would return to the report later.

Closing his laptop, he turned. 'Tell *me* about it.'

She had no idea of the concession he was making—not a clue that a slice of his time was an expensive gift that very few could afford, no idea how many people would give anything for just ten minutes of his undivided attention.

'Oh, it's nothing…' Meg shrugged. 'Just me feeling sorry for myself.'

'Which must be a hard thing to do with a mouthful of wild Iranian caviar…'

He made her laugh—he really did. Niklas really wasn't at all chatty, but when he spoke, when he teased, when she met his eyes, there was a little flip in her stomach that she liked the feeling of. It was a thrill that was new to her, and there was more than just something about him…

It was *everything* about the man.

'Here's to slumming it,' Niklas said. They chinked their glasses and he looked into her eyes, and as he did so somehow—not that she would be aware of it—Niklas let her in.

He was a closed person, an extremely guarded man. He had grown up having to be that way—it had meant survival at the time—yet for the first time in far too long he chose to relax, to take some time, to forget about work, to stop for a moment and just be with her.

As they chatted he let the flight steward put his

laptop away. They were at the back of business class, tucked away and enjoying their own little world.

The food orders were taken and later served, and Meg thought how nice Niklas was to share a meal with. Food was a passion in waiting for Meg. She rarely had time to cook, and though she ate out often it was pretty much always at the same Italian restaurant where they took clients. They'd chosen different mains, and he smiled to himself at the droop of her face when they were served and she found out that steak tartare was in fact raw.

'It's delicious,' he assured her. 'Or you can have my steak?'

At the back of her mind she had known it was raw, if she'd stopped to think about it, but the menu had been incredibly hard to concentrate on with Niklas sitting beside her, and she had made a rather random selection when the flight steward had approached.

'No, it's fine,' Meg said, looking at the strange little piles of food on her plate. There was a big hill of raw minced steak in the middle, with a raw egg yolk in its shell on the top, surrounded by little hills of onions and capers and things. 'I've always wanted to try it. I just tend to stick to safe. It's good to try different things…'

'It is,' Niklas said. 'I like it like this.'

Something caught in her throat, because he'd made it sound like sex. He picked up her knife and fork, and she watched him pour in the egg, pile on the onions and capers, and then chop and chop again before sliding the mixture through Worcestershire sauce. For a fleeting

moment she honestly thought that he might load the
fork and feed her, but he put the utensils down and returned to his meal, and Meg found herself breathless
and blushing at where her mind had just drifted.

'Good?' Niklas asked when she took her first taste.

'Fantastic,' Meg said. It was nice, not amazing, but
made by his hands fantastic it was. 'How's *your* steak?'

He sliced a piece off and lifted the loaded fork and
held it to her. This from a man who had reluctantly
given her a drink, who had on many occasions turned
his back. He was now giving her a taste of food from his
plate. He was just being friendly, Meg told herself. She
was reading far, far too much into this simple gesture.
But as she went to take the fork he lifted it slightly. His
black eyes met hers and he moved the fork to her mouth
and watched as she opened it. Suddenly she began to
wonder if she'd been right the first time.

Maybe he *was* talking about sex.

But if he had been flirting, by the time dessert was
cleared it had ended. He read for a bit, and Meg gazed
out of the window for a while, until the flight attendant
came around and closed the shutters. The lights were
lowered and the cabin was dimmed and Meg fiddled
with her remote to turn the seat into a bed.

Niklas stood and she glanced up at him. 'Are you off
to get your gold pyjamas?'

'And a massage,' Niklas teased back.

She was half asleep when he returned, and watched
idly as he took off his tie. Of course the flight attendant rushed to hold it, while another readied his bed,

and then he took off his shoes and climbed into the flight bed beside her.

His beautiful face was gone now from her vision, but it was there—right there—in her mind's eye. She was terribly aware of his movements and listened to him turn restlessly a few times. She conceded that maybe he did have a point—the flight bed was more than big enough for Meg to stretch out in, but Niklas was eas- ily a foot taller than her and, as he had stated, he really needed this time to sleep, which must be proving dif- ficult. For Niklas the bed was simply too small, and it was almost a sin that he sleep in those immaculate suit trousers.

She lay there trying not to think about him and made herself concentrate instead on work—on the Evans con- tract she had just completed—which was surely enough to send her to sleep. But just as she was closing her eyes, just as she was starting to think that she might be about to drift off even with Niklas beside her, she heard him move again. Her eyes opened and she blinked as his face appeared over hers. She met those black eyes, heard again his rich accent, and how could a woman not smile?

'You never did tell me…' Niklas said, smiling as he invited her to join him in after hours conversation. 'Why is your world too small?'

CHAPTER THREE

THEY PULLED BACK the divider that separated them and lay on their sides, facing each other. Meg knew that this was probably the only time in her life that she'd ever have a man so divine lying on the pillow next to hers, so she was more than happy to forgo sleep for such a glorious cause.

'I work in the family business,' Meg explained.

'Which is?'

'My parents are into real-estate investments. I'm a lawyer…'

He gave a suitably impressed nod, but then frowned, because she didn't seem like a lawyer to him.

'Though I hardly use my training. I do all the paper-work and contracts.'

He saw her roll her eyes.

'I cannot tell you how boring it is.'

'Then why do you do it?'

'Good question. I think it was decided at conception that I would be a lawyer.'

'You don't want to be one?'

It was actually rather hard to admit it. 'I don't think I do…'

He said nothing, just carried on watching her face, waiting for her to share more, and she did.

'I don't think I'm supposed to be one—I mean, I scraped to get the grades I needed at school, held on by my fingernails at university...' She paused as he interrupted.

'You are *never* to say this at an interview.'

'Of course not.' She smiled. 'We're just talking.'

'Good. I'm guessing you were not a little girl who dreamed of being a lawyer?' he checked. 'You did not play with wigs on?' His lips twitched as she smiled. 'You did not line up your dollies and cross-examine them?'

'No.'

'So how did you end up being one?'

'I really don't know where to start.'

He looked at his watch, realised then that perhaps the report simply wasn't going to get done. 'I've got nine hours.'

Niklas made the decision then—they would be entirely devoted to *her*.

'Okay...' Meg thought how best to explain her family to him and chose to start near the beginning. 'In my family you don't get much time to think—even as a little girl there were piano lessons, violin lessons, ballet lessons, tutors. My parents were constantly checking my homework—basically, everything was geared towards me getting into the best school, so that I could get the best grades and go to the best university. Which I did. Except when I got there it was more push, push, push.

I just put my head down and carried on working, but now suddenly I'm twenty-four years old and I'm not really sure that I'm where I want to be…' It was very hard to explain it, because from the outside she had a very nice life.

'They demand too much.'

'You don't know that.'

'They don't listen to you.'

'You don't know that either.'

'But I do.' He said. 'Five or six times on the telephone you said, "Mum, I've got to go." Or, "I really have to go now…"' He saw that she was smiling, but she was smiling not at his imitation of her words but because he had been listening to her conversation. While miserable and scowling and ignoring her, he had still been aware. 'You do this.' He held up an imaginary phone and turned it off.

'I can't.' she admitted. 'Is that what you do?'

'Of course.'

He made it sound so simple.

'You say, *I have to go*, and then you do.'

'It's not just that though,' she admitted. 'They want to know everything about my life…'

'Then tell them you don't want to discuss it,' he said. 'If a conversation moves where you don't want it to, you just say so.'

'How?'

'Say, *I don't want to talk about that*,' he suggested. He made it sound so easy. 'But I don't want to hurt them either—you know how difficult families can be at times.'

'No.' He shook his head. 'There are some advantages to being an orphan, and that is one of them. I get to make my own mistakes.' He said it in such a way that there was no invitation to sympathy—in fact he even gave a small smile, as if letting her know that she did not need to be uncomfortable at his revelation and he took no offence at her casual remark.

'I'm sorry.'

'You don't have to be.'

'But…'

'I don't want to talk about that.' And, far more easily than she, he told her what he was not prepared to discuss. He simply moved the conversation. 'What would you like to do if you could do anything?'

She thought for a moment. 'You're the first person who has ever asked me that.'

'The second,' Niklas corrected. 'I would imagine you have been asking yourself that question an awful lot.'

'Lately I have been,' Meg admitted.

'So, what would you be?'

'A chef.'

And he didn't laugh, didn't tell her that she should know about steak tartare by now, if that was what she wanted to be, and neither did he roll his eyes.

'Why?'

'Because I love cooking.'

'Why?' he asked—not as if he didn't understand how

it was possible to love cooking so much, more as if he really wanted her tell him why.

She just stared at him as their minds locked in a strange wrestle.

'When someone eats something I've cooked—I mean properly prepared and cooked…' She still stared at him as she spoke. 'When they close their eyes for a second…' She couldn't properly explain it. 'When you ate those blinis, when you first tasted them, there was a moment…' She watched that mouth move into a smile, just a brief smile of understanding. 'They tasted fantastic?'

'Yes.'

'I wanted to have cooked them.' It was perhaps the best way to describe it. 'I love shopping for food, planning a meal, preparing it, presenting it, serving it…'

'For that moment?'

'Yes.' Meg nodded. 'And I know that I'm good at it because, no matter how dissatisfied my parents were with my grades or my decisions, on a Sunday I'd cook a meal from scratch and it was the one thing I excelled at. Yet it was the one thing they discouraged.'

'Why?' This time he asked because he didn't understand.

'"Why would you want to work in a kitchen?"' It was Meg doing the imitating now. '"Why, after all the opportunities we've given you…?"' Her voice faded for a moment. 'Maybe I should have stood up to them, but it's hard at fourteen…' She gave him a smile. 'It's still hard at twenty-four.'

'If cooking is your passion then I'm sure you would be a brilliant chef. You should do it.'

'I don't know.' She knew she sounded weak, knew she should just say to hell with them, but there was one other thing she had perhaps not explained. 'I love them,' Meg said, and she saw his slight frown. 'They are impossible and overbearing but I do love them, and I don't want to hurt them—though I know that I'll probably have to.' She gave him a pale smile. 'I'm going to try and work out if I can just hurt them gently.'

After a second or two he smiled back, a pensive smile she did not want, for perhaps he felt sorry for her being weak—though she didn't think she was.

'Do you cook a lot now?'

'Hardly ever.' She shook her head. 'There just never seems to be enough time. But when I do…' She explained to him that on her next weekend off she would prepare the meal she had just eaten for herself and friends…that she would spend hours trying to get it just right. Even if she generally stuck with safer choices, there was so much about food that she wanted to explore.

They lay there, facing each other and talking about food, which to some might sound boring—but for Meg it was the best conversation she had had in her life.

He told her about a restaurant that he frequented in downtown São Paulo which was famed for its seafood, although he thought it wasn't actually their best dish. When he was there Niklas always ordered their *feijoada*, which was a meat and black bean stew that tasted, he told her, as if angels had prepared it and were feeding it to his soul.

In that moment Meg realised that she had not just one growing passion to contend with, but two, because his gaze was intense and his words were so interesting and she never wanted this journey to end. Didn't want to stop their whispers in the dark.

'How come you speak so many languages?'

'It is good that I do. It means I can take my business to many countries…' He was an international financier, Niklas told her, and then, very unusually for him, he told her a little bit more—which he never, ever did. Not with anyone. Not even, if he could help it, with himself. 'One of the nuns who cared for me when I was a baby spoke only Spanish. By the time I moved from that orphanage…'

'At how old?'

He thought for a moment. 'Three, maybe four. By that time I spoke two languages,' he explained. 'Later I taught myself English, and much later French.'

'How?'

'I had a friend who was English—I asked him to speak only English to me. And I—' He'd been about to say looked for, but he changed it. 'I read English newspapers.'

'What language do you dream in?'

He smiled at her question. 'That depends where I am—where my thoughts are.'

He spent a lot of time in France, he told Meg, especially in the South. Meg asked him where his favourite place in the world was. He was about to answer São Paulo—after all, he was looking forward to going back there, to the fast pace and the stunning women—but he paused for a moment and then gave an answer that surprised even him. He told her about the mountains away from the city, and the rainforests and the rivers and springs there, and that maybe he should think of getting a place there—somewhere private.

And then he thanked her.

'For what?'

'For making me think,' Niklas said. 'I have been thinking of taking some time off just to do more of the same…' He did not mention the clubs and the women and the press that were always chasing him for the latest scandal. 'Maybe I should take a proper break.'

She told him that she too preferred the mountains to the beach, even if she lived in Bondi, and they lay there together and rewrote a vision of her—no longer a chef in a busy international hotel, instead she would run a small bed and breakfast set high in the hills.

And she asked about him too.

Rarely, so rarely did he tell anyone, but for some reason this false night he did—just a little. For some reason he didn't hold back. He just said it. Not all of it, by any means, but he gave more of himself than usual. After all, he would never see her again.

He told her how he had taught himself to read and write, how he had educated himself from newspapers, how the business section had always fascinated him and how easily he had read the figures that seemed to daunt others. And he told her how he loved Brazil—for there you could both work hard and play hard too.

'Can I get you anything Mr Dos Santos…?' Worried that their esteemed passenger was being disturbed, the steward checked that he was okay.

'Nothing.' He did not look up. He just looked at Meg as he spoke. 'If you can leave us, please?'

'Dos Santos?' she repeated when the steward had gone, and he told her that it was a surname often given to orphans.

'It means "from the Saints" in Portuguese,' he explained.

'How were you orphaned?'

'I don't actually know,' Niklas admitted. 'Perhaps I was abandoned, just left at the orphanage. I really don't know.'

'Have you ever tried to find out about your family…?'

He opened his mouth to say that he would rather not discuss it, but instead he gave even more of himself. 'I have,' he admitted. 'It would be nice to know, but it proved impossible. I got Miguel, my lawyer, onto it, but he got nowhere.'

She asked him what it had been like, growing up like that, but she was getting too close and it was not something he chose to share.

He told her so. 'I don't want to speak about that.'

So they talked some more about her, and she could have talked to him for ever—except it was Niklas who got too close now, when he asked if she was in a relationship.

'No.'

'Have you ever been serious about anyone?'

'Not really,' she said, but that wasn't quite true. 'I was about to get engaged,' Meg said. 'I called it off.'

'Why?'

She just lay there.

'Why?' Niklas pushed.

'He got on a bit too well with my parents.' She swallowed. 'A colleague.' He could hear her hesitation to discuss it. 'What we said before about worlds being too small…' Meg said. 'I realised I would be making mine smaller still.'

'Was he upset?'

'Not really.' Meg was honest. 'It wasn't exactly a passionate…' She swallowed. She was *so* not going to discuss this with him.

She should have just said so, but instead she told him that she needed to sleep. The dimmed lights and champagne were starting to catch up with both of them, and almost reluctantly their conversation was closed and finally they slept.

For how long Meg wasn't sure. She just knew that when she woke up she regretted it.

Not the conversation, but ending it, falling asleep and wasting the little time that they had.

She'd woken to the scent of coffee and the hum of the engines and now she looked over to him. He was still asleep, and just as beautiful with his eyes closed. It was almost a privilege to examine such a stunning man more intently. His black hair was swept back, his beautiful mouth relaxed and loose. She looked at his dark spiky lashes and thought of the treasure behind them. She wondered what language he was dreaming in, then watched as his eyes were revealed.

For Niklas it was a pleasure to open his eyes to her.

He had felt the caress of her gaze and now he met it and held it.

'English.' He answered the question she had not voiced, but they both understood. He had been dreaming in English, perhaps about her. And then Niklas did what he always did when he woke to a woman he considered beautiful.

It was a touch more difficult to do so—given the gap between them, given that he could not gather her body and slip her towards him—but the result would certainly be worth the brief effort. He pulled himself up on his elbow and moved till his face was right over her, and looking down.

'You never did finish what you were saying.'

She looked back at him.

'When you said it wasn't passionate...'

She could have turned away from him, could have closed the conversation—his question was inappropriate, really—only nothing felt inappropriate with Niklas. There was nothing that couldn't be said with his breath on her cheek and that sulky, beautiful mouth just inches away.

'I was the one who wasn't passionate.'

'I can't imagine that.'

'Well, I wasn't.'

'Because you didn't want him in the way that you want me?'

Meg knew what he was about to do.

And she wanted, absolutely, for him to do it.

So he did.

It did not feel as if she was kissing a stranger as their lips met—all it felt was sublime.

His lips were surprisingly gentle and moved with hers for a moment, giving her a brief glimpse of false security—for his tongue, when it slipped in, was shockingly direct and intent.

This wasn't a kiss to test the water, and now Meg knew what had been wrong with her from the start, the reason she had been rambling. This thing between them was an attraction so instant that he could have kissed her like this the moment he'd sat down beside her. He could have taken his seat, had her turn off her phone and offered his mouth to her and she would have kissed him right back.

And so she kissed him back now.

There was more passion in his kiss than Meg had ever tasted in her life. She discovered that a kiss could be far more than a simple meeting of lips as his tongue told her exactly what else he would like to do, slipping in and out of her parted lips, soft one minute, rougher the next. Then his hand moved beneath the blanket and stroked her breast through her blouse, so expertly that she ached for more.

Meg's hands were in his hair and his jaw scratched at her skin and his tongue probed a little harder. As she concentrated on that, as she fought with her body not to arch into him, he moved his hand inside her top. Now Niklas became less than subtle with his silent instructions and moved his hand to her back, pulling her forward into his embrace. She swallowed the growl that vibrated from his throat as beneath the blanket he rolled her nipple between his fingers—hard at first, and then with his palm he stroked her more softly.

To the outside world they would appear simply as two lovers kissing, their passion indecent, but hidden. Then Niklas moved over her a little more, so all she could breathe was his scent, and his mouth and his hand worked harder, each subtle stroke making her want the next one even more. Suddenly Meg knew she had to stop this, had to pull back, because just her reaction to his kiss had her feeling as though she might come.

'Come.' His mouth was at her ear now, his word voicing her thought.

'Stop,' she told him, even if it was not what she wanted him to do, but she could hardly breathe.

'Why?'

'Because,' she answered with his mouth now back over hers, 'it's wrong.'

'But *so* nice.'

He continued to kiss her. Her mouth was wet from his but she closed her lips, because this feeling was too much and he was taking her to the edge. He parted her lips with his tongue and again she tried to close them, clamped her teeth, but he merely carried on until she gave in and opened again to him. He breathed harder, and his hand still worked at her breast, and she was fighting not to gasp, not to moan, to remember where they were as he suckled her tongue.

Meg forced herself not to push his hand far lower, as her body was begging her to do, not to pull him fully on top of her as Niklas made love to her with his mouth.

She hadn't a hope of winning.

He removed his hand from her breast and prised her knotted fingers from his hair. Then he moved her hand beneath his blanket, his body acting as a shield as he held her small hand over his thick, solid length. Her fingers ached to curl and stroke around him, but he did not allow it. Instead he just flattened her palm against him and held it there. His mouth still worked against hers, and she tried to grumble a protest as her hand fought not to stroke, not to feel, not to explore his arousal.

He won.

He smothered her moan with his mouth and sucked, as if swallowing her cry of pleasure, and then, most cruel of all, he loosened his grip on her hand and accepted the dig of her fingers into him. He lifted his head and watched her, a wicked smile on his face, as she struggled to breathe, watched her bite on her lip as he too fought not to come. And he wished the lights were on so he could watch her in colour, wished that they were in his vast bed so the second she'd finished they could resume.

And they would, he decided.

'That,' Niklas said as he crashed back not to earth but to ten thousand feet in the air, 'was the appetiser.'

She'd been right the first time.

He *had* been talking about sex.

She put on a cardigan and excused herself just as the lights came on.

As she stood in the tiny cubicle and examined her face in the mirror she fastened her bra. Her skin was pink from his prolonged attention, her lips swollen, and her eyes glittered with danger. The face that looked back at her was not a woman she knew.

And she was *so* not the woman Niklas had first met.

Not once in her life had she rebelled; never had she even jumped out of her bedroom window and headed out to parties. At university she had studied and worked part-time, getting the grades her parents had expected before following them into the family business. She had always done the right thing, even when it came to her personal relationships.

Niklas had been right. She hadn't wanted her boyfriend in the way she wanted Niklas, and had strung things out for as long as she could before realising she could not get engaged to someone she cared about but didn't actually fancy. She had told her boyfriend that she wouldn't have sex till she was sure they were serious, but the moment he'd started to talk about rings and a future Meg had known it was time to get out.

And *that* was the part that caused her disquiet.

She wasn't the passionate woman Niklas had just met and kissed—she was a virgin, absolutely clueless with men. A few hours off the leash from her parents and she was lying on her back, with a stranger above her and the throb of illicit pulses below. She closed her eyes in shame, and then opened them again and saw the glitter and the shame burned a little less. There was no going back now to the woman she had been, and even if there were she would not change a minute of the time she had spent with Niklas.

She heard a tap against the door and froze for a second. Then she told herself she was being ridiculous. She brushed her teeth and sorted her hair and washed in the tiny sink, trying to brace herself to head back out there.

As she walked down the aisle she noticed her bed had been put away and the seats were up. She attempted polite conversation with Niklas as breakfast was served. He didn't really return her conversation. It was as if what had passed between them simply hadn't happened. He continued to read his paper, dunking his croissant in strong black coffee as if he *hadn't* just rocked her world.

The dishes were cleared and still he kept reading. And as the plane started its descent Meg decided that she now hated landing too—because she didn't want to arrive back at her old life.

Except you couldn't fly for ever. Meg knew that. And a man like Niklas wasn't going to stick around on landing. She knew what happened with men like him, wasn't naïve enough to think it had been anything more than a nice diversion.

She accepted it was just about sex.

And yet it wasn't just the sex that had her hooked on him.

He stretched out his legs, his suit trousers still somehow unrumpled, and she turned away and stared out of the window, trying not to think about what was beneath the cloth, trying not to think about what she had felt beneath her fingers, about the taste of his kisses and the passion she had encountered. Maybe life would have been easier had she not sat next to him—because now everything would be a mere comparison, for even with the little she knew still she was aware that there were not many men like Niklas.

Niklas just continued reading his newspaper, or appeared to be. His busy mind was already at work, cancelling his day. He knew that she would have plans once they landed. That she probably had a car waiting to take her to her hotel and her parents. But he'd think of something to get around that obstacle.

He had no intention of waiting.

Or maybe he would wait. Maybe he'd arrange to meet up with her tonight.

He thought of her controlling parents and turned a page in the paper. He relished the thought of screwing her right under their nose.

She, Niklas decided, was amazing.

There was no *possibly* about it now.

He thought of her face as she came beneath him and shifted just a little in his seat.

'Ladies and gentlemen…' They both looked up as the captain's voice came over the intercom. 'Due to an incident at LAX all planes are now being re-routed. We will be landing in Las Vegas in just over an hour.'

The captain apologised for the inconvenience and they heard the moans and grumbles from other passengers. They felt the shift as the plane started to climb, and had she been sitting next to anyone else Meg might have been complaining too, or panicking about the prolonged flight, or stressing about the car that was waiting for her, or worried about what was going on...

Instead she was smiling when he turned to her.

'Viva Las Vegas,' Niklas said, and picked up her remote, laid her chair flat again and got back to where he had left off.

CHAPTER FOUR

'IT WAS A false alarm.'

They were still sitting on the plane on the tarmac. The second they had landed in Vegas Niklas had pulled out his phone, turned it on and called someone. He was speaking in Portuguese. He had briefly halted his conversation to inform Meg that whatever had happened in Los Angeles had been a false alarm and then carried on talking into his phone.

'Aguarde, por favour!' he said, and then turned again to Meg. 'I am speaking with my PA, Carla. I can ask her to reschedule your flight also. She will get it done quickly, I think.'

And make sure he'd sit next to her too, Niklas decided.

'So?' he asked. 'When do you want to get there?'

Of course the normal response would be as soon as possible, but there was nothing normal about her response to him. Niklas was looking right at her, and there was undoubtedly an invitation in his eyes, but there was something he needed to know—somehow she had to tell him that what had happened between them wasn't usual for her.

To put it mildly.

Except Niklas made her stomach fold into herself, and his eyes were waiting, and his mouth was so beautiful, and she did not want this to end with a kiss at an airport gate. She did not want to spend the rest of her life regretting what would surely be a far more exciting choice than the one she should be making.

He made it for her.

'It sounds as if there is a lot of backlog. The airport will be hell with so many people having to re-route. I could tell her to book our flights for tomorrow.' Niklas had already made the decision. He had not had twenty-four hours to himself in months, had not stopped working in weeks, and right now he could think of no one nicer to escape the world with.

'I'm supposed to be…' She thought of her parents, waiting for her at the conference, waiting for her to arrive, to perform, to work twelve-hour days and accept weekends constantly on call. Hers was a family that had every minute, every week, every year of her life accounted for, and for just for a little while Meg wanted to be able to breathe.

Or rather to struggle to breathe under him as he kissed her and took her breath.

He looked at her mouth as he awaited her answer, watched the finger that twirled in her hair finally pause as she reached her decision, saw her tongue moisten her lips just before she delivered her answer.

'Tomorrow,' Meg said. 'Tell her tomorrow.'

He spoke with Carla for a couple more moments, checked he had the right spelling of her surname and date of birth and passport number, and then clicked off his phone.

'Done.'

She didn't know what his life was like—didn't really understand what the word *done* meant in Niklas Dos Santos's world...

Yet.

They waited for their baggage and she got to kiss him for the first time standing up, got to feel his tall length pressed against her. He loaded their bags onto one trolley and then he did a nice thing, a very unexpected thing: he stopped at one of the shops and bought her flowers.

She smiled as he handed them to her.

'Dinner, breakfast, champagne, kisses, foreplay...' God, he didn't even lower his voice as he handed her the flowers. 'Have I covered everything?'

'You haven't taken me to the movies,' Meg said.

'No...' He shook his head. 'There was a movie on. You chose not to watch it. I cannot be held responsible for that...'

Oh, but he had been. She felt the thorns of the roses press in as he moved closer again and crushed the flowers.

'Consider yourself dated.'

There was no waiting in long queues for Niklas. Customs was a very different thing in his world, and as his hand was holding hers, she too was processed quickly. Suddenly they had cleared Customs and were walking out—and it was then she got her first glimpse of what *done* meant in a world like Niklas's.

Carla must have been busy, for there was already a driver waiting, holding a sign with 'Niklas Dos Santos' written on it. He relieved them of their bags and they followed him to a blacked-out limousine. She never got a glimpse of Vegas as they drove to the hotel, just felt the brief hit of hot desert sun.

No, she never saw Vegas at all.

She was sitting on his lap.

'I'm going to be the most terrible let-down...' She peeled her face from his.

'You're not,' he groaned.

'I am...' God, her head was splitting just at the attempt to be rational. 'Because I have to ring my mum...'

Her hands were shaking as she dialled the number, her mind reeling, because she *had* to tell him she was a virgin. Oh, God, she really was going to be a let-down! His fingers were working the buttons on her trousers now, his hand slipping in and cupping her bum. His mouth was sucking her breast through her blouse as she was connected to her mother, and she heard only smatters of her conversation.

'Yes, I know it was a false alarm...' She tried to sound normal as she spoke with a less than impressed Ruth. 'But all the flights are in chaos and tomorrow was the earliest I could get.' No, she insisted for a third time, there was simply nothing she could do that would get her there sooner. 'I'll call you when I've sorted out a hotel and things. I have to go, Mum, my battery's about to go flat.'

She clicked off the phone and he turned her so that she was sitting astride him. Holding her hips, he pushed her down, so she could feel what would soon be inside her, and for the first time she was just a little bit scared.

'Niklas…'

'Come on…' He did her blouse up. 'We are nearly there.'

She made herself decent, slipped her cardigan over her blouse to hide the wet patch his mouth had made, and found out once again what it was like in his world.

They breezed through check-in, and even their luggage beat them to their huge suite—not that she paid any attention to it, for finally they were alone. As soon as the door shut he kissed her, pushing her onto the bed. He removed his jacket and pulled condoms from his pocket, placing them within reach on the bedside table, and then he removed her trousers, taking her panties with them at the same time.

God, he was animal, and he moaned as he buried his face in her most private of places. Meg felt the purr of his moan, and this new experience coupled with her own arousal terrified her.

'Niklas…' she pleaded as his tongue started to probe. 'When I said my relationship wasn't passionate…'

'We've already proved it had nothing to do with you.' His words were muffled, but he felt her tense and as he looked up he met anxious eyes.

'I haven't done this before.' She saw him frown. 'I haven't done anything.'

There was a rather long pause. 'Good. I will look after you…'

'I know that.'

'I *will*.'

And then his mouth resumed, and she felt his breath in places she had never felt someone breathe before, but still the tension and fear remained. Niklas must have sensed it too, as he raised himself up on his elbows and looked down at her beneath him, her face flushed.

Niklas was a very uninhibited lover; it was the only piece of himself that he readily gave. Sex was both his rest and recreation, and with his usual lovers there was no need for long conversation and coaxing, no need for reticence or taking his time. But as he looked down at her flushed cheeks he recalled their long conversations on the plane, and the enjoyment of spending proper time with another person. He thought of all the things he had told her that he never usually shared with anyone, and he realised he liked not just the woman who lay beneath him but the words that had come from her mouth.

He kissed it now, as if doing so for the first time.

Not their first kiss. Just a gentle kiss—albeit with his erection pressing into her as he thought about what to do.

His first intention had been to push her on the bed and take her quickly, just so that they could start over again, but he really liked her, and he wanted to do this well.

Thoroughly.

Properly.

'I know…'

He sounded as if he'd had an idea, and he stopped kissing her, smiling down at her before rolling off and picking up the phone. He told Meg that a bath would relax her, and as they waited for a maid to come and run it he wrapped her in a vast white dressing gown. She lay on the bed, watching him as he went through his case, and then he joined her on the bed and showed her some documents, his fingers pointing to the pertinent lines, which she read, frowning.

'I don't get this.'

'I had to get a check-up when I was in Sydney, for my insurance…' he explained.

'So?'

'I wasn't worried about the results. I always use protection…' He was so completely matter-of-fact.

'I'm not on the pill,' Meg replied as she understood his meaning, and she saw his eyes widen just a little as she dampened his plans.

'But still…' He stopped himself, shook his head as if to clear it. What the hell had he been thinking? For a second a baby had seemed a minor inconvenience compared to what they might miss out on. He was, Niklas decided, starting to adore her, and that always came with strong warnings attached—that was always his signal to leave.

'Niklas…am I making a big mistake?'

He was as honest with Meg as he was with all women, because his was a heart that would remain closed. 'If you are looking for love, then yes,' Niklas said. 'Because I don't do that.'

'Never?'

'Ever,' Niklas said. He could not bear even the thought of someone depending on him, could not trust himself to provide for another person, just could not envisage sharing, yet alone caring—except already a part of him cared for *her*.

'Then I want as long as we've got,' Meg said.

When the maid left he took her by the hand and led her to the bathroom. The bath was sunken, and as she slid into the water he undressed, and she was looking up at his huge erection, her cheeks paling in colour. Niklas found himself assuring her that nothing would happen between them just yet—not until she was sure she was ready. The need to comfort her and reassure her was a new sensation for him, and as he looked down at her he decided that for the next twenty-four hours he would let himself care.

He climbed into the water with her and washed her slowly, sensually, smoothing the soap over her silky skin. He dunked her head in the water too, just so he could see the red darken.

'Your last boyfriend—did he try...?' Niklas asked as he soaped her arms, curious because he wondered how any man could resist the beautiful woman he held in his arms.

'A bit...' Meg said.

Even her arms blushed, he noted.

'I just...'

'What?' He loved her blushing, and found himself smiling just watching her skin pinken, feeling the warmth beneath his palms as she squirmed.

'I told him I didn't want to do anything like that till we were really serious. You know...'

His eyes widened. 'Married?'

'Engaged,' she corrected.

'Do people really say that?' He sounded incredulous, his soapy hands moving lower, past her breasts and down to her waist. 'How would you know if you wanted to marry someone if you hadn't—?'

'That had nothing to do with it. I wasn't demanding a ring. I realised I was just making up excuses...'

'Because?' He was sliding his soapy hands between her legs now, and she didn't know how to answer. 'Because?' he insisted.

'Because I didn't have any compulsion to sit in a bath with him and let him wash me *there*...' She couldn't believe he expected her to speak as he was doing what he did. 'And then he started talking rings.'

'I bet he did,' Niklas said, because, naked with her like this, what man wouldn't want his ring on her finger?

Suddenly his brain went to a place it should not, and Niklas tried hard to shut it down. This had to stay as just sex between them. He pulled her straight over to him, hooked her legs over his and kissed her shoulder.

'I loved flying with you...' He said it like a caress as he lifted her hair, and his mouth moved to the back of her neck and sucked hard.

She closed her eyes at the bruise he was making, and then felt his hand move up her thigh. It was his neck she was now kissing, licking away the fragrant water just to get to his skin. As they continued to nip and kiss each other Niklas moved his hand, his finger slipping inside, and when she felt a moment's pain she sucked harder on his neck. He pushed in another finger, stretching her, and again she bit down on his shoulder as pain flashed through her body. She knew he had to stretch her—she had seen that he was huge and this was her first time after all—but he did it with a gentleness that moved her.

He continued to slide his fingers in and out, and then kissed her breast, sucking on her wet nipple. She began to moan and lift herself to his fingers as plea-sure washed over her. Niklas realised that things were moving rather faster than he had intended. He wanted her on the bed—or rather they needed to get back to the condoms.

'Come on…' He moved to stand, except her hand found him first and, yes, she deserved a little play too.

He liked being touched by a woman. He had just never expected to enjoy it as much as he did now. Had never expected the naked pleasure in her eyes and the tentative exploration of her hands, just her enjoyment of him, would make him feel as it did.

For enjoy him, Meg did. It was bliss to hold him, huge and slippery and magnificent in her hands, and she was still scared, but rather more excited at the pros-pect of him being inside her.

'Like this?' she checked, and he closed his eyes and leant his head back on the marble wall behind him.

'Like that,' he said, but then changed his mind. 'Harder.' And he put his hand over hers and showed her—showed her a little too well.

'Come here.' He pulled her up over him. He was seconds away, had to slow down, but he had to have her. He was rubbing himself around her and she was desperate for him to be inside her too.

'We need…' It was him saying it, and he knew he should take her to bed and slip on a condom, but he wanted her this moment, and for once in his life he was conflicted. He knew he could have her now, that he was the only one thinking, and he wanted the pleasure. But as he looked at her, hovering over him, Niklas knew he wouldn't have a hope of pulling out in time.

Her hands were on his shoulders and he was holding her buttocks, almost fighting not to press her down. He wanted to give in, to drive her down and at the same time lift his hips, and he would have—absolutely he would have, in fact—had her phone not rung.

He swore in Portuguese, and then French, and then Spanish at the intrusion.

'Leave it,' he said.

But it rang again, and for a brief moment common sense returned. He stood, taking her wet hand and helping her out as they headed for the bed. He turned off her phone, and checked that his was off too, for he was tired of a world that kept invading his time. Then he looked at the shiny foil packets and realised that the last thing he wanted was to be sheathed when he entered this woman.

'I want to feel you,' he said. 'I want you to feel me.'

And his mind went to a place he never allowed it to go.

He'd been told by plenty of people that he was damaged goods, that a man with his past was not capable of a stable relationship.

Yet he wanted to be stable for a while.

He was tired of the noise and the endless women. Not once had he considered commitment, and he didn't fully now, but surely for a while longer he could carry on caring? He had amassed enough that he could trust himself to take care of another person for a while at least, and if there were consequences to his reckless decision then he could take care of that too.

He could.

In that moment he fully believed that he could.

He would.

No, he did not want others around him today—did not want his thoughts clouded. Usually, to Niklas, rapid thoughts were right, and they were the ones that proved to be the best. He looked at her, pink and warm and a virgin on his bed, and decided he would do this right.

Thoroughly.

Properly.

'Marry me.'

She laughed.

'I'm serious,' he said. 'That's what people do when they come to Vegas.'

'I think they usually know each other first.'

'I know you.'

'You don't.'

'I know enough,' Niklas said. 'You just don't know me. I *want* to do this.'

And what Niklas Dos Santos wanted he usually got.

'I'm not talking about for ever—I could never settle with one person for very long, or stay in one place— but I can help you sort out the stuff with your family. I can step in so you can step back…'

'Why?' She didn't get it. 'Why would you do that?'

He looked at her for a long time before answering, because she was right. Why *would* he do that? Niklas had had many relationships, many less than emotional encounters, and there had been a couple of long high-maintenance ones. Yet not once in his life had he considered marriage before. Not once had he wanted another person close. He had actually feared that another person might depend on a man who had come from nothing, but as he looked at her for the first time he wasn't daunted by the prospect at all.

Around her—again for the first time—he trusted in himself.

'I like you.'

'But what would you get out of it?'

'You,' he replied, and suddenly it seemed imperative that he marry her—that he make her his even if just for a little while. 'I like sorting things out…and I like you. And…' He gestured to the condoms on the bedside table.

'And I don't like them. So,' he said, reaching for the hotel phone, 'will you marry me?'

There was nothing about him she understood, but more than that there was nothing about herself she understood any more, for in that moment his proposal seemed rather logical.

A solution, in fact.

'Yes.'

He spoke on the phone for just a few moments and then turned and smiled at his bride-to-be.

'Done.'

CHAPTER FIVE

IT WAS THE quickest of quick weddings.

Or maybe not.

They were in Vegas, after all.

Niklas rang down to the concierge and informed them of their plans, telling him how they wanted them executed.

'Do you want them to bring up a selection of dresses?' he asked Meg. 'It's your day; you can have whatever you want.'

'No dress.' Meg smiled.

But there were *some* traditional elements.

He ordered lots of flowers, and they arrived in the room along with champagne, and there was even a wedding cake. Meg sat at a table trying on rings as the celebrant went through the paperwork.

He'd arranged music too, but Niklas chose from a selection already on his phone, and Meg found herself walking at his side to music she didn't know and a man she badly wanted to.

The bride and groom wore white bathrobes, and she stood watching as the titanium ring dotted with diamonds she had chosen was slipped onto her finger. Perhaps bizarrely, there was not a flicker of doubt in her mind as she said yes.

And neither was there a flicker of doubt in Niklas's mind as he kissed his virgin bride and told her that he was happy to be married to a woman he had only met yesterday.

'Today,' Meg corrected and, yes, because of the time difference between Vegas and Australia it *was* still the day they'd first met.

'Sorry to rush you.' He grinned.

There was a mixture of nerves and heady relief when everyone had left.

He undid her robe and took off his, and then he pulled her onto the bed.

'Soon,' Niklas promised as his hands roamed over her, 'you will be wondering how you got through your life without this.'

'I'm wondering now,' Meg admitted, and she wasn't just talking about the sex. She was talking about him too. She had never opened up more fully with another person, had never felt more like herself.

Niklas's kiss was incredibly tender—a kiss she would never have expected from him. He kissed her till she almost relaxed, and then his mouth became more consuming. He needed to shave, but she liked the roughness, liked his naked body wrapped around hers.

She was on her back, and he was on top as he had so badly wanted to be on the plane. He could not wait—not for a moment longer. His knees nudged hers apart and he slipped his fingers briefly in, checking she was ready for him, finding that she was.

And now there was nothing between them.

And he was no longer patient.

He warned her it would hurt.

He watched her face as she blanched in pain, then kissed her hard on the mouth.

As he drove into her she screamed into his mouth, because that first thrust seemed to go on for ever, and every part of her felt as if it was tearing just to accommodate his long, thick length. He tried to be gentle, but he was too large for that. But once he had ripped off that Band-Aid he kept moving within her, kept on kissing her mouth, her face, giving her no choice but to grow accustomed to the new sensations she was feeling. He moved within her as his tongue had earlier described that he would, moving deep till he had driven her wild. He wasn't kissing her now, and she looked up to see his face etched with concentration, his eyes closed, his body moving rapidly as hers rose to meet him.

Now it was Meg's hands urging him on, digging her fingers into his tight buttocks, whimpering as she sought relief, and then he opened his eyes and let her have it, spilled every last drop deep into her. Her orgasm followed quickly after, and she was frenzied as she came, almost scared at the power of her body's response, at the things he had taught her to do.

And then he collapsed on top of her, his breathing heavy, and although it felt like a dream somehow it was real. Meg realised that he had been right—she had no idea how she'd got through her life without this.

Without him.

'Shouldn't we be regretting this by now?' Meg asked.

They were lying in a very rumpled bed and it was morning. Her body ached with the most delicious hurt, but Niklas had assured her for this morning's lesson she would need only her mouth.

'What's to regret?' He turned on the bed and looked over to her.

He didn't do happiness, but he felt the first rays of it today. He liked waking up to her, and the rest was mere detail that he would soon sort out.

'You live in Brazil and I live in Australia...'

'As we both know, there are planes...' He looked across the pillow. 'Do you worry about everything?'

'No.'

'I think you do.'

'I don't.'

'So how shall we tell your parents?'

He saw her slight grimace.

'They might be pleased for you.'

As the real world invaded so too did confusion. 'I doubt it. It will be a terrible shock.' She thought for a moment. 'I think once they get used to the idea they'll be pleased.' And then she swallowed nervously. 'I *think*.'

He smiled at her worried face. 'First of all *you* need to get used to the idea.'

'I don't know much about you.'

'There isn't much to know,' Niklas said.

She rather doubted that.

'I don't have family, as I said, so you have avoided having a mother-in-law. I hear from friends they can sometimes be a problem, so that's an unexpected bonus for you!'

He could be so flippant about things that were important, Meg thought, and there was so much she wanted to find out about him. She wondered how he had survived without a family, for a start, how he had made such a success of himself from nothing—because clearly he had. But unlike their wedding some things, Meg guessed, had to be taken more slowly—she couldn't just sit up and fire a thousand questions at him. Somehow she knew it wasn't something he would talk about easily, but she tried. 'What was it like, though?' Meg asked. 'Growing up in an orphanage?'

'There were many orphanages,' he said. 'I was moved around a lot.' Perhaps he realised he wasn't answering her question, because he added, 'I don't know, really. I try not to think about it.'

'But…'

He halted her. 'We're married Meg. But that doesn't mean we need every piece of each other. Let's just enjoy what we have, huh?'

So if he didn't want to talk about himself she'd start with the easier stuff instead. 'You live in São Paulo?'

'I have an apartment there,' Niklas said. 'If I am working in Europe I tend to stay at my house in Villefranche-sur-Mer. And now I guess I'll have to look for somewhere in Sydney…' His smile was wicked. 'If your father gets really cross, maybe I can ask if he knows any good houses—if he would be able to help…'

Meg started to laugh, because it sounded as if he did understand where she was coming from. Niklas was right—a nice big commission would certainly go a long way towards appeasing her father. She realised that the shock would wear off eventually, and that her rather shallow parents would be delighted to find some-where for their rich new son-in-law to live.

As Meg lay there, and the sun started to work its way through the chink in the curtains, she started to realise that this was the happiest she had been in her life. But even with that knowledge there was one part about last night that had been unjustifiably reckless.

'I'll go on the pill…' she said. 'If it isn't already too late.'

He had said this wasn't for ever, and the wedding ring that had seemed a solution yesterday was less than one now.

'If last night brings far-reaching consequences you will both be taken care of.'

'For a while?'

He looked over and knew that, unlike most women, Meg wasn't talking about money. But his bank account was the only thing not tainted by his past.

'For a while,' Niklas said. 'I promise you—we'll be arguing within weeks, we'll be driving each other insane—and not with lust…' He smiled in all the wrong

places, but he made her smile back. 'You'll be glad to
see the back of me.'

She doubted it.

'I'm hard work,' he warned.

But worth it.

Though she *was* going on the pill.

And then he looked over to her again, and for as long
as it was like this she could adore him.

'I am going to write to the airline tomorrow and
thank them for not having a first-class seat,' he said.

'I might write and thank them too.'

'It will be okay,' he told her. 'Soon I will ring Carla
and I will have her re-schedule things. Then we will
meet with your parents and I will tell them.' He grinned
at her horrified expression.

'*I'll* speak to my parents.'

'No,' Niklas said. 'Because you will start apologis-
ing and doubting and I am a better negotiator.'

'Negotiator?'

'How long do you want off for our honeymoon?' Niklas said. 'Of course you will want to give them notice—
you don't want to just walk out—but for now we should
have some time together. Maybe I'll take you to the
mountains…' There was no gap between them now, so
he pulled her across. 'And I will also tell them that we
will have a big wedding in a few weeks.'

'I'm happy with the wedding we had.'

'Don't you want a big one?'

Her hand slid down beneath the sheet and she loved
it that he laughed, not understanding that laughter was

actually rare for him. Then her mouth followed her hands, and he lay there as she inexpertly woke another part of him.

'Don't you want a proper wedding, with family and dancing?'

'I hate dancing…' She kissed all the way down his length and she felt his hand in her hair, gently lifting her to where he wanted more attention.

'I do too.'

'I thought all Brazilians could dance?'

'Stop talking,' Niklas said. 'And I never said I couldn't. I just don't.'

She looked up at the most stunning, complicated man who had ever graced her vision and thought of his prowess and the movement of his body. All of it had been for her, and she shivered at the thought of the days and nights to come, of getting to know more and more of him. Already she knew that she was starting to want for ever, but that wasn't what this was about.

And then she tasted him again.

His hands moved her head as he promised she would not hurt him and told her exactly what to do with her mouth. She was lost in his scent, the feel of him in her mouth, and the shock of his rapid come was a most pleasant surprise. It was a surprise for Niklas too, but this was how she moved him.

He did not want to get out of bed—did not want to get back to the world. Except no doubt it was screaming for him by now—he had never had his phone turned off for so long.

He climbed out of bed and she lay there, just staring at the ceiling, lost in thoughts of him and the time they would take to get to know the other properly.

And Niklas was thinking the same. He had been looking forward to some time off, had been aware that he needed some, now he could not wait to take it.

He showered quickly and considered shaving, and then he picked up his phone, impatient to speak to Carla, to change his plans yet again. He grimaced when he saw how many missed calls he'd had, how many texts, and then he frowned—because there were hundreds. From Carla, from Miguel, from just about everyone he knew…

It was his first inkling that something was wrong.

Niklas had no family, and the only person he had ever really cared about was in bed in the next room, so he didn't have any flare of panic, but there was clearly a problem. Problems he was used to, and was very good at sorting them out.

It just might take a little time, that was all, when really he would far rather be heading back to bed. He dialled Carla's number, wondering if he should tell Meg to order some breakfast. He would just as soon as he made this call.

She could hear him in the lounge, speaking in his own language into his phone. She lay there for ages, twisting her new ring around her finger. Then, as he still spoke on the phone, she realised she wasn't actually terrified at the prospect of telling her parents, and even if this wasn't the most conventional of marriages, even if he had warned her it would end some day, she was completely at peace with what had occurred.

The only thing she was right now, Meg realised, was starving.

'I'm going to ring for breakfast,' she said as he walked back into the room, and then she looked over and frowned, because even though he had been gone ages she was surprised to see that he was dressed.

'I have to return to Brazil.'

'Oh.' She sat up in the bed. 'Now?'

'Now.'

He was not looking at her, Meg realised. What she did not realise was that precisely two seconds from now he was going to break her heart.

'We made a mistake.'

As easily as that he did it.

'Sorry?'

'The party's over.'

'Hold on…' She was completely sideswiped. 'What happened between there and here?' She pointed to the lounge he had come from. 'Who changed your mind?'

'I did.'

'What? Did you suddenly remember you had a fiancée?' Meg shouted. 'Or a girlfriend…?' She was starting to cry. 'Or five kids and a wife…?' It was starting to hit home how little she knew about him.

'There's no wife…' he shrugged '…except you. I will speak with my legal team as soon as I return to Brazil, see if we can get it annulled. But I doubt it…'

He didn't even sit on the bed to tell her it was over,

and she realised what a fool she had been, how easily he had taken her in.

'If it cannot be annulled they will contact you for a divorce. I'll make a one-off settlement,' he said.

'Settlement?'

'My people will sort it. You can fight me for more if you choose, but I strongly suggest that you quickly accept. Of course if you are pregnant…'

He stood there with the sun streaming through the curtains behind him, and all she could see was the dark outline of a man she didn't know.

'It might be a good idea to think about the morning-after pill.'

And then there was a knock on the door and it was a bellboy to take his case.

'I've asked for a late check-out for you, if you want to reschedule your flight. Have breakfast…' he offered, as if this was normal, and then he tipped the bellboy, who left with his luggage.

'I don't understand…' She was turning into some hysterical female, sitting screaming on a bed as her one-night stand walked off.

'This is the type of thing people do in Vegas. We had fun…'

'Fun!' She couldn't believe what she was hearing.

'It's no big deal.'

'But it is for me.'

'It's about time that you grew up, then.'

She had never expected him to be cruel, but she had

no idea what she was dealing with. Niklas could be cruel when necessary, and today it was.

Very necessary.

He could not look at her. She was sitting on the bed in tears, pleading with him, and also, he noted, growing increasingly angry. Her voice rose as she told him that *he* was the one who needed to grow up, that *he* was the one who needed to sort out his life, and her hands were waving. Any minute now he thought she would rise and attack him. He wanted to catch her wrists and kiss the fear away, wanted to feel just for a moment her body writhing in anger and to reassure her—except he had nothing he could reassure her with. He knew how bad things would be shortly, so he had to be cruel to be kind.

'What did you have to marry me for?' she shouted. 'I was clearly already going to sleep with you…'

She was about to lunge at him, Niklas knew. She was kneeling on the bed, still grabbing the sheet around her for now, but in a moment it would be off. Her green eyes were flashing, her teeth bared and with his next words he knew he would end this.

'I told you yesterday.' He went to the bedside and flicked a few foil packets to the floor. 'I don't like condoms.'

He took the clawing to his cheek, stood there as she sprang towards him, then caught and held her naked fury by the arms for a moment. And then he pushed her back on the bed.

And as simply as that he was gone.

* * *

A minute ago the only things on her mind had been breakfast and making love with her new husband.

Now they were talking annulments and settlements.

Or rather they weren't talking.

He was gone.

He had left with cruel words and livid scratches on his cheek and she just lay there, reeling, her anger like a weight that did not propel her, but instead seemed to pin her down to the bed. It was actually an achievement to breathe.

A few minutes later Meg realised she was breathing in through her nose and out through her mouth, as she had done on the plane during take-off. Her own body was rallying to bring her out from the panic she now found herself in. Still she lay there and tried to make sense of something there was no sense to be made of.

He had played her.

Right from the start it had all been just a game to him.

Except this was her life.

Maybe he was right. Maybe she did need to grow up. If a man like Niklas could so easily manipulate her, could have her believing in love at first sight, then maybe she *did* need to sort herself out. She curled into herself for a moment, breathed for a bit, cried for a bit, and then, because she had to, Meg stood.

She didn't have breakfast.

She ordered coffee instead, and gulped on the hot

sweet liquid in the hope that it would warm her, would wean her brain out of its shock. It did not.

She showered, blasting her bruised, tender body with water, for she could not bear to step into the bath where they had kissed and so nearly made love.

Sex, Meg reminded herself. Because as it turned out love at first sight had had nothing to do with it.

She dressed quickly, unable to bear being in a room that smelt of them, and then she looked at the rumpled and bloodstained sheet on the bed where he had taken her and thought she might throw up.

Within an hour she was at the airport.

And just a little while later she was sitting on a plane and trying to work out how to get her life back to where it had been yesterday.

Except her heart felt as bruised and aching as the most intimate parts of her body, and her eyes, swollen from crying, felt the same.

Meg ordered a cool eye mask from the attendant. Before putting it on she slid off her wedding ring and put it on a chain around her neck, trying to fathom what had happened.

She couldn't.

She did her best with make-up in the toilet cubicle just before they came in for landing. She lifted her hair and saw the bruise his mouth had left on her neck and felt a scream building that somehow she had to contain. She covered her eyes with sunglasses and wondered how she would ever get through the next few hours, days, weeks.

'Thank God…' Her mum met her at the baggage carousel. 'The car's waiting. I'll bring you up to speed on the way.' She peered at her daughter. 'Are you okay?'

'Just tired,' Meg answered, and then she looked at her mum and knew she could never, ever tell her, so instead she forced a smile. 'But I'm fine.'

'Good,' said her mum as they grabbed her case and headed for the car. 'How was Vegas?'

CHAPTER SIX

MEG STOOD IN her office, looking out of the window, her fingers, as they so often did, idly turning the ring that still, almost a year later, lived on a chain around her neck.

She wasn't looking forward to tonight, given what she had to tell her parents.

It had nothing to do with Niklas. There had been eleven months of no contact now. Eleven months for Meg to start healing. Yet still she didn't know how to start.

She couldn't bear to think about him, let alone tell anyone what had happened.

And even though she could not bear to think about him, even though it actually hurt to do so, of course all too often Meg did.

It hurt to remember the good bits.

The bad bits almost killed her.

Surprisingly, she couldn't quite work out if she regretted it.

Niklas Dos Santos, for the brief time he had appeared in it, had actually changed her life. Meeting him had

changed her. Hell *did* make you stronger. This was her
life and she must live it, and Meg had decided that she
was finally going to follow her dreams and study to
be a chef. Now she just had to tell her parents. So in a
way tonight did in fact have something to do with him.

The strange thing was, she wanted to tell Niklas
about her decision too—was fighting with herself not
to contact him.

As painful as it was to remember, as brutal as his
departure had been, still a part of her was grateful for
the biggest mistake of her life and, fiddling with his
ring as she so often did, Meg felt tears sting her eyes.

That was the only thing that was different today.

She hadn't cried for him since that morning. Actually, she had, but it had only been the once—the morning a couple of weeks later when she had got her period.
Meg had sunk to her knees and wept on the toilet floor,
not with relief, but because there was nothing left of
them.

Nothing to tell him.

No reason for contact.

Apart from the paperwork it was as over as it could
be.

So for the best part of a year she had completely
avoided it. Had tried not to think of him while finding
it impossible not to.

Every day had her waiting for a thick legal letter
with a Brazilian postmark and yet it had never arrived.

Every night was just a fight not to think.

Sometimes Meg was tempted to look him up on the

internet and find out more about the man who she could not forget—yet she was scared to, scared that even a glimpse of his face on her computer screen would have her picking up the phone to beg.

That was how much she still missed him.

Sometimes she grew angry, and wanted to contact him so that they could initiate the divorce, but that would be just an excuse to ring him. Meg knew she didn't need to speak with him to divorce him, yet she had not even started the simple process, because once she started down that path it would stop being a dream—which sometimes she thought it must have been…

Then her fingers would move to the cool metal of his ring and she'd find out again it was real.

She looked up at the clock and saw that it was time for lunch. Grateful for the chance of some fresh air while she worked out exactly how to tell her parents she was leaving the family business, Meg was tempted to ignore the ringing phone.

She wished she had when she answered it, because some new clients had arrived and were insisting that they be seen immediately.

'Not without an appointment.' Meg shook her head. She was fed up with pushy clients and the continual access she was expected to provide. 'I'm going to lunch.'

'I've told them that you're about to go for lunch.' Helen sounded flustered. 'But they said that they would wait till you get back. They are adamant that they see you today.'

Meg was sick of that word—everyone was *adamant* these days, and because there wasn't much work around her parents insisted more and more that they must jump to potential clients' unreasonable demands.

'Just tell them that they need to book,' Meg said, but as she went to end the call she froze when she heard a certain name.

A name that had her blood running simultaneously hot and cold.

Cold because she had dreaded this day—dreaded their worlds colliding, dreaded the one mistake in her crafted life coming back to haunt her—but at the same time hot for the memories the name Dos Santos triggered.

'He's here?' Meg croaked. 'Niklas is here?'

'No,' Helen answered, and Meg was frustrated at her own disappointment when she heard that it wasn't him. 'It's *regarding* a Mr Dos Santos, apparently, and these people really are insistent…'

'Tell them to give me a moment.'

She needed that moment. Meg really did.

She sank into her chair and poured a drink of water, willed herself to calm down, and then she checked her appearance in the mirror that she kept in her drawer. Her hair was neatly tied back and though her face was a touch pale she looked fairly composed—except Meg could see her own eyes were darting with fear.

There was nothing to fear, Meg told herself. It wasn't trouble that had arrived. It had been almost a year after all. No doubt his legal team were here to get her signature on divorce papers. She closed her eyes and tried to calm herself, but it didn't help because all she could see was herself and Niklas, a tangle of legs and arms on a bed, and the man who had taken her heart with him when he left. Now it really was coming to an end.

She stood as Helen brought her visitors in and sorted out chairs for them. Then Helen offered water or coffee, which all three politely declined, and finally, when Helen had left and the door was closed, Meg addressed them.

'You wanted to see me?'

'First we should introduce ourselves.'

A well-spoken gentleman started things off. He introduced himself and his colleague and then Rosa, a woman whom Meg thought might be around forty, took over. It was terribly difficult to tell her age. She was incredibly elegant, her make-up and hair completely immaculate, her voice as richly accented as Niklas's had been, and it hurt to hear the familiar tone—familiar because it played over and over each night in her dreams. But she tried not to think of that, tried to concentrate on Rosa as she told Meg that they worked at the legal firm Mr Dos Santos used. She went through their qualifications and their business structure, and as she did so Meg felt her own qualifications dissolve beneath her—these were high-end lawyers and clearly here to do business. But Meg still didn't understand why Niklas had felt it necessary to fly three of his most powerful lawyers all the way to Australia, simply to oversee their divorce.

A letter would have sufficed.

'First and foremost,' Rosa started, 'before we go any further, we ask for discretion.'

They were possibly the sweetest words that Meg could hope to hear in this situation.

'Of course' was her response, but that wasn't enough for Rosa.

'We *insist* on your absolute discretion,' Rosa reiterated, and for the first time Meg felt her hackles rise.

'I would need to know what you're here in regard to before I can make an assurance like that.'

'You are married to Niklas Dos Santos?'

'I think we all know that,' Meg said carefully.

'And do you know that your husband is facing serious charges of embezzlement and fraud?'

Ice slid down her spine. Her hackles were definitely up now, and Meg thought for a moment before answering, 'I had no idea.'

'If he is found guilty he will probably never be released.'

Meg ran her tongue over her lips and tasted the wax of the lipstick she had applied earlier. She could feel beads of sweat breaking out on her forehead and felt nauseous at the very thought of a man like Niklas confined and constricted. She felt sick, too, at the thought of what he must have done to face serving life behind bars.

'He is innocent.' The man who had first introduced them spoke then, and Meg couldn't help raising one of her eyebrows, but she made no comment.

Of course his own people would say that he was innocent.

They were his lawyers after all.

She didn't look at Rosa when she spoke. Instead she examined her nails, tried incredibly hard to stop her fingers from reaching for her hair. She did not want to give them any hint that she was nervous.

'We believe that Niklas is being set up.'

What else would they say? Meg thought.

'I really don't see what this has to do with me.' Meg looked in turn at each of the unmoved faces and was impressed by her own voice when she spoke. She possibly sounded like a lawyer, or a woman in control, though of course inside she was not. 'We were married for less than twenty-four hours and then Niklas decided that it was a mistake. Clearly he was right. We hardly knew each other. I had no idea about any of his business affairs. Nothing like that was ever discussed…'

Rosa spoke over her. 'We believe that Niklas is being set up by the head of our firm.'

It was then that Meg started to realise the gravity of the situation. These people were not just defending their client, they were implicating their own principal.

'We have had little access to the case, which in something as big as this is unusual, and without access to the evidence we cannot supply a rigorous defence. For reasons we cannot yet work out, we believe Miguel is intending to misrepresent Niklas. Of course we cannot let our boss know that we suspect him. He is the only one who has access to Niklas while he is being held awaiting a trial date.'

'He's in prison now?'

'He has been for months.'

Meg reached for her water but her glass was empty. Her hands were shaking as she refilled it from the jug. She could not stand the thought of him locked up, could not bear to think of him in prison, did not want those thoughts haunting her. She didn't like the new night-mares these people had brought, and she wanted them gone now.

'It really is appalling, but…' She didn't know how she could help them—didn't know the Brazilian legal system, just didn't know why they were here. 'I don't see how it has anything to do with me. As I said, I'm not involved in his business…' And then she started to panic, because maybe as his wife she had a different involvement with Niklas that they were here to discuss.

'We have made an application of behalf of Niklas for him to exercise his conjugal rights…'

Meg could hear her own pulse pounding in her ears as Rosa continued speaking and she drained her second glass of water. Her throat was still impossibly dry. Her fingers moved to her hair and she twirled the strand around one finger, over and over.

'Niklas is entitled to one phone call a week and a two-hour conjugal visit once every three weeks. He is being brought before the judge in a fortnight for the trial date to be set and we need you to fly there. At your visit with him on Thursday you are to tell him that only when he is in front of the judge he is to fire his law-yer. Before that he is to give no hint. Once he has fired Miguel we will step in for him.'

'No.' Meg shook her head and pulled her finger out of her hair. She was certain of her answer, did not need to think about this for a moment. She just wanted them gone.

'The only way we can get in contact with him is through his wife.'

'I'll phone him.' It was the most she would do. 'You said that he was entitled to a weekly phone call…' And then she shook her head again, because of course the calls would be monitored. 'I can't see him.' She could not. 'We were married for twenty-four hours.'

'Correct me if I am wrong…' Rosa was as tough with the truth as she was direct. 'According to the records we have found you have been married for almost a year.'

'Yes, but we—'

'There has been no divorce?'

'No.'

'And if Niklas was dead and I was here bringing you a cheque would you hand it back and say, *No, we were only married for twenty-four hours?* Would you say, *No, give this to someone else. He had nothing to do with me…?*'

Meg's face was red as she fought for an answer, but she did not know that truth—not that it stopped Rosa.

'And because you have not screamed annulment I am assuming consensual sex occurred.'

Meg felt her face grow redder, because sex had been the only thing they had had between them.

'If you had found yourself pregnant, would you not have contacted him? Would you have told yourself it did not count as you were only married for twenty-four hours? Would you have told your child the same…?'

'You're not being fair.'

'Neither is the system being fair to my client,' Rosa said. 'Your husband will be convicted of a crime he did not commit if you do not get this message to him.'

'So I'm supposed to fly to Brazil and sit in some trailer or cell and pretend that we're…?'

'There will be no pretending—you *will* have sex with him,' Rosa said. 'I don't think you understand what is at stake here, and I don't think you understand the risks to Niklas and his case if it is discovered that we are try-ing to get information in. There will be suspicions if the bed and the bin…'

Thankfully she did not go into further detail, but it was enough to have Meg shake her head.

'I've heard enough, thank you. I will start preparing the paperwork for divorce today.' She stood.

They did not.

'Marrying Niklas was the biggest mistake of my life,' Meg stated. 'I have no intention of revisiting it and I'm certainly not…' She shook her head. 'No. We were a mistake.'

'Niklas never makes mistakes,' Rosa countered. 'That is why we know he is innocent. That is why we have been working behind our own principal's back to ensure justice for him.' She looked to Meg. 'You are his only chance, and whether or not it is pleasant, whether or not you feel it is beneath you, this *must* happen.'

She handed her an envelope and Meg opened it to find an itinerary and airline tickets.

'There is a flight booked for you tomorrow night.'

'I have a life,' Meg flared. 'A job, commitments…'

'A visit has been approved for Thursday. It is the only chance to make contact with him before the pre-trial hearing in two weeks' time. After you have seen him you can go to Hawaii—though we might need you to go back for another visit in three weeks, if things don't go well.'

'No.' How else could she say it? 'I won't do it.'

Rosa remained unmoved. 'You may want this all to go away, but it cannot. Niklas deserves this chance and he will get it. You will see, when you check your bank account, that you are being well compensated for your time.'

'Excuse me?' Meg was furious. 'How dare you? How on earth did you…?' But it wasn't about how they had found out her bank details. It wasn't that that was the problem right now. 'It's not about money…'

'So it's the morality of it, then?' Rosa questioned. 'You're too precious to sleep with your own husband even it means he has to spend the rest of his life behind bars?'

Rosa made it sound so simple.

'For the biggest mistake of your life, you chose rather well, did you not?' Rosa sneered. 'You are being paid to sleep with Niklas—it's hardly a hardship.'

Meg met her eyes and was positive that he and Rosa had slept together. They both stared for a moment, lost in their own private thoughts. Then Rosa stood, a curl on her lip, and another sassy Brazilian gave her opinion of Meg as she upended her life.

'You need to get over yourself.'

CHAPTER SEVEN

WHEN THEY HAD GONE, Meg did what she had spent a year avoiding.

She looked up the man she had married and found out just how powerful he was—or had been before he had been charged. She understood now that the Niklas Dos Santos she was reading about would be less than impressed to find himself in business class. And then she read about the shock his arrest had caused. Niklas might have a reputation in business as being ruthless, but he had always seemed honest—which was apparently why it had made it so easy for him to con some high-flying people into parting with millions. They had believed the lies that had been told to them. His business peers' trust in him had made them gullible, and despite Rosa's and her colleagues' protestations of his innocence, for Meg the articles cast doubt.

She knew, after all, how effortlessly he had read *her*, how easily he had played *her*. Meg had seen another side to Niklas and it wasn't one she liked.

And yet, as Rosa had pointed out, he was her husband, and she was apparently his one hope of receiving a fair trial.

And then Meg clicked on images and wished she had not.

The first one she saw was of him handcuffed and being bundled into a police car.

There were many more of Niklas, but they were not of the man she knew. The suit was on and the tie was beautifully knotted, the hair was as she remembered, but not in one single image did she see him smiling or laughing. Not one single picture captured the Niklas she had so briefly known.

And then she found another image—one that proved the most painful of all to see.

His arrogant face was scowling, there were three scratches on his cheek that her nails had left there, and a deep bruise on his neck that her mouth had made. Meg read the headline: *Dos Santos vira outra mulher!* Meg clicked for a translation. She wanted to know if he had returned that morning and been arrested—wanted to know if that was the reason he had been so cruel to her. Had he known he was about to be arrested and ended it to protect her? She waited for the translation to confirm it, held her breath as it appeared: *Dos Santos upsets another woman!*

And even in prison, even locked up and a world away, somehow he broke her heart again.

There was a knock at the door. Her mother didn't wait for an answer, just opened it and came in. 'Helen said you had visitors?'

'I did.'

'Who were they?'

'Friends.'

She saw her mum purse her lips and knew she would not leave until she found out who her friends were and what they wanted. Even without the arrival of her visitors Meg remembered she had been due for a difficult conversation with her parents today, and now seemed like a good time to get it over with.

'Can you get Dad…?' Meg gave her mum a pale smile. 'I need to speak to you both.'

It didn't go well.

'After all we've done for you' was the running theme, and the words Meg had expected to hear when she told them that she had chosen not to continue working in the family firm.

She didn't mention Niklas. It was enough for them to take in without giving them the added bonus of a son-in-law! And one in prison too.

It should have been a far harder conversation to have, yet she felt as if all her emotions and fears were reserved for the decision that was still to come, and Meg sat through the difficult conversation with her parents pale and upset, but somehow detached.

'Why would you want to be a chef?' Her mother simply didn't get it—didn't get that her daughter could possibly want something that had not been chosen for her. 'You're a lawyer, for God's sake, and you want to go and work in some kitchen—?'

'I don't know exactly what I want to do,' Meg broke in. 'I don't even know if I'll be accepted…'

'Then why would you give it all up?'

And she didn't know how to answer—didn't know how to tell them that she didn't feel as if she was actually giving up *anything*, that she was instead taking back her life.

Just not yet.

She told them she was taking a holiday, though she still wasn't sure that she was, but even without Niklas looming large in her thoughts taking a few weeks off while her parents calmed down seemed sensible.

'And then I'll come back and work for a couple of months,' Meg said. 'I'm not going to just up and leave…'

But according to her parents she already had.

Later, as she sat on the balcony of her small flat and looked at the stunning view, Meg thought about her day. What should have been a difficult conversation with her parents, what should have her sitting at home racked with guilt and wondering if she'd handled things right, barely entered her thoughts now. Instead she focused on the more pressing problem looming ahead.

Quietly she sat and examined the three things she had that proved her relationship with Niklas had actually existed.

She took the ring from the chain around her neck and remembered the certainty she had felt when he had slipped it on—even though he had told her it could never be for ever, somehow she had felt it was right.

And then she picked up the marriage certificate she

had retrieved from her bedside table and examined the dark scrawl of his signature. *Niklas Dos Santos*. She saw the full stop at the end of his name and could even hear the sound his pen had made as he'd dotted the document.

Finalised it.

And then she examined the third thing, the most painful thing—a heart that even eleven months on was still exquisitely tender.

There had been no one since, no thought of another man since that time. She felt dizzy as she peered into her feelings, scared as to what she might find. The truth was there waiting and she hadn't wanted to see it. It hurt too much to admit it.

She loved him.

Or rather she had.

Absolutely she had, or she would never have married him. Meg knew that deep down. And, whether or not he had wanted it, still that love had existed. Her very brief marriage with him had for Meg been the real thing.

And, as Rosa had pointed out, they *were* still married.

It was getting cool, so Meg went inside and read the itinerary Rosa had handed her. Then she looked up the prison he was being held at and could not believe that he was even there, let alone that on Thursday she might be too.

Would be.

Meg slid the ring back on her finger.

A difficult decision, but somehow easily made. Yes, Rosa was right. In legal terms he was still her husband.

But it wasn't in legal terms only that she made her choice. There was a part of herself that she must soon sort out, must work out how to get over, but for now at least, in every sense, Niklas was still her husband.

Though her hotel and flights had been arranged, any problems had to be dealt with by the travel agent, Rosa had told her. Meg must not, under any circumstance, make contact with them. She must not be linked to them in any way—not just to protect them, or even Niklas, they had warned her, but to protect herself.

And she registered the danger but tried not to dwell on it, just tried to deal with a life that had changed all over again.

There was another row with her parents—a huge one this time. They had no comprehension as to why their usually sensible daughter might suddenly up and take off to Brazil.

'Brazil!' Her mother had just gaped. 'Why the hell do you want to go to Brazil?'

They didn't come to the airport to say goodbye. Still, there was one teeny positive to the whole situation: Meg barely noticed the plane taking off. Her thoughts were too taken up with the fact that she was on her way to see Niklas.

And she barely noticed it a second time, when she transferred at Santiago and knew she was on the last leg of her journey to see him. Shortly after take-off the stewards stood, and after a little while she was offered a drink.

'Tonic water…' Meg said, and then changed her mind and added gin.

'Off on holiday?'

She turned to her friendly fellow passenger, an elderly lady who had cousins in São Paulo, she told Meg.

'Yes…' Meg said. 'Sort of.'

'Visiting family?'

'My husband.' How strange it felt to say it, but she was, after all, wearing his ring, and her documents were in her bag, and she might have to say the same thing at Customs, so maybe she'd better start practising.

'Brazil first and then three weeks in Hawaii…'

'Lovely.' The old lady smiled and Meg returned it. Just as Niklas had that first day, she wished her neighbour would just keep quiet.

She could hardly tell her the real purpose for her visit!

Instead she ordered another gin.

It didn't help.

She cried as they descended over São Paulo—she had never seen anything like it. Stretched below her was a sea of city, endless miles of buildings and skyscrapers. The population of this city alone was almost equivalent to the entire population of Australia, and never had Meg felt more small and lost.

The final approach was terrifying—more so because of all he had told her about it, more so now that she could see just how closely the cars and the planes and the city co-existed, more so because she was actually here.

Bizarrely, her eyes searched for him after she'd cleared Customs—a stupid flare of hope that this was a strange joke, that he was testing her, that he might be waiting with flowers and a kiss. Perhaps she might once more feel the thorns press into her skin as he teased her about the lengths she'd go to for just a couple of hours with him.

It wasn't a joke, though. It wasn't a game. There was no one here to greet her.

Meg exited the airport and tried to hire a taxi, but she had never seen a taxi queue like this one. She was exhausted and overwhelmed as once again Niklas pushed her out of her comfort zone.

The driver's music was loud, his windows were down, and he drove her through darkening streets into Jardins. Everything was loud there too. The city pulsed with life. There were food stalls on the streets—unfamiliar scents came in through the windows of the car whenever they stopped at traffic lights—and it was more city than she could deal with. Which made sense, Meg thought with a pale smile. After all it was the city Niklas was from.

All Meg wanted to do was to get to her room.

Dishevelled, confused, *tired*, after they pulled up at a very tall hotel Meg paid the taxi driver. The second she stepped inside she knew she was back in his world.

Modern, cosmopolitan, with staff exquisite and beautiful.

It was a relief to get to her room and look out of the

window at the bewildering streets below, to fathom that she was actually here—that tomorrow she would be taking another taxi to visit Niklas in prison.

Meg scanned the confusing horizon, wondered as to his direction, wondered if he had any inkling at all that she was even here.

Wondered all night how she could stand to face him tomorrow.

'Hi, Mum…' She rang not because they had insisted she did—they were hardly talking, after all—she rang because, despite their problems, Meg loved her parents and wanted the sound of normality tonight.

'How's Brazil?' Her mother's voice was terse, but at least she spoke.

'Amazing,' Meg said. 'Though I haven't seen much of it…'

'Have you booked any trips?'

'Not yet,' Meg said, and was quiet for a moment. She didn't like lying, especially to her parents, but she found herself doing it at every turn. Tomorrow she would be ringing her parents again to tell them that she had changed her mind about Brazil and was going to spend the rest of her vacation in Hawaii—how would they react to that?

More than anything Meg just wanted tomorrow over with, so that she could lie on a beach and hopefully heal once and for all. She hadn't dared risk putting her divorce application in her luggage in case it caused questions at Customs, but the second she landed home it would be posted.

Her heart couldn't take any more of him.

'How's Dad?'

'Worried,' her mum said, and Meg felt her heart sink—because she hated that they were worried about her. 'It's going to cost an arm and a leg to hire a new lawyer...'

Meg knew her mum didn't mean to hurt her, but unintentionally she had. The business was always the biggest thing on their minds.

'I've told you that I'll work for a couple of months when I get back. You don't have to rush into anything. And you don't need a full-time lawyer; you can contract out. We'll go through it all properly when I get back.'

'You *are* coming back?'

And Meg gave a small unseen smile, because maybe it wasn't just about the business. As difficult as they could be at times, they did want what they thought was best for her, and they did love her—that much Meg knew.

'Of course I am. I'm just taking a few weeks to sort out my head—I'll be back before you know it.'

It was impossible to sleep. She was dreading tomorrow and seeing him again, dreading the impact of seeing him face to face. It was emotionally draining just thinking about him, let alone seeing him.

Let alone having sex with him.

If Meg slept, she didn't sleep much, and she was up long before her alarm call. She ordered breakfast, but her stomach was doing somersaults and she could hardly manage to hold down a small piece of bread and grilled cheese.

The coffee she was more grateful for.

Had she not loved him, she doubted she could do this.

But had she not loved him she would not have married him in the first place and wouldn't be in this mess.

Except she remembered his cruel words from that morning long ago and knew that love had no place in this.

She gave up on breakfast and lay in the bath, tried to prepare herself for what lay ahead, but had no idea how. As she picked up a razor and shaved her legs she did not know if her actions were for his pleasure or for her pride. It was the same with the body oil she rubbed in. She wore simple flesh-coloured underwear and an olive green shift dress with flat leather sandals. Her hand was shaking too much to bother with make-up so she gave in.

Rosa had given her the name of a good car company to use, rather than getting a taxi, and the desk rang to tell her that her driver was here. As she left the room she glanced around and wondered how she would feel when she returned. This time tomorrow she would be on a plane on her way to Hawaii. This time tomorrow it would be done—for despite what Rosa had said she would not be returning to him.

Once was enough.

Twice might kill her.

So she looked at her room and tried not to think too much about what had to happen before she returned.

They drove through the most diverse of cities, passed the Court of Justice, where in two weeks Niklas would be, and in daylight Meg saw more of this stunning city. There was beauty and wealth, and such poverty too. She thought of Niklas growing up on the streets, and of how much he had made of himself only to fall. She didn't know enough to believe in his innocence. She might be a fool for love, but she wasn't a blind fool. Still, he deserved a fair trial.

Meg had never known such fear in her life as they approached the jail. The sight of the watchtower, the sounds when she entered, the shame of the examination… Her papers were examined and her photograph taken and she was told her rights—or rather her husband's rights. She could return in three weeks; she could ring him once a week at a designated time and speak for ten minutes. And although Meg took the paper with the telephone number on it, she knew that she would never use it.

Then a female guard examined her for contraband and Meg closed her eyes, thinking she would spit at her if she ever faced Rosa again, before being allowed to pull her knickers back up. Maybe she did need to get over herself, but as she was led through to an area where two guards chatted she heard the Dos Santos name said a few times, and even if Meg didn't understand precisely what they were saying she got their lewd drift. As she stood waiting for Niklas to arrive Meg knew that, yes, she might have to get over herself—but right about now she was completely over *him*.

CHAPTER EIGHT

THE SLOT ON the door opened and lunch was delivered. Niklas ate beans and rice. It was tepid and bland and there were no herbs to pick out, but he was hungry and cleared his plate in silence.

His cellmate did the same.

It was how they both survived.

He refused to let the constant noise and shouts from other inmates rile him. He made no comment or complaint about the bland food and the filth. From the first day he had arrived here, apart from the odd necessary word, he had been silent, had conformed to the system though some of the guards had tried to goad him.

As he had entered the jail they had told him of the cellmate they had for him, of the beatings he could expect. They'd told the rich boy just how bad things would be in there for him as he'd removed his suit and shoes and then his watch and jewellry before they searched him and then hosed him.

Niklas had said nothing.

He had been hosed many times before.

There was no mirror to look in, so after his hair was

shaved he'd just run a hand over his head. He wore the rough denim without real thought. He had worn harsher clothes and been filthier and hungrier than this on many occasion.

Niklas was streetwise. He had grown up in the toughest place and survived it. He had come from nothing and he'd returned to nothing—as he had always silently feared that he would. This anonymous, brutal world was one that he belonged in, and the one he truly deserved. Perhaps this was actually his home, Niklas had realised—not ten thousand feet in the air, swigging champagne as caviar popped in his mouth; not considering a home in the mountains and a family to take care of. He had been a fool to glimpse it, a fool to let down his guard, for those things were not his to know.

Assets frozen, friends and colleagues doubting him… The eventual snap of cuffs on his wrists had provided temporary relief as Niklas went back to the harsh world he had known one day would reclaim him. He'd returned to another system and navigated it seemingly with ease. But the temporary relief had soon faded and a sense of injustice had started to creep in. His head felt as if it would explode at times, and his body was so wired that he was sure he could rip the bars from the cell window with his bare hands or catch bullets with his teeth—but then, as he had long ago taught himself to, he simply turned those thoughts off.

Not for a second did he show his anger, and rarely did he speak.

His cellmate was one the most feared men in the

prison. He ran the place and had contacts both inside and out. The guards had thought it would be like two bulls put in the same paddock. The motto of São Paulo was *I am not led. I lead.* So they had put the rich boy who led the business world in with the man who led the inmates and had waited for sobs from Dos Santos. But Niklas had held Fernando's eyes and nodded when he had been placed in his cell. He had said good evening and got no answer, and from that point on Niklas had said nothing more to him. He had ignored his cellmate—as suited Fernando, as suited him—and over the months the tension had dissipated. The silence between the two inmates was now amicable; both men respected the other's privacy, in a friendship of no words.

Niklas finished his lunch. He would exercise soon.

They had not been let out to the yard in over a week, so in a moment he would use the floor to exercise. He paced himself, sticking to routines to hold onto his mind. For while he slotted in with the system, while he followed the prison rules, more and more he was starting to reject them. Inside a slow anger had long been building and it was one that must not explode, because he wanted to be here when his trial date was set—did not want solitary till then.

He lay on his bunk and tried not to build up too much hope that he might be bailed in a fortnight, when he appeared for the pre-trial hearing. Miguel had told him that he thought bail was unlikely—there were too many high-profile people involved who did not want him to have freedom.

'But there is no one involved,' Niklas had pointed out at their last meeting. 'Because I did not do anything. That is what you are supposed to prove.'

'And we will,' Miguel said.

'Where's Rosa?' Niklas had asked to see Rosa at this visit. He liked her straight talking, wanted to hear her take on things, but yet again it was Miguel who had come to meet with him.

'She…' Miguel looked uncomfortable. 'She wants to see you,' he said. 'I asked her to come in, but…'

'But what?'

'Silvio,' Miguel said. 'He does not want her in here with you.'

And Niklas got that.

Rosa's husband, Silvio, had complained about Rosa working for him. Niklas and Rosa had once been an item for a few weeks, just before she had met Silvio, and though there was nothing between them now, her working for Niklas still caused a few problems.

As he lay there replaying conversations, because that was all he was able to do in this place, Niklas conceded that Silvio was right not to want Rosa to visit him here.

Nothing would happen between them, but it was not just Rosa's sharp insight he wanted. The place stank of testosterone, of confined angry male, and Rosa was open enough to understand that his eyes would roam. She would let them, and he knew that she would dress well for him.

He tried not to think of Meg—did not want even an

image of her in this place—but of course it was impossible not to think of her.

As his mind started to drift he turned those thoughts off and hauled them back to his pre-trial hearing. His frustration at the lack of progress was building—his frustration at everything was nearing breaking point.

He climbed down from his bunk and started doing sit-ups, counting in his head. And then he changed to push-ups, and for those he did not bother to count. He would just work till his body ached. But anger was still building. He wanted to be on the outside—not just for freedom but because there he could control things, and he could control nothing here except his small routines. So he kept on doing his sit-ups and as a guard came to the door Niklas carried on, ignoring the jeering, just kept on with his workout.

'Lucky man, Dos Santos.'

He did not miss a beat, just continued his exercise.

'Who did you pay?'

Still Niklas did not answer.

'You have a beautiful wife.'

Only then did he pause, just for a second, mid-push-up, before carrying on. The guard didn't know what he was talking about. No one knew of Meg—they were winding him up, messing with his head, and he chose not to respond.

'She's here waiting to see you.'

And then the slot in the door opened and he was told to get up. There was no choice now but to do as he was told. So Niklas stood, met Fernando's eyes for just a second, which was rare. The change in routine was notable for both of them.

Niklas put his hands through the slot and handcuffs were applied, then he pulled his cuffed wrists back as the cell door was opened. He walked along the corridor and down metal steps, heard the jeers and taunts and crude remarks as he walked past. There were a couple of shoves from the guard but Niklas did not react, just kept on walking while trying to work things out.

Miguel must have arranged a hooker, finally pulled a few strings.

Thank God.

Maybe now his mind would hold till the trial date.

Not that he showed any emotion as they walked. He'd learnt that many years ago.

Show weakness and you lose—he'd learnt that at eight.

He had walked through the new orphanage he'd been sent to—he had been on his third orphanage by then—and this one was by far the worst. Still, there was good news, he had been told—his new family were waiting to meet him. A beautiful family, the worker had told him. They were rich, well fed and well dressed and had everything they wanted in the world except children. More than anything they wanted a son and had chosen Niklas.

His heart had leapt in hope. He'd hated the orphanage, a rough home for boys where the staff were often cruel, and he had been grinning and excited as the door had been pushed open and he had prepared himself to meet his new family.

How the workers waiting for him in there had laughed at his tears—how they had jeered him, enjoying their little joke long into the night. How could he have been so bold as to think that a family might want him?

It was the very last time that Niklas had cried.

His last display of true emotion.

Now he kept it all inside.

He would not give the prison guards the same pleasure. Whatever their plan, he would not give them the satisfaction of reading his face.

But then he saw her.

It had not properly entered his head that it might actually be Meg.

He had not allowed it to.

She did not belong in here. That was his first thought as he saw her dressed in a linin shift dress. Her hair burned gold and copper, the colour of the sun at night through his cell window, and then he saw the anxiety in her eyes turn to horror as she took in the shaved head and the rough clothing. A lash of shame tore through him that he should be seen by her like this, and his expression slipped for just a second. He stared ahead as his cuffs were removed, and though he remained silent his mind raced. To the left was Andros, the guard he trusted the least, and he thought again how Meg did not belong here. He wanted to know who the hell had arranged this, who had approved this visit, for even though he was confined and locked up he still had a system in place, and he had told Miguel that everything was to be run by him.

He could feel Andros watching as she walked towards him, heard the fear and anxiety in her voice as she spoke.

'I've missed you so much.'

She was playing a part. Niklas got that. But as her lips met his cheek it did not matter. Her touch was the first reprieve for his senses in months. Her skin on his cheek was so soft that the contact actually shocked him. He wanted to know the hows and whys of her visit here, wanted to know exactly what was going on, yet his first instinct was not to kiss her, but to protect her— and that meant that he too must play a part, for Andros was watching.

It was a kiss for others, and his mind tried to keep it at that—except her breath tasted of the outside and he drank her in. The feel of her in his arms allowed temporary escape and it was Meg who pulled back.

Meg stood with her cheeks burning red, tears of shame and hurt and anger in her eyes, and her lips pressed closed as one guard said something that made the other laugh. Then a door opened and they walked into a small, simply furnished room. The guard shouted something to them, and whatever language you spoke it was crude, before closing the door behind them. Meg stood and then realised that she couldn't stand for very much longer, so she sat on a chair for a moment, honestly shaken.

It wasn't just shock at the sight of him—seeing Niklas with his hair cropped almost as short as the dark stubble on his chin, dressed in rough prison denim. Even like this he was still the most beautiful man she had ever seen. It was not just the shock that she had again tasted his mouth, felt his skin against hers, relighting all those memories from their one night together. It was everything: the whole journey here, the poverty in the streets she had driven through, the sight of the prison as she had approached, the watchtower and the guns on the guards and the shame of the strip-search. Surely all of those things had severed any feelings she had for him?

But, no, for then she'd had to deal with the impact of seeing him again, of tasting him. For a moment she just sat there and wondered how, after all she had been through, she could still hear her heart hammer in relief to be back at his side. She wanted to be over him—had to be for sanity's sake—so she tried not to look at him, just drank from the glass of water he offered her.

He stood and watched her and saw her shock, saw what just a little while in this place had done to her, and thought again how she did not belong here.

'Why?' He knelt down beside her and spoke in a rough whisper. 'Why would you come here?'

She didn't answer him—Meg couldn't open her mouth to speak.

'Why?' he demanded, and then she looked at him and he was reminded of the last time he had seen her. Because even with the absence of her bared teeth he could feel her anger, could see her green eyes flash with suppressed rage and hear the spit of her words when finally she answered him.

'You're *entitled* to me, apparently.'

Niklas remembered the first time he had met her. She had been anxious, but happy, and he knew that it was he who had reduced her to this. He could see the pain and the disgust in her eyes as she looked at the man she had married, as she saw the nothing he really was.

And he did not want her charity.

'Thanks, but no thanks.'

He moved to the door, preparing to call for the guards. He might regret it later, but he did not want a minute more in this room.

As he moved to go he heard her voice.

'Niklas.' She halted him. This was not about what had happened between them, not about scoring points, she was here for one reason only. 'Your people told me...' He turned to face her. 'I'm to tell you...'

He silenced her by pressing his finger to his lips and nodded to the door. He trusted no one—never had in his life, and wasn't about to start in here. But then he closed his eyes for a second, for that was wrong. Because for a while he had trusted *her*, and did still. He came over to her, knelt down again and moved his head to her mouth, so she could quietly tell him the little she knew.

'Miguel is working against you. You are to ask for a change of representation at your trial...'

His head pulled back and she watched as he took in the news. Quietly she told him the little she knew. His face was grey and his eyes shone black. He swallowed as if tasting bile and she heard his rapid angry breathing. His whisper was harsh when it came.

'*No.*'

It had to be a lie, because if his own lawyer was working against him he was here for life.

She *had* to be lying.

'How?' he demanded. 'Why?'

'I don't know anything more than that,' Meg said. 'It's all I've been told.'

'When?' he insisted, his voice an angry whisper. 'When were you told?'

And she told him about the visit—how on Monday morning Rosa and her colleagues had arrived at her place of work. He thought of her momentarily in Sydney, getting on with her life without him, and now here she was in Brazil.

'They should never have sent you…' He was livid. 'It's too dangerous…'

'It's fine…'

It was so *not* fine.

'Niklas…' She told him *all* they had told her—that they had to have sex, about the bed and the bin, and that the guards could not know she was here for any other reason.

He saw her face burn in shame, and she saw his disgust at what he had put her through.

'It's fine, Niklas,' she whispered. 'I know what I'm doing…' She could feel his fury; it was there in the room with them.

'You should not be here.'

'It's my decision.'

'Then it's the wrong one.'

'I'm very good at making those around you, it would seem. Anyway,' she whispered harshly, 'you don't have to worry—you're paying me well…'

'How much?'

She told him.

And he knew then the gravity of his situation, understood just how serious this was—because he had no money any more. Everything had been frozen. He thought of his legal team paying her with money of their own and it tempered the bitterness that sometimes consumed him a little. Then he looked at the woman he might even have loved and tasted bitterness one again, for he hated what the world had done to him.

'So you're not here out of the goodness of your heart?'

'You've already had that part,' Meg said. 'So can we just get it over with?'

She looked over to the bed and he saw the swallowing in her throat, knew that she was drenched in fear. He looked to the door again, knowing there was a guard outside, one he did not trust, who must never get so much as a hint as to the real reason she was here.

Paid to be here, Niklas reminded himself.

He trusted no one again.

He stood and ripped the sheet from the bed, and she sat there as he twisted it in his hands before throwing it back. She heard his anger as he took the bedhead in angry hands and rocked the bed against the wall. He felt his anger building as he slammed the bed faster and faster. He had never paid for sex in his life. Yes, he'd have been grateful for a hooker, but he'd never taken Meg as one and his head was pounding as the bed hit the wall again and again. He did not know who to believe any more, and as the bed slammed faster he shouted out.

Meg sobbed as he shouted, but it did nothing to dissipate the fury still building, and then he picked up the condoms by the bedside and went to the small wash area and got to work to make sure evidence of their coupling was in place. Meg sat there, listening and crying. She understood his anger but she did not understand her own self, for even here, amidst this filth and shame, she wanted him. So badly she wanted to be with the man she had so sorely missed. Not just the sex, but the comfort he somehow gave.

'Niklas…' She walked into the washroom and ignored him when he told her, less than politely, to go away. His back was to her. She moved to his side and saw his fury, saw his hand working fast. He repeated his demand for her to leave him, and when it was clear that she didn't understand just how much he meant the words he told her in French and then Spanish.

'How many ways do you need to hear it…?'

How deep was his shame to be seen like this, to be reduced to this? His back had been to Meg, for he could not face her, yet she'd slipped into the space between him and the wall and her mouth was on his. One of her hands joined his now.

'Leave me.'

'No.' She stroked him too.

'Leave me,' he said as her other hand slipped off her panties.

'No.'

And she put her hands around his neck and pressed herself against him, tried to kiss him. He spat her out.

'You don't know the fire you are playing with.'

'I want to, though.'

She wanted every piece of him—wanted a little more of what she could never fully have. Because a man like Niklas could only ever be on loan to her. She had flown to him not because she had to, not for the money, and not for the morality of doing the right thing by her husband. Purely because of him, and not once did his anger scare her.

Not once, as rough hands pulled her dress up, did she fear him.

He lifted her up and onto him and positioned her, pulling her roughly down to him. The most basic sex was their only release and she wrapped her legs tight around him, locked her arms around his neck. His kiss was violent now, and she felt the clash of their teeth and tongues and the rapid angry stabs of him. The rough feel of denim on her thighs was nothing compared to the roughness deep inside, and her back was hard against the wall. Meg could feel his anger, it blasted deep inside her, and it let Meg be angry too—angry at so many things: that she was here, that she still wanted him, even that this man still moved her so.

Her moans and shouts that he blocked with his mouth

shocked Meg even more—scared her, almost—but she was not scared of him as he pulled her down on him, as she felt the bruise of his fingers in her hips. She could feel her orgasm building rapidly, as if she had waited eleven months just to come to him, as if her body had been waiting for him to set it free.

There was a flash of confusion for Niklas too, for her cries and the grip of intimate muscles, the arch of her back and the spasm of her thighs, could never be faked. He had thought this was charity, a paid act at best, a sympathy screw at worst, but she was craving him again, the way she once had, and as he shot into her he remembered all the good again—the way they had been. He never cried, but he was as close to it now as he had ever been. They were both drenched in brief release and escape and his kisses turned softer now, to bring her back to him. Then he heard the drizzle of the tap and his eyes opened to his surroundings, to the reality they faced. There were no more kisses to be had and he lifted her off.

Stood her down.

But she would not lose him to his pride and she carried on kissing him, opened his shirt and put her palms to his chest. He felt as if her hands seared him, for there had been no contact, no touch of another on his skin for many months, and he loathed the exposure, the prying of her hands. It was just sex he wanted, not her, but her hands were still moving, exploring the defined muscles. Her fingers were a pleasure and he did not want her to be here—yet he wanted her for every second that they had.

There would be hours later for thinking, for working out what to do about Miguel. For now he wanted every minute he had left with her.

He took her to the bed and undressed her, took his clothes off too, and she looked at all the changes to his body. He was thinner, but more muscled, and his face wasn't the one she had turned to on the plane—it was closed and angry, and yet she had felt his pain back there, felt him slip into affection, and for a small moment had glimpsed the man she had once met.

'Is that why you ended things?' She looked over to him as he joined her on the bed, but he just lay and looked up at the ceiling. 'Did you find out the trouble you were in?'

'I didn't know then.' It would be easier for her if he lied.

'So what happened that morning to change things?'

'I spoke to my people at work, realised how much I had on…'

'I don't believe you.'

'Believe in your fairytale if you want.' Niklas shrugged.

'Are you going to tell me to grow up again?' she asked. 'Because I grew up a long time ago—long before you met me. I've realised that I wasn't being weak staying in my job—I simply won't ride roughshod over the people I care about. And I don't believe that you would either and,' she finished, 'I *do* believe that you cared about me.'

'Believe what you want to.'

'I will,' Meg said. 'And I care about you.'

'It makes no difference to me.'

She had been paid plenty to be here with him so he should turn and start things. She had told him what she had came to say and the clock was counting down. He should use every minute wisely. They should not bother with talking—there were more basic things to be getting on with. Except this was Meg, and she didn't know how to separate the two.

'How are you dealing with being in here? How—?' she started, but he soon interrupted.

'I was right the first time.' He turned to look at her face—the face he had first seen on a plane. 'You talk too much. And I don't want to talk about me.' But before he moved to kiss her he allowed himself the luxury of just one question. 'Are you still working for your parents?'

'I resigned…' Meg said. 'I'm trying to choose my course at the moment…'

'Good,' Niklas said. He should push her hand down to where he was hardening again, but first there was something else he wanted to know. 'Are you okay?'

'Of course.'

'Are you happy?'

'Working on it.'

'Do your parents know you are here?'

'They know that I am in Brazil…' he saw tears pool in her eyes '…they don't know I have a husband that I'm visiting in prison.'

'You need to get away from here,' Niklas said. 'As soon as this visit is over.'

'I fly to Hawaii tomorrow.'

'Okay.' Tomorrow should be okay, he told himself, but he wasn't sure. 'Maybe change it to tonight...'

'I fly out at six a.m.'

He saw her grimace at the thought, remembered the first time they had met and the conversation they had had.

'How was your landing?' And for the first time he smiled. He didn't care how much they'd paid her, that she'd flown into Congonhas was enough for him to know that this had nothing to do with money.

'It wasn't so bad...' she attempted, and then told him the truth. 'I was petrified. I thought I was going to throw up. Although,' she added, 'that might have been the gin!'

He laughed, and so did she. He hadn't laughed for almost a year, but this afternoon he did. She kicked him and they fought for a bit—a nice fight, a friendly fight—and he took her back to when they'd been lovers so easily, far, far too easily. But, given this was the last time she would be here, she let him. No one could kiss like he did. It was quite simply perfect, and the feel of him hard in her hands was perfect too.

This time he would be gentle, Niklas decided, worried that he had been too rough before. He didn't just kiss her mouth, he kissed her everywhere—her hair and her ears and down to her neck, breathing in her scent. He kissed down to her waist and then further, to where he wanted to be. He had been too rough, for she was hot and swollen, but Meg lay there and felt his soft kiss and was lost to it.

When he couldn't hold on any more he reached for the condom that was a requirement in here. Her hands reached for it too, and he let her put it on, but before she did she kissed him there, and he closed his eyes as she did so. Two hours could never be enough for all they wanted to do. She slid it on. He should roll her over and take her, but he let her climb on top of him, because if he looked up to her hair and her body for a little while he could forget where he was.

And she looked down as she moved on him and knew exactly why she was here. She loved him. Still. Her real fear at coming here had nothing to do with the flight or the prison or the danger, it was *him*—because she'd known all along that this was the only way she would ever be over him.

She should be grilling him about his involvement in the charges, insisting she find out, or just lying on her back martyred as he took her, ready to get the hell out once he'd finished. Instead she'd told him she cared about him. Instead she was riding him, and his hands were busy elsewhere, roaming her body. He was watching her. She was moaning, and he told her to hush, for he would not give the guards the turn-on of the sounds that she made. He put his hand over her mouth and she licked it, bit it, and he pushed his fingers into her mouth. He was coming, and so was she, and when the moment finally came she folded on top of him, buried his face with her hair, and he felt the silent scream inside her as she clutched him tightly over and over till it ended.

That was when she told him she loved him.

'You don't know me,' he said.

'I want to, though.'

'Divorce me,' he said, still inside her, and pulled her close. 'Send the papers to Rosa and I'll sign them.'

'I don't want to.'

'You do.'

She didn't.

'I can see you again in three weeks...' She was drunk on him. 'I can come to the trial.'

'You are to *leave*!'

'I can ring you on Wednesday each week...'

He was scared now as to what he'd unleashed. Scared not of her passion, but that she might stay.

'No.'

'I can. I'm allowed one phone call a week.'

He looked up at her and all he knew was that she was not coming back here. With his own lawyer working against him he was probably done. Here was where he would always be and he would not do this to her. Even with new lawyers, trials took for ever in Brazil. Even with the best legal team he would be here for years at best. He lifted her off him and swore in three languages when he saw the condom was shredded. 'Get the morning-after pill and when I speak with my new lawyers I will have them file for divorce...'

'No...'

'You are to go to Hawaii.'

'Niklas—'

The guards were knocking at the door. Their time was up. He stood and threw her clothes at her, telling her to dress quickly for he did not want them getting one single glimpse of her. She continued to argue with him as he picked up her bra and clipped it on her, before lifting each leg into her panties, followed by her dress, and even as he zipped it up still she argued.

'We're finished,' he told her.

And he wasted time telling her that they *had* to be over when he should have told her how dangerous this was, just how little he knew about what was going on, and that he was scared for her life. But the guards were here now and he could not say.

He gave her a brief kiss, his eyes urging her. 'Have a safe flight.'

CHAPTER NINE

SHE DIDN'T WANT to lie on a beach in Hawaii.

There could be no healing from him.

She wanted to be close to him, wanted to be there for his trial hearing at least. She hoped for a miracle.

He would not want her there. Meg knew that.

But he was her husband, and she could at least be here in the city for him. Could watch it on the news, could be close even if he didn't know it.

And then she could visit him again before she left. She did not want a divorce from him now, and she wanted one more visit to argue her case.

She was probably going insane, Meg realised as she cancelled Hawaii and stayed on in Brazil, but that was how he made her feel.

She ventured out onto the busy streets and toured the amazing city. The sights, the smells, the food, the noise—there was everything to meet her moods.

And without Niklas she might never have seen any of this—might never have visited the Pinacoteca, a stunning art museum, nor seen the sculptured garden beside it.

At first Meg did guided tours with lots of other tourists around her, but gradually she tuned in to the energy of the place, to the smiles and the thumbs-up from the locals and ventured out more alone. She was glad to be here—glad for everything she got to see, to hear, to feel. Every little thing. She could have lived her whole life and never tasted *pamonah*, and there were vendors selling them everywhere—from the streets, from cars, ringing triangles to alert they were here. The first time Meg had bought one and had sunk her teeth into the new taste of mashed and boiled corn she had been unable to finish it. But the next day she had been back, drawn by the strange sweet taste—inadvertently she'd bought savoury, and found that was the one she liked best.

There were so many things to learn.

So badly she wanted to visit the mountains, to take a trip to the rainforests Niklas had told her about, yet it felt too painful to visit the mountains without him.

She didn't dare ring him that first week. Instead when six p.m. on Wednesday neared she sat in a restaurant the concierge had told her was famed for its seafood and ordered *feijoada*. Maybe it wasn't the same restaurant Niklas had told her about, but she felt as if angels were feeding her soul and that she was right to be there.

As the days passed she fell more and more in love with the city—the contrasts of it, the feel of it and the sound of it. The people were the most beautiful and elegant she had seen, yet the poverty was confrontational. It was a world that changed at every turn and she loved the anonymity of being somewhere so huge, loved being lost in it, and for two weeks she was.

As instructed, she did not contact Rosa. The only people she spoke to were her parents, and she gave Niklas no indication that she was there until the night before his trial date.

His face was on the TV screen, a reporter was already outside the court, and Meg had worked out that *amanhã* meant tomorrow. Until *amanhã* she simply could not wait. She just had to hear his voice. She had fallen in love with a man who was in prison and she should be signing paperwork, should be happily divorced, should be grateful for the chance to resume her life—but instead she sat in her hotel room, staring at the phone…

Confused was all she was without him. The passion and love she felt for him only made real sense when he was near her and she had an overwhelming desire to talk to him. She counted down the moments until she could make that call.

He knew that she would call.

Niklas could feel it.

Andros came and got him from his cell and he sat by the phone at the allotted time. The need for her to be safe overrode any desire to hear her voice.

His teeth gritted when he heard the phone ring, and he wondered if he should let it remain unanswered, but he needed her to get the message—to get out of his life and leave him the hell alone.

And then he heard her voice and realised just how much he craved it, closed his eyes in unexpected relief just to hear the sound of her.

'I told you not to ring.'

'I just wanted to wish you good luck for tomorrow.'

'It is just to arrange a trial date…' He did not trust the phones. He did not trust himself. For now he wanted her to visit him again. He wanted her living in a house in the mountains right behind the prison and wanted her to ring him every Wednesday, to come in to see him every three weeks. What scared him the most was that she might do it. 'You did not need to ring for that. It will all be over in ten minutes.'

She understood the need to be careful. 'Even so, I hope they give you a date soon.'

'What are you doing now?'

'Talking to you.'

'Is everything okay?'

She knew what he was referring to—had seen his face when he'd removed the condom.

'It's fine.'

'Did you go to a *pharmacia*?'

He closed his eyes when she didn't answer, thought again of her in a home in the mountains, but this time he pictured her with his baby at her side and selfish hope glimmered.

'How's Hawaii?'

He heard her pause, heard that her voice was a little too high as she answered him. 'You know…' She attempted. 'Nice.'

'I *don't* know,' Niklas said, and it was not about what he wanted, it was not about him, it was about keeping her safe. His words were harsh now. 'I've never been and I want a postcard,' he said. 'I want you, *tonight*, to write me a postcard from Hawaii.'

He was telling her what to do and she knew it.

'Niklas,' she attempted, 'I still have some holidays left. I thought maybe next week…'

'You want to be paid again?'

'Niklas, please—' She hated that he'd mentioned money. 'I just want to see you.'

'You've already earned your keep…go spend your money on holiday.'

'Niklas…I know you don't mean that.'

'*What* do you know?' His voice was black. 'We were married for one day; we screwed an awful lot. You know nothing about me.'

'I know that you care. I know when you saw me—'

'Care?' he sneered down the phone. 'The only way I can get sex in here is if they bring in my wife—that's it. I am sick of conversations, and you seem to want just as many of those as you give of the other.'

'Niklas, please…'

But he would not let her speak. He had to get her away from here. Did she not get that she could be in danger? He had no idea what was happening on the outside, had no idea what was going on, and he wanted her safely away—had to make sure she was safe.

So again he drowned her with words.

'Meg, if you want to come back and suck me, then do. But just so long as you know you mean nothing to me.'

He slammed down the phone—not in fury but in fear. He put his hands through the door and felt the cool of the cuffs. His mind was racing. Since her visit, since getting the information that Miguel was working against him, his mind had been spinning, trying to work out what the hell was going on, trying to figure things out. But now he had a head full of *her*, and he had more to be concerned with than that she was still here in Brazil.

He needed to speak with Rosa—had to work out what the hell was going on.

As he was walked back to his cell his face was expressionless, but his mind was pounding like a jackhammer and he cursed under his breath in Portuguese as Andros made some reference to his wife, about his nice little family, and asked how scum from the streets had managed that. Then Andros pushed him up the stairs and Niklas cursed again, but in French this time.

'Watch it, Dos Santos…' Andros told him, sensing his prisoner's rising anger and slamming him up against the wall.

The move was not meant to overpower him, Niklas realised, simply to provoke him, because Dos Santos was an orphan's name. Niklas went to swear again, in Spanish, but his brain was working quickly, far more quickly than his mouth, and in that second he knew what was happening.

Dos Santos meant something different in Spanish.
And it was a Spanish nun who had named him.
Dos Santos in Spanish meant two saints.
He had a twin.

In that very second it was as if a bomb had exploded
in his brain and he worked it all out. He knew instantly
how he had got to be here. Knew that his double was out
there and had been working with Miguel against him.
And with a lurch of fear that was violent to his soul he
knew that Meg was in serious danger.

Niklas said nothing when Andros jeered again, just
stood silent against the wall as Andros spoke filth about
his wife. He stood still and refused to react as another
guard came over. A decent guard this time, because
there were plenty of them around.

'Trouble?' the guard asked.

'No trouble,' Niklas said, because he did not want to
go to solitary tonight. He really needed to get to his cell.

He stood compliant as his cuffs were removed and
went quietly into his cell. There he met the eyes of Fernando, and for the first time since his arrival he spoke
with the other man.

'I need your help,' Niklas said, for he had worked
out what was happening and urgent help was required.
'I need you to make contact on the outside.'

CHAPTER TEN

ANOTHER NIGHT CRYING over Niklas Dos Santos and Meg swore it would be the last.

Part of her could almost convince herself that he was just trying to get her to leave, that that was the reason behind his cruel words, but the more sensible part of Meg soon talked herself round. Her sensible side reminded her that this was a man she knew nothing about—a man who had caused her nothing but heartache and trouble since the day that they had met.

Hawaii sounded pretty good to Meg right now.

A week lying on the beach concentrating on nothing but how best to forget him.

It was well after lunchtime now, and Meg was *still* waiting for the travel agent to return her call. When she did, Meg would ask to be booked onto the earliest flight that could be arranged, and she packed her suitcase in preparation. Very deliberately she did not turn on the vast television to see how his trial was going, or to catch a glimpse of him on the news, because one glimpse of Niklas and she was lost to him—that much she knew.

She wanted her divorce now, wanted to be the hell

away from him, would not waste even one more single minute on him.

But as she packed up her toiletries Meg threw tampons into her make-up bag and suddenly realised that it might be rather more complicated than that.

She looked at the unopened packet, an Australian brand because she hadn't bought any since she had arrived here, and tried to remember when she'd last had a period.

She tried to remember the days in Australia before her life had been changed so dramatically by the visit from Niklas's lawyers. No, she hadn't had her period for a while.

There should be the reassurance that they'd used condoms, but the last one hadn't held.

Could she be pregnant?

Would she tell him if she was?

Meg looked in the mirror and decided that, no, she could not deny him that. Even if his life was to be spent on the inside, he would have to know the truth, and it wasn't the kind of news she could reveal in a letter— maybe she would have to visit him again.

Maybe not.

A letter was probably more than he deserved.

But first she had to know for sure.

She was probably overreacting, Meg told herself as she headed out of her hotel room and to the elevators. Worrying too much, she tried to convince herself as she headed onto the street. With all that she'd been through these past weeks it was no wonder that her period was late.

The streets were busy, as always—the cars jammed together, horns blaring, and sirens blazing as police tried to thread their way through the impossible madness that was downtown São Paulo. She found a *pharmacia* and inside it was the same as the world over, with numerous pregnancy testing kits sitting on the shelves. Meg didn't need to speak the language to know she was making the right purchase.

What was different from Australia, though, was that instead of being pounced on by an assistant the second she entered the store, here Meg was pretty much ignored. Even when she tried to pay the pharmacist and his checkout assistants were all taking an impromptu break and watching the television, and Meg could feel mounting impatience. She really had to know now if she was pregnant. Had to make the decision of facing Niklas and telling him while she was still here.

Finally someone came over to serve her, still talking to her colleagues, and Meg froze when she heard one of them shout the name Dos Santos. She felt sweat bead on her forehead as she paid, because despite herself—despite all this—she wanted to turn the television on, wanted to know how he was.

She almost ran back to the hotel, terrified of her feelings for him, that even a mention of his name could reduce her to this petrified state.

It was blissfully cool and quiet in her room—such a contrast to the chaos down below. She fought not to turn on the television, picked up the remote and hurled it, tried not to look where it landed. The light on the phone said she had a new message. She hoped it was the travel agent and played it back, but heard her mum's voice instead. Meg honestly didn't know how she could ever begin tell her parents all that had happened. She had always hoped she would never have to, but if this test proved positive…

She could feel the tears starting again but refused to give in to them—just bit them back and headed to the bathroom, put her purchase in its bag on the bench, ready to find out. Then there was a knock on the door and Meg assumed it was the cleaner. She didn't want her coming in now. She wanted privacy for this at least.

So she went to tell them. She didn't even look through the peephole, just opened the door, and what was left of the sensible part of her mind struggled to remain calm because standing at her door was Niklas. She froze for a moment, unable to respond to seeing him in such an ordinary setting. She wanted to sob at him, to rage at him, to ask him how on earth he was here—except she just stood there.

'It's okay…' He stepped in. 'I know it must be a shock to see me here.'

'I don't understand…'

'The judge understood,' he said. 'Didn't you see it all on the news?'

'I haven't been watching it.'

'That is good.' He gave her a smile. 'I get to tell you the good news myself.'

'I don't want to hear it.' She was so very angry with him, and now finally she could tell him. 'I haven't been watching it because I'm sick of this, Niklas. I'm sick of how you make me feel at times. I can't do this any more.'

'You're upset.'

'Do you blame me?' She looked at him. She could smell his cologne—the same cologne he had worn the day they had met. He was dressed in a stunning suit now, just as beautiful as the day they had met, just as cruel as the day he had ended things between them, but she wanted to know. 'You've been let off?'

'I've been bailed while they take some time to review new evidence.'

'Well, after the way you spoke to me last night I need some time for a review too,' Meg answered. She refused just to go back to loving him. He had hurt her too much. And she could not find out if she was pregnant while he was near. She needed to do that part alone.

'Come here…' He moved to pull her into his arms.

'Just leave.' It took everything she had to shake her head. 'Just go, Niklas. I'm doing as you told me. I'm going to Hawaii…'

'You're upset.'

'Why do you keep saying that? Of *course* I'm upset!' she flared. 'Did you think I wouldn't be? How the hell do you justify speaking to me like that?'

'Meg…'

He walked over and she did *not* want him to take her in his arms, did not want him to melt her all over again.

'I say stupid things at times. You know that…'

'Stupid things?' There were so many other ways she could describe his words. 'It was more than stupid, it was foul…' She would not be fobbed off. 'Why?' she demanded. 'Why did you speak to me like that?'

'I've said I'm sorry.'

'No, you haven't, and you're clearly not as sorry as I was to hear it.' She went to open the door, to tell him to get out of here, but he stopped her and wrapped his arms around her shoulders. Meg just stood there, tears rising, remembering the love they had made and all the ways he made her feel. But she could not go back there. 'Get out!' She pushed him off her. 'I mean it, Niklas…'

'Meg…' His mouth was on her cheek and she pulled her head away. His hands were in her hair but she brushed them off.

'Please,' she said, 'can you just leave me? I'll call you later. I'll—'

His phone rang then, and it annoyed her that he took the call. Yes, of course he was busy, she knew that, and maybe she should be flattered that he had come straight to her, but it annoyed her that in the middle of a row he could just stop and take a call. It made her even more angry, and she was tired of making excuses for him. She wanted him gone and she told him so when he ended his call.

'You are cross…' He smiled at her. 'You look beautiful when you are cross…'

He aimed his phone at her and she blinked at the flash. 'What the hell are you doing?'

'I've missed things like this. I want to capture everything...'

'I just you want you to leave.'

But he simply refused to listen. 'Let's go for a walk.'

'A walk?'

The last thing she wanted was a walk. She wanted him to leave. She looked at his lips and not even his beautiful mouth could silence her doubts now. She just wanted him gone.

'A walk to clear the air...' Niklas said.

'No.' She shook her head. 'I'm waiting for the travel agent to ring me back.'

'She'll call back if you're not here.' He shrugged. 'Come,' he said. 'I want to taste the fresh air. I want to feel the rain...'

She looked out of the window. Yes, it was raining, and she realised that he wouldn't have felt the rain in a long time. She was relieved that he wasn't all over her, trying to kiss her back to confusion as he so often did, but she didn't feel she knew him at all.

'Meg, after all we have been through will you at least come for a walk with me?'

'You hurt me last night.'

'I apologise.' His black eyes met hers. 'Meg, I truly apologise. We can start again, without all this hanging over us...'

But she was stronger than she'd thought she could be.

She looked into his eyes and quite simply no longer wanted him—didn't want to get back on the roller-coaster ride beside him. It was then that she made a decision that was surprisingly easy; she looked at the man who had broken her heart and knew that he would break it all over again. She simply refused to let him.

It was over.

Whatever the pregnancy test told her, Meg knew it was far better that she find out well away from him. She would fly to Hawaii today, search for the clarity he so easily clouded and make better decisions alone.

'Come…' he said. 'I want to taste my freedom.'

Maybe it would be easier to tell him that they were finished while they were walking. Maybe it would prove easier out there. Because she knew his kisses made her weak. So she nodded and she went to get her jacket, to comb her hair.

'Don't worry about that…' he said. 'Your hair is fine…'

Niklas was right. Her hair really didn't matter right now—it was her heart Meg had to worry about. They rode down in the lift together and Meg looked at him more closely. She hated her swollen eyes. Even more she hated that she had let him cause them.

They headed out through the foyer and into the street and she felt the warm rain that was so regular here. His hand reached for her, but she pulled hers back, refusing to give this man any more chances. He'd already used his last one with his filthy words to her the previous night and now his pathetic attempt at an apology.

'I'm ending it, Niklas.' He kept on walking. 'I'm going to file for divorce.'

'We'll go to a bar and talk about it.'

'There's nothing to discuss.' Meg stopped—which wasn't the most sensible thing to do on such a busy street.

There were moans from a few pedestrians and he took her hand and they kept walking. She really was sure that she was making the right choice, because she did not know him, and he did not know her, and a walk would not clear the air. Only his kiss could possibly have given them a chance, because sex was the only thing they had going for them. Maybe she was mad for thinking it, but shouldn't that be the way a man celebrated his freedom? If he loved her, if he wanted her, wouldn't the first thing he wanted be taking her to bed, not out for a walk?

'There's a bar up here that I know,' Niklas said. 'It's not far—just a couple of blocks away…'

'I don't want to go to a bar…'

'The street is too noisy. Come on, we can talk properly there.'

'I don't want to talk.'

Meg was starting to panic now, and she didn't really know why. His hand was too tight on her wrist, and he was walking her faster, and she had the most appalling thought then that he hadn't been bailed at all. There was an urgency in the steps he was taking. She looked over to him and his head was down, and it dawned on Meg that maybe he had escaped from jail. She recalled the screams of the police cars and bikes. They were screaming in the streets even louder now. She remembered too the pharmacy staff all huddled around the television, saying his name. Maybe it was because Niklas Dos Santos had escaped. Still he walked her ever faster.

'Niklas…'

She could hear the thud of music as they turned into a side street, could hear the clang of triangles and the smell of *pamonah*. There were so many people around; surely she was safe. She pulled her hand from his and stopped walking, but he turned and put a hand to her cheek. She shivered, but not with pleasure. There was something dark and menacing in his eyes. She was a fool to have got involved with this man, a fool to follow her heart, for look where it had led her—to a dingy side street in Brazil with a man she was now terrified of.

'Come,' he said. 'We will talk about where our relationship is going later. Right now I want to celebrate my freedom and I want you to celebrate it with me.' His hand was tight on her arm. 'You wouldn't deny me that?'

'I do,' she said. 'And I want you to let me go.'

'Don't spoil this day for me, Meg—it's been a hell of a long year for both of us. Now we can drink *cachaca*, unwind, dance. Later we can talk, but first…'

He lowered his head to kiss her, but it was too late for that and she moved her head back from his, suddenly confused. Because Niklas didn't dance. It was one of the few things that she *did* know about him—or had that been just another of his lies? Suddenly she was scared, and with real reason now.

Meg turned to go but he pulled her roughly back and

pushed her against the wall. Then he opened his jacket and she saw that he had a gun.

'Try to run and it will be the last thing you do…'

'Niklas…' she begged, and when Meg heard her own voice she heard the way she sounded when she pleaded for her life. She was trying to show him that she wasn't panicked, trying to reason with a man she absolutely didn't know, trying to get away. 'Why do you need me?' she said. 'If you've escaped…'

People were turning to look at them, maybe alerted by the panic in her voice even though she wasn't screaming. Or perhaps it was that if he had just escaped then his picture would be everywhere, being flashed over the news. Perhaps that was why he lowered his face to her.

'Why do you need me with you?'

'Because you're my last chance.'

And his mouth came down on hers.

She could hear a car pulling up beside them and Meg knew this was *her* last chance to get away. She knew instinctively that when the car doors opened she would be shoved in, that that was why he had taken the call—to arrange all this. Terrified, Meg did the only thing she could think of to survive. She bit hard on his lip with all she had—took that beautiful mouth and bit it as hard as she could. In the second when he recoiled, as he cursed her in Portuguese and reached for his gun, Meg ran—ran as she never had—ran and ran faster as she heard gunshots.

She kept running till rough arms grabbed her and pulled her down, slamming her to the ground. She felt her cheek hit the pavement and the skin leave her leg as she rose to run again, heard another volley of gunshots and looked behind her. She saw police cars screeching up. Whoever had shielded her from him had gone. Then she stared at the body on the ground and it was the only thing she could see.

'Niklas!' she screamed, and tried to run back to him, for she hated the man but it was agony to see him lying dead and riddled with bullets.

She could not stop screaming. Not even when other arms wrapped around her and her face was buried in rough prison denim and she smelt him again—not his cologne, but the scent of Niklas, her drug of choice, a scent that till now had been missing. She heard him saying over and over that she was safe, that he was here, that now it would all be okay, but she still did not believe it was him—until he lifted her face and she met his eyes, saw that the beautiful mouth had not been bitten and knew that somehow it was him.

That she was safe.

It was just her heart that was in danger again.

CHAPTER ELEVEN

MEG DID NOT get to see him again. Instead she was taken to a police station. There were press clamouring outside as she was taken in to give a statement, and while she was waiting for a translator Rosa arrived.

Meg gave her statement as best she could. They kept talking about twins, and although she had already worked that out when she was being held in Niklas's arms, her brain was so scrambled and confused that even with a translator she could hardly understand the questions, let alone answer them.

Every time she closed her eyes she saw Niklas—or rather the man she had thought was Niklas—lying there dead. The raw grief and panic, the *knowing* in that moment that she would never see him again, that the man she had fallen so heavily in love with was now dead, was not a memory or a feeling she could simply erase.

Fortunately Rosa had told the police she would return with Meg tomorrow, but that for now she needed peace, and thankfully they accepted that.

'We will return at ten tomorrow,' Rosa told her.

They stepped out into the foyer and she saw him

standing there, still dressed in prison denim. He took her in his arms and she knew then that she had to be careful, because the one thing she had worked out before this embrace was that she wasn't strong around him—that she'd only been able to break up with Niklas when it hadn't actually been him.

'I'm still angry with you.'

'I thought you might be.' He kissed her bruised cheek and didn't let her go as he spoke. 'We can row in bed.'

Which sounded a lot more like the Niklas she knew. He held her tight and pressed his face into her hair and she could feel his ragged breathing. For a moment she thought he was crying, but he just held her a moment longer and spoke into her hair.

'The press are outside so we have to go out the back. I am taking you far away from here. I need to stay in the city, but—'

'*Não*,' Rosa said.

Meg heard the word *amanhã* again, and realised Rosa was telling him that Meg must return to the police tomorrow.

'I'll ring Carla, then.'

With his arm still around Meg he took Rosa's phone and started to dial the number. Whilst he was occupied Meg stepped out of his embrace, and a little later, when they climbed into a waiting car, she sat on the back seat far away from him, needing some time alone.

Even though they went out the back way the press still got some photos and it was horrible. They scrambled over to the car and blocked their exit, but the driver shook them off. Niklas told her it might be like this for a while, and that he was taking her to a hotel. He saw the start in her eyes.

'We're not going back *there*—I've asked Carla to book us into a different one.'

Us.

So easily he assumed.

They entered the new hotel the back way too, and were ushered straight to a waiting lift where Niklas pressed a high number. They stood in silence till Meg broke it.

'Did you get off?'

'I've been released on bail.'

'So why are you still wearing…?' And then she shook her head, because she was simply too tired for explanations right now.

They stepped out of the lift and there was hotel security in the corridor—'For the press,' Niklas said, but it felt a lot like prison to her, and no doubt to him too, but he said nothing, just swiped open a door, leading her into a plush suite.

Meg stood there for a moment, only knowing for certain the city she was in and that Niklas was alive. She remembered her feeling at seeing him dead, and the fear that had gripped her in the moments before, and started shaking.

'I wanted to take you away from the city tonight, but because we need to go back to the police station tomorrow it is better that we stay here. I've had your stuff packed up, but it is in the other place…you'll have to make do for now…'

It was hardly 'make do'; there was food and soon she would take a bath, and then she sat and had a strong coffee. Niklas offered her *cachaca*—the same drink she had been offered a little while ago—and she shuddered as she remembered. He opened the fridge and opened a bottle of champagne instead.

Which seemed a strange choice and was a drink she hadn't had it in almost a year.

Not since their wedding.

It was the drink they had shared on the day they had met, and he poured her a glass now, kissing her forehead as they chinked glasses and celebrated that somehow they were both here. It was a muted celebration, and there was still so much to be said, but Niklas dealt with the essentials first.

'You need to ring your parents.'

'I don't know what to say to them,' Meg admitted. She felt like crying just at the thought of them, was dreading the conversation that had to be had—and how much worse it was going to be now, after not telling them anything.

'Tell them the truth,' Niklas said. 'A bit diluted.' He nudged her. 'You need to speak to them now in case they hear anything on the news, or the consulate might contact them. Have they tried to ring *you*?'

'I didn't even bring my phone with me,' Meg said.

'It will be at the other hotel,' Niklas said. 'For now

they just need to know you are safe. I will speak to them if it gets too much.'

'No.' She shook her head—not at phoning them, but at the thought of him talking to them. She knew how badly things were going to go. 'I'll do it...'

'Now.'

'I still don't really know what happened.' But she took the phone, because he was right. They needed to know she was safe. 'Leave me,' she said, and was glad that he didn't argue.

Niklas headed into the bedroom and she dialled the number, then looked out of the window to a very beautiful, but very complicated city. She held her breath when she heard the very normal sound of her mum.

'How's Brazil?' Ruth asked. 'Or is it Hawaii this week?'

'Still Brazil,' Meg said, and because Ruth was her mum straight away she knew.

'What's wrong?'

It was the most difficult of conversations. First she had to tell her how Vegas had been and how she had married a man she had only just met. She diluted the story a lot, of course—an awful lot—but she still had to tell them how, the morning after their wedding, Niklas had upset her, how she had been trying to psyche herself up to divorce him.

And her mum kept interrupting her with questions that her father was shouting—questions that weren't really relevant because they still didn't know half of the story. So she told them she was here to visit him, that he had been arrested a while ago, but was innocent of all charges. Her mother was shouting and sobbing now, and her dad was demanding the phone, and they were simply getting nowhere, and then Niklas was back and she was so glad to hand the phone over to him.

She found out for certain then just how brilliant he was, how clever he was with people, for somehow he calmed her father down.

'My intention when I married your daughter was to take proper care of her. I was on my way to tell you the same when I found out that I was being investigated.'

He said a few more things, and she could hear the shouts receding as he calmly spoke his truth.

'I was deliberately nasty to her in the hope she would divorce me—of course she was confused, of course she was ashamed and did not feel that she could tell you. I wanted to keep her away from the trouble that was coming—in that I failed, and I apologise.'

They didn't need to know all the details, but he told them some pertinent ones, because as soon as they hung up they would be racing to find out the news for themselves. So he told them about the shooting, but he was brief and matter-of-fact and reiterated that Meg was safe. He told them that they could ring any time with more questions, no matter the time of day or night, and that he would do his best to answer them. Then he handed the phone back to Meg.

'You're safe,' her mum said.

'I am.'

'We need to talk…'

'We will.'

When she hung up the phone she looked at him. 'You could have told me the truth that day.' She was angry that he hadn't.

'What? Walk back in and tell you that I am being investigated for fraud and embezzlement? That the man you met twenty-four hours ago is facing thirty-five years to life in jail…?' He looked at her. 'What would you have said?'

'I might have suggested you didn't go back till you found out the case against you…' she flared. 'I might not be the best one in the world, but I *am* a lawyer…'

'My own lawyer was telling me to get straight back.' He kicked himself then, because had he confided in her—had he been able to tell her—he might not have raced back, might have found out some more information before taking a first-class flight to hell.

'I had to return to face it,' Niklas said. 'Would you have stood by me?'

'You never gave me that chance.'

'Because that was what I was most afraid of.' He was kneeling beside her and she could hear him breathing. 'You never asked if I did it.'

'No.'

'Even when you visited…even when you rang…'

'No, I didn't.'

'Did you believe I was innocent?'

'I hoped that you were.'

'There was too much love for common sense,' Niklas said.

She sat there for ages and was glad when he left her alone and headed to the bathroom. She heard his sigh of relief as he slipped into the bath water and thought about his words—because while she had hoped he was innocent, it hadn't changed her feelings towards him and that scared her. After a little while she wandered in to him.

'I am so sorry.' He looked at her. 'For everything I have put you and your family through.'

'It wasn't your fault.'

'No,' he said. 'But still, I have scared you, and nearly cost you your life…'

And then he looked at her and asked the question the police had asked her earlier.

'Did he do anything to you?'

'Apart from hold a gun at me…' she knew what he meant '…no.'

She watched him close his eyes in relief and knew then that he *had* cried.

'He wanted to walk,' Meg said. 'That was when I started to worry.' She gave him a pale smile. 'Not quite the Niklas I know.' And then there wasn't a pale smile. 'I'm still cross about what you said on the phone.'

'I wanted you to leave,' he said. 'I wanted you to be so angry, so upset, that you got on the next plane you could…'

'I nearly did.'

'Do you want me tell you what happened?'

She wanted to hear it now, and he held his hand out to her. Yes, he assumed she would join him—and for now he was right. Her clothes and her body were filthy, and she wanted to feel clean again, to hear what had happened, and she wanted to hear it as she lay beside him. So she took off her clothes and slid into the water, with her back to his chest, resting on him, and he held her close and washed all her bruises and slowly he told her.

'There was bedlam in court,' Niklas said as he washed her gently. 'The place erupted when I asked for a new lawyer, and then Rosa presented the evidence implicating Miguel. He was arrested immediately, but of course I had to go back to prison…I knew they were never going to release me just like that. I told them that you were in danger, but they would not listen, and then, as they were taking me back, *he* made contact with Carla, asking for money. He said that he had my wife and texted a photo. The police only believed me then that I had a twin.'

She frowned and looked up to him. 'You *knew* you had a twin?'

'I guessed that I did last night, after I spoke to you.'

'How?'

'It made sense. I knew I was innocent.'

'But how did you work it out?'

'I swear in several languages…' She smiled, because that *was* what he did. 'I was angry after speaking to you—worried that you would not leave—and I swore in Portuguese. The guard warned me to be careful, he called me Dos Santos and I heard the derision in his voice, in his tone. I thought he was referring to me having no one, and I swore again, and then he said something about you. I went to curse again, but in Spanish…'

He was soaping her arms and his mouth was at her neck—not kissing, just breathing.

'The first nun who looked after me, till I was three, she taught me Spanish…'

Still Meg frowned.

'Dos Santos means something different in Spanish,' Niklas explained. 'In Portuguese it means "from the saints", in Spanish it means…'

'Two.' She turned and looked to him. '"Two saints".'

'There were two of us… That is why the Spanish nun chose our surname. It made sense. Apparently in the month before I was arrested I was having meals and meetings with very powerful people, persuading them to invest.…'

'My God!'

'He and Miguel were rorting every contact I have made. A couple of months before it happened I thought I had lost my phone, but of course they had it and were diverting numbers. Both of them knew that they didn't have long before I found out, or the banks or the police did, so they were busy getting a lot of money based on my reputation. My lawyer had every reason to want me to be convicted and spend life in jail—every reason not to tell me about the evidence that would convict me. Because as soon as I saw it, I would know the truth. It was not me.'

She felt him breathe in deeply.

'I can see how people were fooled. When I saw him

lying there I felt as if I was looking at me.' He elaborated on his feelings no more than that, and told her the little he knew. 'His name was Emilios Dos Santos. The police said he had lived on the streets all his life but had no criminal record—just a few warnings for begging. I guess he was tired of having nothing. When he found out Miguel had been arrested he must have seen you as his last chance to get money from me...'

'How did he know I was here? How did he know what hotel...?'

'The prison guards, maybe.' He shrugged. 'Miguel would have been paying someone to keep an eye on me. You would have had to give your address for the prison visitors' list.'

She knew then how dangerous it had been not to listen to him, not to leave when he had told her to.

'I should have gone to Hawaii.'

'Yes,' he said, 'you should have.' But then he thought for a moment. Because without her here, without his fear that she was in danger, he might not have worked things out.

'It doesn't matter anyway,' Meg said. 'It's over now.' He didn't answer, and she turned and saw the exhaustion and agony still in his face. She could have kicked herself, for at the end of the day he had lost his twin, and Meg knew that despite all that had happened it had to hurt.

'Maybe he did want to talk to you when he found out he had a twin—perhaps Miguel dissuaded him, saw the chance to make some serious money and told him it was the only way.'

'I don't want to speak about that.'

So quickly he locked her out.

And then the phone rang—trust the hotel bathroom to have one.

Niklas answered it.

'It's your father.' He handed it to Meg, and she spoke with her parents. Neither shouted this time, just asked more questions—and, more than that, they told her how much they loved her, and how badly they wanted her to come home as quickly as possible.

She was glad she was facing away from him, but glad to be leaning on him as they spoke and he held her. Later her father asked to speak with him, and he held out his wet hand for the phone and listened to what her father was saying.

'We have to give some more statements to the police, so Meg needs to be here for a few more days,' he said, 'but I will take her somewhere quiet.' He listened for a moment and then spoke again. 'She's tired now, but I will see what she wants to do in the morning, once she has spoken to the police.'

And then he said goodbye, and she frowned because they almost sounded a little bit friendly.

'He's coming around to me.'

It was, as Meg knew only too well, terribly easy to do so.

'They want you home, Meg.'

'I know that, but I want to be here with you.'

'Well, they need to see you,' Niklas said. 'They need to see for themselves that you are not hurt.'

'I know that…' She wanted him to say he'd come with her, wanted him to say he would never let her go, but he didn't. She wanted more from him, wanted to be fully in his life, but still he would not let her in.

She turned her head and looked at him—looked at this man who'd told her from the start that they'd never last.

'This doesn't change things, does it?'

He didn't answer.

She surprised herself by not crying.

'You'll never find another love like this.' She meant it—and not in an arrogant way—because even if he didn't accept it, even if he refused to believe it, whether he wanted it or not, this really *was* love.

'I told you on the first day that it would not be for ever.'

'We didn't love each other as much then.'

'I have never said that I love you.'

'You did earlier.'

'I said there was too much love for common sense,' Niklas said. 'Too much love for you to think straight…'

'I don't believe you.'

'Believe in fairytales if you want to.' He said it much more nicely than last time, but the message was the same. 'Meg, I told you I could never settle in one place, that I could not commit to one person for ever. I *told* you that.'

He had.

'And I told you that I don't do love.'

He had.

'You said you wanted this for as long as it lasted.'

His voice was the gentlest and kindest she had heard it.

'In a few days, once all the questioning is over, you need to go home to your family.'

And even if she'd promised herself not to cry she did a bit, and he caught her tear with his thumb before lowering his head and tasting it. She could hear the clock ticking, knew that every kiss they shared now might be their last, that soon it would be a kiss goodbye.

'It could last…' She pulled her head away and opened her mouth to argue, but he spoke over her.

'I don't want to wait for the rows and the disenchantment to kick in. I don't want to do that to us because what we have now is so good. But, no, it cannot last…'

Which was why she'd accept his kisses—which was why, tonight, she would shut out the fact that this was temporary. Because tonight maybe she just needed to escape, and maybe he did too.

And even if he wouldn't admit it, even if he chose not to share his feelings, Niklas felt as if he'd just stepped out of hell's inferno into heaven as his mouth met hers.

Her mouth was bruised, but very gently he kissed it. Her cheek was hurting and her legs were grazed where she'd fallen. She knew she could never keep him, that for now guilt and fear would drive his kisses, and that later this man she didn't really know would return to a life she had never really been in. This wasn't love they were making. It was *now*.

Over and over she told herself that.

She thought he'd make love to her in the water, but he took her wet to the bed and dried her with a towel, every inch of her, and then he kissed her bruises, up her legs, and he kissed her *there* till she was crying and moaning in frustration. His hand was over her mouth again, because there were still guards outside, but she wanted him—wanted all of him. Then he slipped inside her, and it was incredibly slow, a savour in each thrust, but the words she needed were not in her ears. She bit down as she came, and gave him her body while trying to claim back a heart this man didn't want but already had.

CHAPTER TWELVE

MEG WOKE IN the night, crying and scared, and Niklas held her tightly before he made love to her again.

And he would have had her again in the morning—was pulling her across the mattress when the phone rang to tell them that Rosa was on her way up.

'Later!' he said, and kissed her. 'Or just really, really quickly now?'

She looked into black eyes that smiled down at her and simply could not read him—couldn't be his sex toy any more.

'Later,' Meg said, and climbed out of bed.

She let Rosa in. She had brought fresh clothes for both of them. Surprisingly, she gave Meg a hug and told her that she would accompany them to the police station.

'I am very sorry for the way I spoke to you,' Rosa said.

'What way?' Niklas checked.

She looked at Niklas. 'I gave her a hard time.'

'You weren't the only one,' Meg said, and then went purple when Rosa laughed. God, was that the only place minds went in Brazil? 'What I meant,' she said in her best cross voice, 'was that I do understand why you said what you did.'

'I am grateful,' Niklas said to Rosa. 'To all three of you, but especially to you. I will repay you just as soon as I get my assets back.'

'Hopefully it won't be long now,' Rosa said, and then smiled as she scolded, 'But did you *have* to drink the most expensive champagne in the fridge? I just paid your room bill.'

'*You* paid?' Meg blinked. She wasn't talking about the champagne. 'That was your money?' Meg had assumed it came from Niklas's funds, but of course she now realised that while he was being investigated they would all be frozen.

'I put up my home,' Rosa said. 'I believed in him.'

'You're the richest one of us in the room,' Niklas said to Meg, and even Rosa laughed.

'I'll buy you all a coffee on the way to the station.' Meg smiled, but it was strained. She headed to the bathroom to get changed and thought about Rosa's belief in Niklas. It was clear to Meg that in the past Rosa and Niklas had slept together, but it wasn't that fact that riled her. It was the friendship they had that ate at her—a friendship that would not waver, one that would always last.

It was the longevity that riled her.

Meg opened the bag of fresh clothes and noticed that Rosa had chosen well for her. There was a skirt that was soft and long and would cover the grazes on her legs, a thin blouse and some gorgeous, albeit completely see-through, underwear. Meg inspected the underwear more closely and saw that there wasn't an awful lot of it, and when she pulled the knickers on she was silently mortified to realise that there was a hole in the middle—which was intentional. They were the most outrageous things she'd ever worn, but she could hardly complain to Rosa.

There were sandals too, because hers had broken yesterday.

She dressed and brushed her teeth, and combed her hair, and looked in the mirror and examined her solemn face. She should be happy and celebrating, except she couldn't quite rise to it. Memories of yesterday were still too raw, and she didn't understand how Niklas and Rosa could be smiling and chatting.

Didn't understand how Niklas could just turn his pain off.

But she had to learn how to, because soon she had to go home.

Had to.

She could not hang around and watch as his guilt for what he had put her through and the attraction he clearly had for her faded. She couldn't bear the thought of his boredom setting in as she waited for the news that she was to be dismissed from his life.

If Niklas didn't want for ever, then she couldn't carry on with it being just for now.

'Ready?' Niklas checked, looking over as she walked out of the bathroom.

'I guess so.' There was nothing to pack, after all.

'Do you want me to take your clothes and have them cleaned?' Rosa offered.

'I'll bin them.' Meg headed back to the bathroom to do so. 'I never want to see them again.'

'Okay.' Rosa hitched up her bag and headed off. 'I'll go and make sure the car is ready.'

When she'd left Meg picked up all the clothes from the wet bathroom floor and took them through to the bin in the lounge, but as she went to throw them in he stopped her.

'Not those.'

She looked at the denims he was retrieving and he turned and smiled.

'You might want me to shave my head again one day…'

She wasn't smiling back.

'It's all a game to you, isn't it?'

'No, Meg.' He shook his head, and he wasn't smiling now. 'It's not.'

But as they took the lift down she noted that he was holding a bag. He hadn't binned the denim clothes he'd worn in prison.

He pulled her into him and shielded her from the press as they left the hotel, did it again when they got to the police station, but she was actually shielding herself from him. He gave her a thorough kiss before she headed in to give her statement, but all it did was make her want to cry, because she wanted more than just sex from him.

'You'll be fine.' He wiped a tear with his thumb. 'Just tell them what happened. Rosa will be there…'

'I know.'

'It's nothing to be scared of,' he said. 'And then I'm going to get you right away from here—just us…' He smiled as he said it, gave her another kiss to reassure her.

She returned neither.

The statement was long and detailed, and she felt as if she were going over and over the same thing.

No, she had never met Miguel, and nor had Emilios mentioned him.

She didn't know who had called Emilios, but it had been after that call that he had suggested they go for a walk.

'They ask,' Rosa said, 'when did you realise it was not Niklas?'

'I never realised,' she said again.

'But you said you started to panic long before you saw the gun?'

She nodded, but Rosa told her she had to answer. 'Yes.'

They made her go over and over it, and she tried to explain things but it was so hard. It was hard to understand herself. She didn't want to say in the police station that she was surprised he hadn't taken her to bed, that perhaps that had been the biggest clue that it wasn't Niklas—which for Meg just rammed home how empty their relationship really was.

'So what made you panic?' Rosa checked again.

'I realised what a mistake I'd made marrying him,' Meg said, in a voice that was flat as she relived it. 'That there was no real basis for a relationship, that he'd always said it wouldn't last. All I wanted was to be away from him.'

'From Emilios?'

She shook her head. She remembered her swollen eyes and flinging things in a suitcase, the pleasure and pain of the last year, mainly the pain, and still, *still* he delivered it.

'From Niklas.' As she said it she saw Rosa's slight frown.

And then they took her further back, to her first meeting with Niklas on the plane and their late-night conversation.

'I asked how he'd been orphaned and he said he wasn't sure.'

'You asked if he had ever tried to look for his family?'

'Yes.'

'And what was his response?'

'He said that he had got Miguel, his lawyer, onto it, but he had got nowhere.'

'He said that?' the police officer checked via Rosa. 'He definitely said that?'

'Yes.'

The officer looked long and hard at her, and then Rosa asked if Meg was sure, as this was from a conversation a year ago. 'He asks if you are sure this is not the conversation you had with Niklas last night.'

Meg blinked.

'I told the police.'

'You remember this conversation exactly?' the officer checked, and she said yes, because she had been replaying every second of their time over and over for close to a year now.

'Exactly.' She nodded. 'And then I asked what it had been like, growing up in an orphanage, but he didn't respond,' Meg said. 'He told me he didn't want to speak about that sort of thing.'

But the police weren't interested in that part.

Only Meg was.

She went over and over everything again. She said that, no, she hadn't been aware she was being followed at the time, and looked to Rosa for explanation, but she gave a brief shake of her head. Then her statement was read back to her. She listened and heard that basically they had had an awful lot of sex and just a few conversations, but he had definitely mentioned that he had asked Miguel to look for his family. She signed her name to it.

'That is good,' Rosa said as they walked out. 'You have a good memory. They will jump on that part in court if Miguel denies that he was asked to find Niklas's family,' she warned. 'Just stay with that.'

'Am I free to fly home?' Meg asked. She saw the brief purse of Rosa's lips. 'My family's worried about me.'

'It might be better for Niklas's case if you were here.'

'What case?' Meg asked. 'It's clear he's innocent.'

'To you,' Rosa said. 'And it is to me. But dead men

can't speak.' She gave a thin smile. 'I correct myself. When I said that Niklas never makes mistakes, he has made one—he hired Miguel, and he is a brilliant lawyer. He might say it was both of them that were conning people. He might insist he believed it was Niklas giving him instructions, or that the directions came from both of them…'

'No!'

'Yes,' Rosa said. 'I will fight it, but it might look better for Niklas if his wife was here beside him—not back home, counting the money his legal team has placed in her account.'

'You know it isn't like that.'

'Tell the judge,' Rosa said, and she was back to being mean. 'I get that your family is worried about you, but if you can pretend for a little while longer that Niklas is a part of your family…'

'Niklas doesn't want me to,' Meg retorted. 'Niklas doesn't want a family…'

'He doesn't even know what one is!' Rosa shouted. 'Yet he has done everything right by you.'

'Everything *right* by me?' It was Meg who was shouting now. 'Are we talking about the same man?'

It wasn't the best choice of words, given the circumstances—especially as Niklas appeared then.

'My mother had triplets, maybe?' he quipped.

It was her poor choice of words, perhaps, but his response was just in bad taste. She did not understand how he could be so laid-back about it. How could he have his arm around her and be walking out of the po-

lice station as if the nightmare of the last year hadn't
even happened?

It was the same circus of cameras as before, and
then they left Rosa to give the press a statement. A
car was waiting for them. It's driver handed the keys
over to Niklas, who sat behind the wheel as Meg sat in
the passenger seat. The moment she was seated Niklas
accelerated away at speed—away from the crowds of
press. After a while the car slowed, and the drive was
a long one, taking them out of the city and through the
hills. There was little conversation, just an angry silence from Meg, whereas with every mile the car ate
up Niklas seemed more relaxed.

'You're quiet,' he commented.

'Isn't that what you want me to be?'

Sulking didn't work with Niklas. It didn't bother him
a bit. He just carried on driving, one hand on the wheel,
the other out of the window. Any minute now he'd start
whistling, just to annoy her further. She was still bristling from Rosa's words. The first thing she would do
when she got back to Sydney was send back all the
money that she had been paid.

He looked over at her tense profile. 'We'll be there
soon.'

She didn't answer him.

Nothing made sense: the policeman's questions had
confused her, Rosa had angered her, and as for him…
She turned and could not fathom how calm he was after
all that had happened. He was fiddling with the sound

system now, flicking through channels. She did not need background music, and her hand snapped it off.

'The police said I was being followed. That it wasn't the police who shot him…'

'It was a bodyguard.'

'Bodyguard?'

'Just leave it.'

'No,' Meg snapped. 'I will not.'

'He will not do any prison time. I have my lawyers working for him. I had a couple of people following you when I realised you were still here—when I guessed I had a twin. I did not know exactly what was happening, but I knew you would not be safe, so I arranged to have people protect you.'

'How?'

'I owe a favour to a very powerful man,' Niklas said. 'He got a message to the outside after you rang me.'

And then he stopped talking about it, and she felt his hand come to rest on her leg, and she could not understand how easily he dismissed the fact that it was a bodyguard *he* had arranged who had shot his twin.

Did nothing get to him?

He gave her thigh a squeeze, which she guessed meant they were nearly at their destination and would be off to look at another bedroom any time soon.

'We're here.'

It was the most stunning house she had ever seen, with dark wood, white furniture and screens on the windows so the sun and the sounds of the mountains could stream in. It was gorgeous and, Niklas said, the place he had dreamt of when he was on the inside.

'You like it?'

'It's gorgeous.'

'Look…'

He took her by the hand and led her to the bedroom, then walked and opened huge glass doors, revealing lush grass that rolled towards another mountain. The sound of birds was all that could be heard. In a place like this, Meg thought, you could start to heal.

'There are servants, but I have told them not to come till I call them. They've left us lots of food…'

And there were her things, hanging in the wardrobe, and there were his arms around her, and again he was holding her close.

She started crying and he didn't seem surprised at all.

'You're exhausted,' he said.

She was.

From nearly a year of loving him.

'Are you about to suggest we go to bed?'

'Meg…' He saw her anger and he didn't blame her. 'I don't care how cross you are. You deserve to be. If you want to shout, go ahead. I have put you through hell and I am just trying to make you feel better, to say the right thing. I'm probably getting it wrong, but for now you are here, and safe.'

It was the 'for now' part that was killing her, but she wasn't going to go there again. 'I don't know what's wrong,' she said. 'I'm so angry! I'm so confused…'

'It's shock,' he said. 'You were nearly kidnapped. You saw a man shot.'

'I saw your *twin* shot!' she shouted. 'I thought it was you.'

He did not react—he just held her.

'Shouldn't it be the other way round?' She pulled away from him, so angry. 'Shouldn't *you* be the one crying? He was your brother.'

'That's for me to deal with,' Niklas said.

'Can't you deal with it with me?'

'I prefer to do things like that alone.' He was nothing if not honest. 'I don't want to talk about me. Right now I want to be here for you.'

He said all the right things, but they were the wrong things too. He took all of her, but didn't give himself back, and maybe she had better just accept it. He felt nothing for anyone, and as she looked out to the mountains she hoped here she might find a little peace before she left him.

'I hope the press don't find us here.'

'Not a chance,' Niklas said. 'I told you that.'

'If they know that you own it they soon will.' She looked down the mountain and hoped there were no cars loaded with press following them up, because she was beyond tired now, could not face moving again. She just wanted a moment to gather her thoughts. 'They'll be going through all your assets…'

'I don't own it,' Niklas said. 'It's not listed in my assets. This is in your name…' He lifted up her face and kissed her frowning forehead. 'I bought this for you before I got arrested. I wanted the divorce, I knew I might be going away for a very long time, and this was to be part of your settlement. The sale went through the day before my finances were frozen…' He gave her a smile. 'They could not seize this because it is yours…'

'You bought this for me?'

'It is big enough for a bed and breakfast…' He shrugged. 'If that is what you want to do with it. I knew you would probably sell it…'

He had known he was about to be arrested and go to prison and yet he had still looked after her—had come to this place and chosen it. It was more than she could take in.

'Why are you crying?'

'Because of this.'

'I said I would take care of you.'

'And you have…'

He had kept every promise he had made, had listened to all her dreams.

They walked through the house and he showed her every room before he took her into the kitchen, with its massive ovens and benches, and huge glass doors that opened to let in the sound and the breeze of the mountains. He had chosen the perfect home—except he hadn't factored that he might live in it.

'I might have to stay here a while,' Niklas said. 'You can be my landlady.'

He came over for a kiss, because that was what he always did.

'I'll send you the rent I owe when I get it.'

'Send it?' Meg said.

'You need to go back.'

He did care about her. She knew it then—knew why he was sending her away. 'And you can't come with me.' It wasn't a question, she was telling him that she knew why.

He tried to hush her with a kiss.

'You can't come to Sydney even for a little while because you're still on bail.'

'Meg…'

When that didn't work, she was more specific. 'And you won't let me stay because you think you might go back to jail.'

'More than might,' Niklas said. 'Miguel is the best legal mind I have met…' He smiled. 'No offence meant.'

Always he made her smile, and always, Meg knew then, he had loved her—even if he didn't know it, even if he refused to see it. Rosa was right. He had always been taking care of her and he was trying to take care of her now.

'I'm on bail,' he said, 'and I doubt the charges will be dropped. Miguel will not simply admit his guilt. There will be a trial, there could be years of doubt, and then I might be put away again. You need to go back to your family.'

'*You're* my family.'

'No…' He just would not accept it. 'Because as much as I might want you here, as much as I thought of you here in this home while I was in that place, as much as a three-weekly visit might keep me sane, I will *not* do that to you.'

'Yes.'

'No,' Niklas said. 'We will have a couple of nights here and then, as I promised your father, I will make sure you get home. By the time you are there I will have divorced you.'

He was adamant.

And she both loved and loathed that word now. She wanted to kiss the man she was certain now loved her, yet she wanted to know the man she loved. He kissed her as if he would never let her go, yet he had told her that she must.

'You're so bloody selfish…' She could have slapped him. She pulled her head back, would not be hushed with sex. 'Why don't I get a say?' She was furious now, and shouting. 'You're as bad as my parents—telling me what I want and how I should live my life…'

'What?' he demanded. 'You *want* to be up here, living in the mountains, coming to prison for a screw every three weeks?'

'Your mouth can be foul.'

'Your life could be,' Niklas retorted. 'Barefoot and pregnant, with your husband—'

She didn't hear the next bit. It was then that Meg remembered—only then that she remembered what she had been preparing to find out before Emilios had come to her door. He watched her anger change to panic, and in turn she watched the fear that darted in his eyes when she told him that she might already be.

It was not how it should be. Meg knew that.

He just stood there as she walked off, as she walked into the bedroom and went through her things. Yes, there was her toiletry bag and, yes, Rosa had packed everything. The pregnancy testing kit was there.

She kicked off her shoes when she returned to the kitchen, because barefoot and pregnant she *was*.

'You need to go home to your family.'

'That's all you have to say?'

'That's it.'

She couldn't believe his detachment, that he could simply turn away.

'You'd let us both go, wouldn't you?'

'You'll have a far better life…'

'I probably would,' Meg said. 'Because I am sick of being married to a man who can't even talk to me, who sorts everything out with sex. Who, even if he won't admit it, *does* actually love me. I'm tired of trying to prise it out of you.'

'Go, then.'

'Is that what you want?' Meg persisted. 'Or are you telling me again what I *should* want?'

'I could come out of this with nothing!'

And if Meg thought she had glimpsed fear before, then she had no idea—because now that gorgeous mouth was strung by taut tendons. His black eyes flashed in terror as he saw himself searching bins for food—not just for himself but for the family she was asking him to provide for. Meg knew then that she had never known real fear…would never know the depth of his terror.

She would not die hungry.

She would not leave the earth unnoticed.

She would be missed.

'I might not be able to give you anything...'

She glimpsed the magnitude of his words.

'We might have nothing.'

'We wouldn't have nothing,' Meg argued, with this man who had no comprehension of family. 'We'd have each other.'

'You don't know what nothing is.'

'So tell me.'

'I don't want to discuss it.'

'Then I *will* leave, Niklas, and I *will* divorce you. And don't you dare come looking for me when the charges are dropped. Don't you dare try to get back in my life when you think the going can only be good.'

He just stood there.

'And don't bother writing to find out what I have, because if I walk out now I will do everything I can to make sure you can't find out. I will write "father unknown" on the birth certificate and you really will be nothing to your child.'

And she was fighting for the baby she had only just found out about, and the family she knew they could be, and as she turned to go Niklas fought for them too.

'Stay.'

'For what?' Meg asked. 'Shall we go to bed?' she demanded. 'Or shall we just do it here? Or...' she looked at him as if she'd had a sudden idea '...or we could talk.'

'You talk too much.'

He pulled her to him and kissed her mouth, running his hands over her, down her waist to her stomach. He pressed his hands into it for a second and then, as if it killed him to touch her there, he slid his hands between her thighs and moved to lift her skirt. He tried desperately to kiss her back to him, but she halted him and pulled her head away.

'And you don't talk enough.'

She would not let him go this time, and he knew he could not kiss her back into his life. And she *would* walk—he knew it. She was a thousand times stronger than she thought, and so must he be—for without her and his baby he was back to nothing.

'Don't waste time in fear, Niklas,' Meg said. 'You told me that.'

So he stood there and slowly and quietly told her what it had been like to be completely alone, to be moved on to yet another boys' home when he caused too much trouble, to boys' homes that had made living on the streets preferable.

And she *was* stronger than she'd thought she was, because she didn't cry or comment—just stood in his arms and listened. She'd asked for this, she reminded herself a few times at some of the harder parts.

'You would make a friend and then you would move on. Or he would steal from you and you would decide to go it alone. Then you might make another friend, and the same would happen again, or you would wake up and he would be lying dead beside you. But you keep on living, and you get a job, and it turns out you are clever—more clever than most—so you start to make money and you start to forget. Except you never do. But you make a good life for yourself, make new friends, and you would not change it, this new life, but still you taste the bitterness of your past. You make more money than you can spend because you're scared of having nothing again and, yes, you're happy—but it still tastes bitter.'

He didn't know how to explain it neatly, but he tried. He looked at her and could not fathom why she wanted to get inside his messed-up head.

'You never forget—not for one minute. You remember eating from bins and beatings, and running away, and the smell of sleeping on the streets, and you trust no one. You remember how people will take from you the second your back is turned—would steal from a beggar who sleeps on the streets. So you relish each mouthful you take and you swear you will never go back to being nothing. But always you fear that you will.'

And then he stopped.

'You want to hear the rest?'

'Yes.'

He paused, took a deep breath before continuing. 'Then you meet a woman on a plane, and this woman feels worried because in living her own life and following her dreams she might hurt her family, and you know then that there are people who do worry about others, who do care. And this woman changes your life.'

'I didn't.'

'More than that—you saved my life. Because when

I did go back to having nothing I survived. More than I should have, I thought of you. Every night I saw the sun, and it was the colour of your hair. Then last night I got to hold you, and look back, and I realised that it is a good world. There are people you cannot trust, but there are also people you can—people who help you even if you don't know it at the time.'

She didn't understand.

'That a woman you only dated for a while would put up her house…' He hesitated. 'Rosa and I…'

'I worked that out.'

'It was before she was married, and there has been nothing since, but her husband is still not pleased that she works for me. That she should go to him, that Silvio should trust her and me enough—that is real friendship,' he said. 'That does not let you taste bitterness.'

And that part she understood.

'Then you look back further and realise that the nun who taught you Spanish, the woman who named you, was the one good thing you can properly remember from your childhood and will end up saving the life of the woman you love—how can you not be grateful for that?'

'You can't not be.'

'And that woman you met on the plane—who your gut told you was right—who you married and then hurt so badly—would fly into Congonhas Airport to come and have paid sex with me…'

She thought of his anger in the prison, and the roughness of the sex, and then his tenderness afterwards, and she was so glad that he'd known he was loved, that she'd told him.

'I'd have done it for nothing.'

'I know,' he said, and he was honest. 'You loved me when I had nothing, and you will never properly appreciate what that means. But I might again have nothing, and I thought that was my worst nightmare, but to have nothing to give you or my child…'

'We've got a home that you chose for us,' Meg said. 'And I can work, and I have parents who will help me. Your child—our child—will never have nothing, and neither will you, so long as we have each other.'

He still could not really fathom it, but maybe he was starting to believe it.

'It might not mean prison…the charges could be dropped…' he said. 'Rosa thinks they have enough already to prove I was not involved. They are going through the evidence now.'

'And, unlike your wife, Rosa's got a good legal brain!' Meg said.

He didn't smile, but he gave a half-smirk.

'Rosa thinks it was Miguel who suggested the plan to my brother.' He tested this new thing called love. 'I want him to have a proper funeral. I want to find out more about him. I want to know about his life. Do you understand that?'

'Yes.'

'I might not talk about it without you.'

And still he said all the wrong things, but they were the right things for them.

'Whatever feels right for you.' And now she understood him a little better. She didn't have to know everything, didn't have to have all of him—just the parts that he chose to give. They were more than enough. And when he did choose to share, she could be there for him.

'Can you accept now that, even though I don't tell you everything, there are no secrets that might hurt you between us?'

'Yes.'

And then he did what Niklas did when he had to: he simply turned the pain of his past off. He smiled at her, held her, and then for the longest time he kissed her—a kiss that tasted deeper now, a kiss that had her burning.

But, unusually for Niklas, he stopped.

'And just to prove how much I love you,' he said, 'there will be no more sex for a while, so we can talk some more.'

'I didn't mean that.'

'No.' He was insistent. 'I can see what you were saying. We can go for a walk in the mountains.' He smiled and it was wicked. 'We can get some fresh air and we can talk some more...'

'Stop it.' His mouth had left her wanting.

She tried to kiss him, tried to resume, but Niklas shrugged her off and found a basket, started loading it from the fridge.

'We're going to have a picnic,' Niklas said. 'Is that romantic?'

He was the sexiest guy she had ever met, Meg realised, and she'd been complaining because they were having too much sex…

'Niklas, please.' She didn't want a picnic in the mountains, didn't want a sex strike from her Brazilian lover, and she told him so.

'Husband,' he corrected. 'I married you, remember?'

'Yes.'

'How can you say it was all about sex? I was nothing but a gentleman that day…I could have had you on the plane, but I married you first!'

'Hardly a gentleman,' she said. 'But, yes, you *did* marry me, and I get it all now. So can you put the basket down and…?'

'And what?' Niklas said.

Seemingly shallow, but impossibly deep, he was gorgeous and insatiable, and he was hers for ever.

His sex strike lasted all of two minutes, because now he was lifting her onto the kitchen bench even as he kissed her. His hands were everywhere and his mouth was too, but so were her hands before he slapped them away. '*I'm* doing this.'

He was the most horrible tease.

He whistled when he lifted up her skirt. 'What are you wearing?'

She writhed in embarrassment at his scrutiny. 'They're new.'

'You didn't buy these, though.' He smiled, because he couldn't really imagine his seemingly uptight girl buying knickers you didn't even have to take off.

'I might have.'

'Meg…' He was very matter-of-fact as he pulled down his zipper. 'You wore sensible knickers the day I met you. You even wore sensible knickers when you came to visit me in prison.' And then carefully he positioned her. 'Watch.'

And when he slipped straight into her the outrageous knickers she was wearing seemed like a sensible choice now.

'Never think I don't love you.' He would say it a hundred times a day if he had to. 'Never think that this is not love.'

And she knew then that he *did* love her, and that what they shared was much more than just sex. He was very slow and deliberate, and it was Meg who couldn't stop. He kept going as the scream built within her, and she waited for his hand to cover her mouth, waited for him to hush her—except they were home now, as he told her, and he pushed harder into her.

'We're home,' he said again, and moved faster, and for the first time she could scream, could sob and scream as much as she wanted, could be whoever and however she pleased.

And so too could he.

He told her how much he loved her as he came, and over and over he told her that he would work something out, he would sort this out.

And as he looked over her shoulder to the mountains he knew how lucky he was—how easily it could have been him lying dead on the pavement instead of his brother. His twin who must have tasted so much bitterness in his life too and been unable to escape as Niklas had done. When still he held her, when he buried his face in her hair and she heard his ragged breathing, for a moment she said nothing.

And then, because it was Niklas, he switched off his pain and came to her, smiling. 'Do you know what day it is today?'

'The day we found out we—' She stopped then, and blinked in realisation as her husband moved in to kiss her.

'Happy anniversary.'

CHAPTER THIRTEEN

SHE LOVED BRAZIL more and more every day she spent there, but it was the evenings she loved the most.

Meg lay half dozing by the pool, then stretched and smelt the air, damp from the rain that often came in the afternoon, washing the mountains till they were gleaming, and thought about how happy she was.

The charges had been dropped, but it had taken a couple of months for them to get back on their feet. They had paid Rosa back her money and lived off Meg's savings, but only when the nightmare of his returning to prison had stopped looming over them and Meg's pregnancy had started showing had Niklas really begun to think this was real.

There were now regular trips into São Paulo, and Niklas came to each pre-natal visit, and she loved that her family adored Brazil as much as Niklas did Australia when they were there.

She saw her parents often—they had only just left that day—and, thanks to a few suggestions and more than a little help from their new son-in-law, business was going well in Sydney.

They had surprised her—after the shock of finding out had worn off, they'd been wonderful. Niklas had flown them over to Brazil and the first day he'd met them he'd begun to work out why sometimes you couldn't just hang up the phone or shut someone out. He'd started to get used to both the complications and the rewards of family.

They hadn't shared their good news about Meg's pregnancy on that visit—it had seemed all too new and too soon to give them another thing to deal with, and there had also been a funeral to prepare for.

She had thought Niklas would do that on his own, except he hadn't.

Only a few other people had been invited. Meg had met Carla for the first time, and she was, of course, stunning, and there had been Rosa and her colleagues, and Rosa's husband Silvio too. And, even if they hadn't wanted to attend at first, her parents had come too, because they loved Meg and Niklas, and Niklas had told them how much it was appreciated. There had been flowers sent from Fernando—a fellow *paulistano* who knew only too well how tough it was on the streets, who knew that sometimes it was just about surviving.

Meg had been a bit teary, saying goodbye to her parents that morning, but they'd reassured her that they'd be returning in a month's time, so that they could be there for the birth of their grandchild.

If she lasted another month, Meg thought as she felt a tightening again and picked up her baby guidebook.

No, it wasn't painful, and they were ages apart. So

she read about Braxton Hicks for a while. But then another one came, and this time she noted the time on her phone, because though it didn't quite hurt she found herself holding her breath till it passed. Maybe she should ring someone to check—or just wait because Niklas would be home soon? It probably was just Braxton Hicks...

Her pregnancy book said so...

Meg loved being pregnant. She loved her ripening belly, and so too did Niklas. And she loved *him* more than she had thought she was capable of.

No, she'd never fully know him. But she had the rest of her life to try and work out the most complicated man in the world.

The nightmares had stopped for both of them and life had moved on, and more and more she realised how much he loved her.

There was plenty of happiness—they had friends over often, and many evenings she got to do what she adored: trying out new recipes.

Meg looked at her phone. It had been ages since the last pain, so she should be getting started with dinner really. They had Rosa and her husband and a few other guests coming over tonight, to cheer Meg up after saying goodbye to her parents.

They had such good friends. She could even laugh at things now, and she and Rosa had become firm allies. Rosa would sometimes tease Meg about the earlier conversations they had shared—not to mention the outrageous knickers.

God, she'd been such an uptight thing then.

She lay blushing in her bikini at the thought of the lovely things they did, and then she felt another tightening. She looked at her phone again, noting the time. They were still ages apart, but as she heard the hum of the helicopter bringing Niklas home she was suddenly glad he was here. She walked across the lush grounds to meet him and picked a few ripe avocados from the tree to make a guacamole. As she did so she felt something gush.

It would seem the book was wrong. These weren't practice contractions, because there was real pain gripping her now—a tightening that had her blowing her breath out and feeling the strangest pressure.

Niklas saw her double over as he walked towards her. He could hear the chopper lifting into the sky and was torn between whether to ring and have the pilot return or just to get to her. He walked quickly, cursing himself because they had been going to move to his city apartment at the weekend, so that they could be closer to the hospital.

'It's fine…' He was very calm and practical when he found her kneeling on the grass. 'I'll get the chopper sent back and we will fly you to the hospital. Let's get you into the house…' He tried to help her stand but she kept moaning. 'Okay…' he said. 'I will carry you inside…'

'No…' She was kneeling down and desperate to push—though part of her told her not to, told her it couldn't be happening, that she still had ages, must keep the baby in. And yet another part of her told her that if she pushed hard enough, if she just gave in and went with it, the pain would be gone.

'It's coming!'

She was vaguely aware of him ringing someone, and frowned when she heard who it was.

'Carla?'

She wasn't thinking straight, the pain was far too much, but why the *hell* was he calling Carla?

'Done,' he said.

'Done?'

'Help is on the way…'

She could see him sweating, which Niklas never did, but his voice was very calm and he was very reassuring.

'She will be ringing for the helicopter to come back and for an ambulance…'

He saw her start to cry because she knew they would be too late—that the baby was almost here.

'It's fine…' He took off his jacket and she watched him take out his cufflinks and very neatly start to fold up his sleeves. 'Everything will be okay.'

'You've delivered a lot of babies, have you?' She was shouting and she didn't mean to.

'No,' he said, and then he looked up and straight into her eyes, and he turned her pain and fear off, because that was what he did best. 'But I did do a life-skills course in prison…'

And that he made her smile, even if she was petrified, and then she started shouting again when he had the gall to answer his ringing phone.

'It's the obstetrician.'

She must remember to thank Carla, Meg thought as he pulled down her bikini bottoms. From what she could make out with her limited Portuguese he was telling the doctor on speakerphone that, yes, he could see the head.

She could have told the doctor that!

But she was sort of glad not to know what was being said—sort of glad just to push and then be told to stop and then to push some more. She was *very* annoyed when he said something that made the obstetrician laugh, and she was about to tell him so when suddenly their baby was out.

'*Sim,*' he told the doctor. '*Ela é rosa e respiração.*'

Yes, her baby was pink and breathing. They were the best words in the world and, given he had said *ela*, it would seem they had a baby girl.

The doctor didn't need to ask if the baby was crying for it sang across the mountains—and Meg cried too.

Not Niklas—he never cried. Just on the day he'd found out she was safe she had seen a glimpse, and then the next day she had guessed he might have been, but he was in midwife mode now!

He did what the doctor said and kept them both warm. He took his shirt off and wrapped his daughter in it, and there was his jacket around Meg, and then he got a rug from beside the pool and covered them both with it. He thanked the doctor and said he could hear help arriving, and then he turned off his phone.

'She needs to feed,' he told her, and he must have seen her wide eyes. He was an expert in breastfeeding now, was he? 'The doctor said it will help with the next bit…'

'Oh…'

'Well done,' he said.

'Well done to you too.' She smiled at her lovely midwife. 'Were you scared?'

'Of course not.' He shook his head. 'It's a natural process. Normally quick deliveries are easy ones…'

He said a few other things that had her guessing he'd been reading her book—the bit about babies that come quickly and early.

'She's early…' Meg sighed, because she had really been hoping that this would be a very late baby, that somehow they could fudge the dates a little and she would never know she'd been made in prison.

'It will be fine,' he said. 'She was made with love. That's all she needs to know.'

They had a name for a boy and one for a girl, and he nodded when she checked that he still wanted it. She tasted his kiss. Then she saw him look down to his daughter and thought maybe she glimpsed a tear, but she did not go there—she just loved that moment alone, the three of them, just a few minutes before the helicopter arrived—alone on their mountain with their new baby, Emilia Dos Santos.

The Portuguese meaning, though.

From the saints.

* * * * *

EXPECTING HIS LOVE-CHILD

To

Anne Marie, Helen, Leanne, Raelene and Tracy

For *always* being available for lunch x

CHAPTER ONE

THEY HAD TO be breaking up, Millie decided.

Or rather *he* was breaking up with her.

To keep her brain from freezing over as she served patrons long into the night at the terribly exclusive Melbourne restaurant, Millie Andrews invented a background for each of the tables she waited on.

And now, as the clock edged past midnight, there were just three tables left.

One was a rather boozy celebratory business dinner, which thankfully, now that the bar was closed, was starting to wind up. The second consisted of a rather strained couple. The lady had duly eaten her way through fish and salad, minus dressing, and was clearly uncomfortable in her very tight black velvet dress. Millie decided she had probably just had a baby and was feeling horribly self-conscious at being out with her very good-looking but extremely passive-aggressive husband— 'You don't really want dessert, do you, darling?'

And then there was the beautiful pair.

Blonde, svelte and jangling with nerves, a stunning woman was imploring her dining partner to 'just, please, listen'—reaching for his hand, her throaty voice urgent as her... Millie couldn't quite make this one out—husband, fiancé...? No, neither fitted. Boyfriend? Or just lover, perhaps...? As he sat and listened impassively, utterly unmoved by her desperate pleas.

'Please, if you would just listen to me—really listen...'

They were too rich to notice or care that a waitress was clearing away their barely touched plates, and Millie's ears were on elastic as the blonde beauty begged for her chance, her bright, blue eyes glittering with tears as she choked the words out and reached for his hand again. 'Before you say it cannot happen, just hear what I have to say first...please.'

'Perhaps *you* should try listening...' he growled. His voice was accented, deep, low and just divine, but since till then the only words he'd growled in Millie's direction had been 'Rare steak, fresh tomato salad,' so far she hadn't been able to place it. 'All night I have told you no, yet still you persist.'

'Why do you think I persist, Levander?'

Russian, Millie finally recognised, lingering rather too long over clearing the table. His salad had barely been touched; his steak was only half eaten. If she'd followed protocol, she should have asked then if everything had been to his satisfaction—if, by chance, there was a problem with his meal—but the intense conversation and his mood certainly didn't encourage interruption, and, given that it was her last night in Melbourne, protocol went where it belonged.

Straight out of the window.

'You persist because you hope I change my mind. How many times do you have to hear me say it to understand that I never will?'

Even as she backed away, and even though the kitchen had long ago closed, Millie was tempted to offer them the dessert menu. Prepared even to whisk up dessert herself if it meant she could listen on.

They fascinated her.

Fascinated her.

From the second they had walked in she had been entranced.

By him.

As he'd walked through the door, standing tall, brooding and vaguely familiar in a charcoal suit, loosening his tie as his eyes scowled over the room, a low murmur had gone around and every head had turned—especially Millie's, as she'd tried and failed to place him. Ross, the manager, had raced over and steered them to the most private table at the back of the restaurant, then delivered Millie a quick warning before he dispatched her to take their orders.

'Nothing's too much trouble, okay?'

His date was beautiful, yes—on any other night she'd be a fascinating subject—but the glamorous woman faded into insignificance beside her date, because he was...

...exquisite.

As an artist Millie was often asked where her inspiration came from—and here was a fragment of the answer.

Inspiration came in the most unexpected places and at the most unexpected times. Twelve hours before she left Australia—twelve hours before she headed home for London—her head should be buzzing with "to do" lists. She should be adding up her tips and working out if she could afford the night in Singapore she'd booked *en route*. Instead she was consumed with this fascinating man—his beauty was, quite literally, inspiring.

His bone structure was impeccable, and his features had Millie's fingers aching to pull out a sketchpad and capture them: in perfect symmetry, as with all true beauties, his high cheekbones razored through his face, a strong jawline was dark and unshaven against his pale skin. His thick, longish hair was charcoal, not quite black, but too dark to be called brown, and whatever palette his creator had used, the brush had been dipped twice in the same well—his eyes held the same bewitching hue, only deeper and glossier.

His date was gorgeous—possibly one of the most beautiful women Millie had seen—yet she dimmed beside him. The whole restaurant dimmed a touch, and she wanted to capture that, make him the sole focus—like endless Russian dolls, Millie mused, seeing the germ of the picture she would create in her mind's eye: him—the biggest, most stunning, most exquisitely featured—and the rest—his date, the other clients, the staff, the street outside—ever diminishing objects, growing smaller and smaller till there was nothing left.

'You are a cold bastard.' His date hissed the words out, almost spat them across the table. But he didn't flinch and neither, Millie noted, did he attempt to dispute the fact.

'It must be hereditary.'

'So that's it? After all I've told you—you can just sit there?' Still he didn't answer—utterly bored, he had the audacity to yawn as she promptly burst into tears. 'You're not even going to think about it?'

Again he didn't answer, and even though Millie still hadn't managed to pin a label on her as, sobbing yet somehow elegant, the blonde stumbled out of the restaurant, it was clear that whatever her title had been a few minutes ago it had just been superseded. As of this moment she was an ex.

'She waits now for me to run after her...' Those charcoal eyes stared up at her, his lashes so thick, his gaze so intense, that for a second Millie's world stopped.

I'd wait, Millie thought, stunned that he was talking to her, that he didn't seem remotely embarrassed that she'd witnessed this intensely personal moment.

'I will sit here for a while longer—hopefully she will get the message and go home.'

'Or she might ring you on your mobile,' Millie said, blushing furiously as she did so, because even if it seemed to be idle conversation, as a lowly waitress it was inappropriate to comment. Management's orders were very clear: she should merely smile politely and move on.

Only she didn't.

Instead she hovered on the giddy line of propriety. His eyes pinned her, and the impact of him close up, of actually conversing with him, was utterly, fabulously devastating—and he surely knew it. Knew it because instead of looking away, instead of dismissing her, he responded with a question.

'Would you wait?'

'Perhaps…' Her voice when it came was breathy, her shirt suddenly impossibly tight as she struggled to drag air into her lungs, her skin on fire—and not because Ross, her manager, was looking on and frowning at the exchange. 'Once I'd calmed down, once I'd…' She didn't get to finish as, almost on cue, his phone rang. And at that point she crossed the line. Instead of turning and discreetly walking away, instead of heading back to the bar to let him take his call, she stood there, watching transfixed as he picked up his phone with long, pale, slender fingers that had Millie wondering if he was also an artist—wondering if that might be the reason she was so drawn to him.

'Thank you for the warning,' he said, turning off the phone.

'You're welcome,' Millie croaked, her cheeks flaming as attraction fully hit, and she was, for the first time, privy to that unscrupulous face breaking into a smile.

'Another.' He gestured to his glass, and Millie was about to say no, that the bar had closed about ten minutes ago. But glancing over to her boss, and seeing him frantically nodding, Millie gave a smile and, slipping away, headed over to the bar.

'What was that all about?' Ross asked the second she was within earshot.

'What?'

'Come on, Millie, don't play games with me. What was that cosy little exchange you were having with Levander?'

'He was just talking.' Millie flushed, and not just at being caught flirting—even his name was sexy. 'You were the one who said that nothing should be too much trouble. It would have been rude to walk away.'

'You know how to handle things.' Ross shot her a warning look. 'Do you want me to take his drink over for you?'

'Of course not.' Millie shook her head, quickly changing the subject as Ross poured a generous dash of vodka into a glass. 'Should we get the port those businessmen wanted? They might get upset if they see us still serving him.'

'The bar's closed,' Ross said, placing the drink down for Millie to take over. 'At least to anyone who isn't a Kolovsky.'

'Kolovsky?' Mille frowned, trying to place the familiar name and hoping he'd elaborate, but Ross just grinned.

'It's Russian for money!'

Placing his drink in front of him, Millie was curiously disappointed when he didn't look up, when he didn't even give a distracted thanks. Instead he stared across the room and out onto the street, drumming his fingers restlessly. Never had it taken so long to place a drink on a table, to clear away a few stray glasses and wait—wait for him to bring her into his delicious focus, to once again, even for a moment, be the woman who held his attention.

Only he didn't.

'You might as well go home, Millie.' Ross came over as the last of the rowdy businessmen finally tipped out onto the street, but the words she'd been waiting to hear all night didn't sound quite so sweet now. Despite her tiredness, despite an empty suitcase waiting to be filled and a flight to be caught back to London in the morning, suddenly she didn't want to go. Staring over at the table, she watched as he leant back in his chair and took a slow sip of his drink. Ross did the same. 'I might as well get started on some paperwork—he looks as if he's settled for the night.'

Millie couldn't help but frown—an extra drink for a special customer was one thing, but for Ross to happily sit and while away an hour or two was unprecedented. This time Ross was only too happy to elaborate. 'He's a great tipper—as you're about to find out.' He held out a black velvet folder and peeled out an indecent amount of notes, taking his cut and handing the rest to Millie. 'Looks like you'll be staying in Singapore after all!'

'Goodness.'

'You deserve it. You've been a great worker—a real asset to the restaurant.' He went over to the till and handed her an envelope. 'There are your other tips and your wages, and there's a reference in there, too. If you're ever back in Melbourne, know that there's always a job here for you.'

More than anything Millie hated goodbyes. Ross wasn't even that much of a friend, but still tears filled her eyes as she took the envelope. Maybe it was emotion catching up, maybe it was the fact that no doubt she'd never be back, her dream trip to Australia to showcase her art having been nothing but a flop, but for whatever reason, she gave him a small hug.

Without this job she'd have been home weeks ago.

Without this job she'd still be wondering if she might have one day made it.

Like it or not, at least now she knew the answer.

There were a million things she had to do, but instead of turning left as she exited the restaurant Millie turned right, noisily clipping along Collins Street on black stilettos that needed re-heeling, barely even glancing into the exclusive shops as she headed to the gallery for one final glimpse of her work in the window.

And then she saw it. Millie's head turned so abruptly that she was positively whiplashed as she put a very beautiful face to a very beautiful name.

House of Kolovsky.

The cerulean blue frontage and the embossed gold lettering were familiar the world over—yet so far removed from Millie's existence that till now she'd barely even given the building a glance. Unable to resist now, though, she teetered forward, gazing into a magnificent window, dressed with ream after ream of the heavy silk that was so much the Kolovsky trademark, with opals as big as gulls' eggs seemingly casually tossed in—but the effect was so stunning Millie was in no doubt that each jewel had been placed with military precision, along with the tiny lights that were twinkling and catching the fluid colour of the fabric.

Kolovsky was renowned for its stunning fashion collections as well as the fabrics themselves: rich, heavy silks that were supposed to have the same magical effect as opals—capturing the light and even, it was rumoured by devotees, changing colour according to a woman's mood. Millie had raised her eyebrows in rather bored disbelief when she'd read that in a magazine, but standing with her nose practically against the window, seeing the heavy, fabulous tones and sumptuous attention to detail, Mille could almost believe it. What she was finding rather more difficult to fathom, though, was what had taken place earlier. She had flirted with none other than Levander Kolovsky.

She *had* seen him before—it was all coming to her now: notorious bad boy, the darling of the tabloids here in Melbourne, his every move, his every comment, his every encounter faithfully and libellously documented.

Millie let out a gurgle of laughter. She'd been flirting with the biggest rake in Melbourne. Just wait till she told Anton!

Peeling herself away from the window, Millie allowed herself just one final glimpse. She would have loved to feel her body draped in something so exquisite. Not that she could ever afford it. Millie sighed, picking up her pace and walking the few doors down to the gallery. She could barely afford anything at the moment—which is how a tortured artist was supposed to start, Mille reminded herself. But her usual pep-talk was starting to lose its oomph—cold reality hitting home as she stood on the pavement outside the gallery.

Very soon she wouldn't be a struggling artist.

Instead she'd be a teacher.

Seeing a light on inside, Millie stood well back, not wanting Anton, the owner, to see her tears as she bade goodbye to her dream.

'Which one is yours?' How long she'd stood there staring Millie had no idea. She'd been so lost in her own world she hadn't noticed someone approaching, hadn't heard him next to her. Only now that he was, every nerve sizzled with awareness.

'That one.' Millie pointed to a tiny oil painting with a shaking hand, wondering what his take would be. It was a field of flowers and grass, every blade smiling, every flower wearing a different expression, and in the middle was a wooden child bearing no features—it was quite simply her favourite piece, evoking for Millie such emotion and memory that it would truly break her heart if it ever did sell. Yet it was the one she had hoped would launch her career.

'Were you on drugs when you painted this?'

'No.' Millie let out a little laugh, not just at the question but at the pronunciation. His English, though excellent, was laced with a heavy dash of fabulous accent, and that he could make such an offensive remark sound somehow sexy was certainly a credit to him.

She glanced over at him. His face was at the window, and he was peering at her work with a frown. For an artist it was actually a compliment—someone trying to fathom her work, instead of a brief, cursory glance and then on to the next one.

'My brother's autistic—when I was younger I remember the doctor explaining to me that the reason he didn't cuddle or kiss or show affection was because of the way he saw the world. The clouds, the trees, the grass and animals were in his eyes just as important as us—to him, people were the inanimate objects. That's me.' She pointed to the frozen lifeless object in the middle, waited for his comment. For an age it didn't come. He was looking, really looking, at her picture.

'I knew a child once—he screamed if he had to go to bed. Not just screamed...' Slate eyes turned to hers and Millie was lost. 'Every night it was as if he was terrified. Do you think to him the bed was real? That perhaps he thought he would hurt it...?'

'Maybe.' Millie was flustered, wondering who he was referring to, wanting to know more. But it didn't matter anyway. The fact that her work had provoked such thought, a memory, such a question, was reward enough in itself. 'I don't know, but I guess it's possible.'

'And may I ask the name of the artist?'

'You may. It's Millie.' She smiled. 'Millie Andrews.'

'Your accent?' He frowned just as Millie had when trying to place his. 'England? London?'

'That's right.'

'Are you here on holiday?'

'A working holiday…' Millie gave a rueful smile. 'I go home tomorrow.'

'Shame.'

She'd been flirted with on many occasions, but never so blatantly and never by anyone so divine.

'Millie?' He pondered on her name for a moment. 'I am not familiar with that. Is it short for something?'

'Do we have to go there?'

'Sorry?'

'Millicent.' She winced. 'My parents must have been—' She didn't get to finish. Anton was frantically waving in recognition as he came to the window, gesturing for her to come inside. It would have been rude to say no, to shake her head and carry on this delicious conversation. So, extremely reluctantly, she turned to bid Levander goodnight.

Clearly he had other ideas. As the door opened, instead of walking away, instead of concluding their time together, he blatantly extended it, moving to the door, then stepping back to allow her to go first, his hand taking her elbow. It wasn't just his boldness that startled Millie but the contact itself—the firm, warm, incredibly male contact that had her more flustered than she cared, or rather dared to admit.

'Ready for the off?' Anton's effeminate voice rang out as he scooped her into a hug, but it lasted about point three of a second. He dropped her like a hot coal as he clapped eyes on her companion.

'My, my, Millie. And I thought you were supposed to be working tonight.'

'I—I am.' Millie stammered. 'I was. Anton, this is…'

'I know who it is.' Anton beamed. 'Welcome, welcome, Levander—and may I say I just love your new range?'

'It is not my range.' Levander smiled tightly. 'I deal with the business, not the fashion.'

'Well, I adore it anyway,' Anton gushed, but Levander wasn't listening. Instead he wandered around the gallery, squinting as he peered closely at the paintings, some holding his attention, others barely meriting a cursory glance.

'Do you know him?' Millie whispered, which was more than a touch rude, but she just had to know more about him.

'Everyone knows who the Kolovskys are.'

'I mean do you *know* him?'

'I wish,' Anton sighed. 'The boutique may be a couple of doors down from me—but the Kolovskys are a million miles away. I did used to talk to the twins, though…' Anton smiled at her frown. 'They're just as gorgeous. Millie have you any idea who you're dealing with? They're practically royalty here,' Anton breathed, 'and your beau tonight is first in line.'

His voice trailed off as Levander made his way back to them, and Anton spectacularly saved the rather awkward moment, rolling his eyes dramatically at Levander.

'I'm scolding Millie for even considering being seen with you in her waitress garb. Mind you, perhaps it's just as well—I assume you've seen her when she's not working?'

'Not yet.' Levander turned and gave Millie a slow, lingering look, unashamedly undressing her with his eyes for an indecent amount of time as she stood there squirming. Not even turning back to Anton, he carried on talking. 'But I am very much looking forward to it.'

'Well, don't get too excited,' Anton sighed. 'Millie has no end of paint-splattered shorts and T-shirts, but not much else.'

'I see you have only one of Millie's paintings in the window—while other artists there have two.'

'The other artists have sold.' Anton held his palms up to the air in a helpless gesture. 'Actually, Millie, darling…' He gave a little wince. 'I'm not going to take you out of the gallery, but space is at a premium, and with this new exhibition I'm going to have to move—'

'You have more of Millie's work?' Levander interrupted. 'I would like to see it if I may.'

'Of course.' Anton gave Millie a wide-eyed look as he gestured him to the back of the gallery, to the tiny piece of wall that—for now at least—displayed her work.

'Your price is too low…' Levander ran a quick eye through Millie's bio and gave a shake of his head. 'And you come across too needy—too grateful that anyone should even stop to look at your work, let alone buy it. You need to raise your price.'

'It was higher,' Millie answered, 'and I still didn't sell.'

'This is an exclusive gallery—yes?' Levander waited for Anton's hesitant nod. 'People do not want rubbish on their walls—and at this price that is what they think they are buying.'

'She's an unknown.' Anton's bubbly demeanour dimmed a touch as his judgement was challenged, but Levander held firm.

'*Today* she is unknown.' He turned to Millie. 'Change it before you leave. Rewrite your bio…' He turned the page. 'Each painting is now the cost of your air ticket—the price you paid to share your talent.'

'It won't work…'

'So you have lost nothing. And she should have at least two in the window…'

'Levander…' Anton was blushing, flirting, and trying to be assertive all at the same time. 'Millie's already had three months on display in the window. I simply cannot—'

'When is this exhibition you mentioned?' Levander interrupted. 'I remember my stepmother saying she wanted another nice piece for the boutique. Perhaps I should suggest that she comes for a look?'

'I already sent an invite,' Anton said dubiously, 'and as usual it was politely declined.'

'Nina wouldn't have even seen it,' Levander said dismissively. 'It would have been her assistant who declined on her behalf. If I tell her about it myself, I can assure you she will come—and possibly my father too. Though I am not sure if *I* will be available.'

Anton was right—clearly Millie hadn't a clue. Because at just the hint that they were coming to the preview Anton was a gibbering wreck, promptly dispatching her to choose another piece to go in the window before a 'bored now' Levander took her by the hand and led her outside.

'You—you didn't have to do that...' Millie stammered, once they were out on the street.

'No one *has* to do anything.' Levander shrugged. 'Your work deserves its chance.'

'Thank you.' Millie shook her head to clear it. 'Your stepmother *will* go to the exhibition?' she checked. 'I mean, if she's already declined... I'd hate for Anton to be disappointed—especially if he's giving me so much of a prime position. He's already been more than generous...'

'She will be there,' Anton said assuredly. 'She will not want to go, of course. But when I tell her she is expected—that I have accepted on her behalf—she will have no choice but to go.'

'Sorry?'

'It would appear rude to not turn up—and in my family appearance is everything.'

'Well, thank you...' Millie said. 'You've no idea how much it means.'

'I have a very good idea what it means,' Levander corrected her. 'I know how important that first sale is—and, yes, I could have bought your painting—given you the red dot on your work for the world to see—but that would be cheating, yes?'

On so many levels, Millie realised, staring up at him. His skin was white in the street light, contrasting with the hollow shadows of his cheeks, his eyes two dark, unreadable pools.

'It will sell—some things that are truly beautiful don't always catch the eye first time around.' Levander's voice was a caress. 'Sometimes you need to actually stop and take another look.'

He was certainly taking a good look now. His gaze was so intense, his face so close she could feel the heat of his breath on her face. She thought for a blissful second that he was going to kiss her, but instead it was his rich deep voice that bathed her senses, his eyes quizzical as they assessed her. 'So, you leave tomorrow?'

'In the morning.'

'And have you enjoyed your time in Melbourne?'

'I haven't really seen anything of it.' She gave a tiny shrug. 'I've been to a few galleries, a couple of shows— but mainly I've been working...' Her voice trailed off, her simple answer somehow giving him an opening she'd never intended. Millie's breath caught in her throat as Levander took it.

'Then we'd better get started. Come...' He pointed to where a pony and trap was pulling in across the deserted street, tourists climbing down, the weary trap rider about to dismantle and head off home. He shook his head when Levander called for him to wait.

'Sorry, mate. That was the last ride for the night—back again tomorrow.'

'I will talk with him.' Levander turned to go, but she shook her head.

'It doesn't matter. It's late…' Millie attempted, struggling in quicksand as she stared into his eyes. 'And I've got a plane to catch tomorrow…'

'Plenty of time to sleep on the plane, then.'

But a blip of sensibility was invading now. She was playing with fire here, and her assessment was based on not just what she had read—Anton himself had warned her, and Levander's own dining companion hadn't exactly given him a glowing reference.

'You're a cold bastard.'

The pain in her voice had been real, the emotion that had choked out those words hadn't been manufactured—and Levander's response had done little to dispute the accusation.

What the hell was she doing?

It would be madness to go with this man.

'Really…' Millie swallowed hard. 'It's probably not such a good idea. I've got so much to do, and you—well, you…'

'Don't worry about me.'

'You just broke up with your girlfriend, Levander…' She wasn't going to play games. 'You're probably feeling a bit…'

'You have no idea how I am feeling…' Instead of walking away, he stepped closer, took her face in his hands, his warm skin actually cool on her stinging cheeks. 'And I did not break up with my girlfriend—Annika is my half-sister...'

'It was your *half-sister* you were rowing with?'

Levander nodded, his eyes narrowing. 'What did you hear?'

'Nothing.' Millie blushed. The only thing she had heard was that he was a cold bastard, but she could hardly tell him that. 'I just saw her flounce off.'

'And that is all?'

After a beat of hesitation she nodded.

'Siblings fight.' His breath mingled with hers, and that cynical mouth was so close Millie could almost taste it—like a chocolate cake cooking in the oven, teasing her senses...

'She's really your half-sister?' Millie checked, wanting to believe him but scared to at the same time. Wanting him to kiss her but worried that he would.

'Who else would I allow to talk to me like that?' Levander answered. 'Now, you wait here.'

What had she heard?

Levander's hackles were raised, his mind, eternally vigilant, racing as he recalled not just his conversation with Annika, but the times Millie had been present.

At first he'd barely noticed her—a waitress not meriting even a glance from him, especially with the tense subject matter that had been forcing his attention—and then she'd moved to clear his plate.

Her heavenly scent had reached him, her tiny embarrassed smile as she'd caught his eyes, and from that second on he'd thanked her for the distraction—thanked this unknown woman who had allowed his mind to detour as Annika delivered the fatal news and shrilled the family's demands.

So much more pleasant to stare over Annika's shoulder and watch the woman, the pink flush on her cheeks, her blonde curls tumbling further out of their hair tie with each swoosh through the kitchen door, her slight exasperation as she dealt with a rowdy table. He had felt surprising pleasure as he'd watched that full, pretty mouth nibble on the end of her pen between writing down orders. And later, when still Annika had persisted, when it had all been just too much to deal with—his battle to remain outwardly calm despite the emotions churning within—it had been a welcome relief when she'd returned to his table. Her soft fragrance had been such a contrast to the bitter musk of the Kolovsky perfume Annika had doused herself in—a delicate hint of vanilla and something he couldn't define, like a breath of fresh air—and as she'd leant forward to clear his table he'd tried and failed not to notice the slight tug of her blouse as it strained over her breasts. He had actually had to look away when she'd stooped to retrieve a dropped napkin and he'd caught a glimpse of the creamy flesh of her cleavage.

He wanted her.

Handing the rider a sizeable wad of notes, he bought them a little more time—but somehow he knew it wasn't enough. That if he made a move too soon—she'd run like a squirrel up a tree.

And yet if it was sex he wanted there were easier ways. He could head back to the hotel, return any one of the endless messages that would undoubtedly be on his answering machine and lose himself tonight.

How he wanted to lose himself.

Like a judge summing up, he bitterly assessed the conversation that had taken place with Annika—the family demands that had been delivered by the sweetest, the most vulnerable of them all.

His father was dying.

Which, according to the family, meant there was now no question of Levander leaving—no question of him turning his back on the people who had apparently given him everything he possessed.

Five more years of hell was what they were demanding.

Levander had gritted his teeth at the prospect, but the sentencing hadn't ended there—a wife and child had been added to the non-parole period.

Well, they could all go to hell!

He'd more than served his time—he had saved the House of Kolovsky from financial suicide almost the second he'd joined the firm. That they now had the audacity to think he actually owed them anything made Levander's stomach churn with loathing.

To think that that bastard, after all he had done—

'Hey.' Her sweet voice broke into his black thoughts, her smiling, trusting face such an engaging contrast with the hard-nosed women he was too used to dealing with. 'Did you manage to persuade him?'

'Of course,' Levander answered calmly, though his mind was anything but. 'I am a very good persuader.' He watched her eyes widen a touch, registered the tiny nervous swallow in her throat at the slightly provocative statement, and so badly he wanted to kiss her—to push that soft body against a wall, to press his lips to hers, to feel her soft, fragrant skin beneath his hands, to take her up to his hotel and make love to her...

To somehow take refuge from the savage sleet of his thoughts... But strangely, for Levander, it wasn't *all* he wanted from her.

For the first time Levander wanted more than the passion of a woman to fill his night.

He wanted her company.

CHAPTER TWO

IT WAS THE strangest first date she'd ever been asked on—but one thing was sure: it was a date.

Millie knew that—knew from the way he was looking at her and the fact that she couldn't stop looking at him—knew from the butterflies dancing in her stomach and the shrill of pleasure that there was definitely romance in the air.

If it had been with anyone else a romantic horse and cart ride around the city would have been tacky, but with Levander it didn't feel that way. With the feel of the cool night air on her cheeks, the noise of the horse as it clipped through the semi-deserted streets and the warmth of Levander by her side, it felt amazing. It was a whirlwind Monopoly board tour of Melbourne. They clopped past Flinders Street Station, the famous old building stunning by night and lit up like a fairground, and Levander pointed out the sights as they went, from a vibrant Southbank that was still awake despite the hour, and the casino glittering and beckoning, to the smart theatre district and lavish hotels at the top end of town.

'This is where I live.'

He had to lean into her to say it. Her skirt had already ridden up a touch, and, feeling his suited thigh against her bare one, it was almost all she could do to look up instead of down. Her whole focus was on his body against hers.

'It's a hotel.'

'Up there,' Levander elaborated. 'On the top floor.'

'You actually *live* there?'

'Why not?'

He stared down at her and she forgot her question, sure he was about to kiss her. She almost wept in frustration when the cart halted somewhat abruptly, lurching them both backwards into their seats, but Levander gave a small lazy smile as he climbed out—a smile that told her there was plenty of time for that later. And as he stepped down and took her hand to help her down, just his touch confirmed what they both knew.

There *would* be a later.

'You like to dance?'

'No,' Millie admitted, gulping as they descended steep stairs into a tiny smoky and very exclusive private club that she wouldn't have known existed even if she'd been walking on the street outside.

Exclusive because only the most beautiful or famous seemed to be present—faces that had Millie frowning as she tried to place them, then jolting in recognition as the social pages she devoured in magazines came to life before her very eyes.

'Do you?'

'Sometimes.' Levander shrugged, pushing her through the crowd with one arm around her.

The slow, heavy thud of the music was out of time with her rapidly beating heart as he led her to a small, plush, impossibly sexy booth that was clearly designed for intimacy. Like some erotic confessional, the purple velvet-lined seats went up to the ceiling, dulling the chatter and noise enough to allow conversation so long as one leant forward. And as he sat opposite her the table was so narrow it was impossible not to touch knees—impossible to look anywhere but at him.

He ordered their drinks—didn't even ask her what she wanted—and some strange red cocktail appeared that tasted icy and delicious, burning her throat and stomach as she sipped it. But it didn't compare to the sensations Levander evoked.

'Relax,' he ordered, as if she should be able to on command. Only Millie couldn't.

Even here, amongst Melbourne's most beautiful, Levander caused a stir—she'd seen the ripple effect wash through the crowd as they'd walked to their table. Like a mini Mexican wave going through the bar, heads had turned and conversations had paused; Millie had half expected oxygen masks to drop from the ceiling as every female sucked in her stomach *en masse*—but all eyes were most definitely on Levander. His questionable choice of date tonight didn't even merit a second uninterested glance.

Clearly there'd be a new one tomorrow.

Clearly every woman present hoped it might be them.

'You are here to sell paintings, I take it, not for a holiday?'

'That was the plan,' Millie sighed.

'So why are you going back now?'

'I gave myself three months. It was Anton who suggested I come out here.'

'You knew Anton before you came?'

'I met him last year, when he was in London.' Millie nodded. 'I was just finishing my degree and he came as a guest speaker.'

'He is not an artist?' Levander checked.

'No—but he's extremely well known for showcasing new talent, and I was fortunate because he liked my work. We got on well, and he said if I was ever interested in coming over... So here I am—at least until tomorrow. I really can't afford to stay on any longer.'

He pulled back just enough to squint down at his watch. 'It is already tomorrow,' Levander pointed out. 'So what happens now—when you go back, I mean? If your work is not selling...'

'I studied teaching as well.' Millie sighed at the prospect. 'As something to fall back on. I suppose it's just as well I did.'

'You can do both,' Levander pointed out. 'Just because you cannot make a living from your art, it does not mean that you have to give it up completely.'

'I know that.' Millie sighed again. 'It's just...' Her voice faded. Melancholy musings were not really the correct form for a first date, but Levander pushed her to continue and, given that nothing about tonight had even bordered on normal, Millie decided to tell him—to reveal just a little more of herself than she otherwise might. 'When I work…well, it's sort of hot and cold. Yes, in theory it would be fabulous to work Monday to Friday, and save my art for the weekends and evenings—I know it's what a lot of people do—but…'

'But?'

'The picture you saw tonight?' Millie said, and Levander nodded. 'It was sort of brewing in my head for a couple of weeks, and finally—when I could see it, when I was actually ready to put my vision onto the canvas—I locked myself away for a more than a week. I just can't imagine that I'd ever have done that piece if I'd had to slot in the real world. My focus is totally on my art; it's like I just turn on and everything else is off. Except for occasionally surfacing for food and showers I just live and breathe to paint. Actually…' she gave a tiny embarrassed giggle '…come to think about it, nutrition and hygiene weren't exactly at the top of my agenda.'

And if that revelation wasn't correct form either, Levander didn't seem to mind a bit. In fact he leant closer, if that were possible, so close she could feel his breath on her cheek, could feel his knee and the lower part of his thigh against hers as he dizzied her with his thoughts.

'Now you are *really* turning me on!'

Shocked, wondering if she'd misheard, misunderstood, perhaps, Millie tipped back a fraction, wide eyes meeting his, flushing under his lazy scrutiny as he told her without a word that she hadn't misheard.

'Do you come here a lot?' Millie croaked, taking a desperate slug of her drink and wondering if she'd been spirited into a very early menopause as for the millionth time that evening a hot flush sent another searing blush up to her face. The heat between them was so stifling surely someone must have turned off the airconditioner—and had there been a menu handy Millie would have grabbed it as a fan.

'Occasionally,' Levander answered easily—so pale and elegant and utterly calm it made her want to weep at the injustice. His eyes shifted momentarily as he glanced at the beautiful crowd. 'But really I don't like it much: too many people with empty minds who think they are interesting.'

'Oh.'

He mesmerised her—every word reeling her in, every feature captivating her. How long she stared, how long they held eye contact, Millie had no idea—but it seemed to go on for ever. Another entirely separate conversation was taking place, without a single word, and though his eyes never left hers, though his hands were safely on the table, he might just as well have been touching her—because her body seared at his beckoning, the dull red of her cheeks stealing down over her bosom as still they didn't speak, blood fizzing through her veins. It seemed to engorge her body, swelling her most feminine places. Her nipples were thrumming against her flimsy blouse as somewhere deep inside—low, so low in her stomach—a delicious knot tightened. Her panties were damp now as still he stared on. She couldn't move, didn't dare even to run a dry tongue over her lips so intense was the arousal, and all Millie knew was that if she didn't break the spell, didn't literally force herself to speak, then she'd surely lean over and kiss him, or take him by the hand and run…

'How long have you been in Melbourne?' Her voice was a croak.

'Does it matter?' Still he stared.

'Do you like your work?' Millie attempted vainly.

'Is this a job interview?' He was watching her mouth intently now, making it almost impossible to form a sentence. God, what did this man do to her? With one look she was a shivering mass of lust—and with one crook of his finger, Millie knew, she'd follow him gladly to wherever he wanted to take her. It both excited and terrified her. Supremely cautious with men, supremely cautious with her emotions, it was as if she had suddenly dropped the rule book she'd lived her life by in the bath, leaving its pages damp and illegible, all its moral guidelines so deeply entrenched utterly indecipherable in Levander's heady presence.

She wanted him to make love to her—wanted him now, this very minute. Wanted him to take her out of this bar, take her anywhere, just so long as he ravished her…

…wanted him to be her first.

Oh, she hadn't held on to her virginity for some prudish reason—work, study, the strains of family life had meant she'd never let anyone particularly close, had never actually invested the energy to take a relationship to that next level, had never trusted another enough to give that part of herself.

But she'd give it to Levander.

In a heartbeat.

And that thought alone shocked her to the very core.

'I came to Australia as a teenager.' Levander's voice broke her introspection, broke the sensual spell. Maybe he had sensed the shift in her, the shock that had ricocheted through her, but suddenly things were, if not normal, then safer, and her mind scrambled to remember the question she had first voiced. 'I studied finance and business—as well as learning English, of course.'

'You didn't speak English when you came?'

'Not a word.'

'Your brothers and sisters here spoke Russian, though?' Millie checked, appalled at how it must have been for him to land in a family and not even be able to communicate.

'*Half*-brothers and sisters,' Levander corrected. 'And, no, they did not speak much Russian. But language was the least of our barriers.'

'What do you mean?'

'We had different childhoods.' Levander flicked away the question with his hand, then reached for a drink. But even if he wanted that part of the conversation over, even if clearly she'd wandered into forbidden territory, Millie wanted to know more.

'What about your mother?' Millie asked, remembering that here he had a stepmother. 'Do you get back to see her? Is she still in Russia?'

'She is dead.' Just like that he said it—his expression not changing, his voice completely even—as if the detail was so trivial it was hardly worth a mention. 'So there is no reason at all to go back. As I was saying, when I finished my degree I assumed the role of Financial Director at the House of Kolovsky.'

'It must be quite a job.' Millie blinked. 'I mean, the name's everywhere.'

'We have outlets all over the world. Melbourne is really just kept on for sentimental reasons—this is where my father came when he emigrated from Russia. Our main outlets are in Europe, and of course the US, so I travel a lot—which is good.'

'Must be interesting?'

'Sometimes.' Levander shrugged. 'But the people in the industry leave a lot to be desired.' He curled his lip and made a small hissing sound. 'It is full of bitches—and I am not only talking about the women. It is the most narcissistic environment to be in. Like here—' His hand gestured to the heaving room. 'Everyone here would happily claim to be my best friend—would that be the case if I worked in a lower profile job?'

'I don't know...' Millie mused. Because even if the answer was seemingly obvious—even if his position *must* ensure a never-ending stream of hangers-on—long before she'd known his name, in fact from the second Millie had laid eyes on him, she'd been captivated. And from Millie's perspective it wasn't hard to afford others the benefit of the doubt. 'You can't know that either...' She gave a helpless shrug, not sure how she could tell him that even if he took away the suit, the money, the name—he was still far and away the most exciting, breathtaking company she'd ever kept.

'I *do* know, though,' Levander said firmly. 'From the day I set foot in Australia I have had endless friends— yet no one wanted to know me when I was a Detsky Dom kid.'

'Detsky Dom?' Millie frowned. 'Is that where you're from?'

It was an innocent question, clarifying things in her own mind as she pieced together his history. She expected him to nod, to just say yes and move on. But instead those brooding features shifted into a wry smile, and she didn't know if it was her attempt at pronunciation or if he was laughing at some sort of private joke. 'That is right, Millie—I am from *Detsky Dom*. Come…' Standing abruptly, he offered her hand. 'You do not belong here—let's go somewhere where we can properly talk.'

Which was easier said than done. As he guided her through the throng, his hand on her waist, his broad shoulders acting as a buffer, his name was called from every direction. Not that he deigned to respond—even when a rather ravishing Latina woman grabbed him by the sleeve of his jacket, Levander merely shrugged her off.

'Levander, please…' She caught up with them just as they stepped out of the lobby. Millie's foot was almost on the pavement outside when her tearful voice pleaded her case. 'You cannot walk out like this... We made love last night—please talk to me.'

Which was a pretty good case to plead, Millie thought, as with a grim half-smile Levander excused himself and led the dark beauty to a corner of the lobby—leaving Millie to stand making polite small talk with the doorman. Her cheeks burned with humiliation—not just because of the paper tissue way he clearly treated women, not just because she was obviously the next one in the box, but because of the very fact she wasn't walking away.

It was hell to watch.

Like some gory bit in a film, where you wanted to peek from behind a cushion, it was just horrible, listening to her plead her case, begging him for another chance, promising to change and more. But far worse for Millie was Levander's response—not cool and detached, as she'd expected, instead he bordered on sympathetic, seeming understanding of her plight even as he patiently explained why he hadn't returned her calls and reiterated what he had already told her—that it was over.

Still, when her glittering eyes fell on Millie, when a few choice words were said, his Latina lover must have crossed Levander's questionable line of moral conduct—because he stalked off, taking Millie firmly by the arm and leading her out onto the street.

'Levander...' the brunette sobbed. 'We need to talk.'

'What is the point?' Levander snarled, and never had his Russian accent been more pronounced as he bundled Millie into a taxi. 'When you're too drunk to remember what was said in the morning?'

'I'm sorry you had to see that.' They'd ended up at St Kilda Beach, and as they wandered along the fore-shore it was the first time since the incident that either of them had spoken.

'Perhaps it's better that I did,' Millie answered tightly—the sobbing spectacle had been a rather timely reminder of what she'd almost let herself in for.

'We went out for a few weeks—but we were having problems...'

'Clearly you weren't having too many problems last night.' She sniffed.

He had the nerve to laugh at her response. The bloody nerve to *laugh!*

'Stop it,' Millie demanded. 'That's completely ir-redeemable....' Only it wasn't; Levander was so un-ashamedly bad, his behaviour so utterly and completely reprehensible, that inexplicably after a moment or two Millie was laughing too. Oh, not out loud laughing—but a very reluctant smile was wobbling on her lips as he took her in his arms. The whole thing was so awful, so far from anything she'd ever experienced, it was ei-ther that...

...or cry.

'Millie, I do not as a rule have...er...*problems* in that department. But Carla was wrong when she said we had made love last night.'

'I don't need the details...'

'In fact, though last night wasn't lacking in physicality, I could say that Carla and I, while we enjoyed each other, never "made love".'

'Please.' Millie closed her eyes against his gaze—because that wasn't the concern right now. Here she stood, with the most beautiful man she had ever met, listening as he told her, quite clearly, that he, unlike others, had no trouble separating sex from love—which should make perfect sense. After all, nestled in the club, feeling his legs pressing against her, all she had wanted was him, and love surely hadn't entered the equation...

Love *couldn't* have entered the equation because she barely knew him...

And yet...

Troubled eyes opened on his—and he was still there, still just as divine, still just as confusing.

'I am sorry...' His breath mingled with hers, his lips a mere fraction away, and she stiffened, terrified of the dizzying effect he had on her. But somehow she didn't relax when he broke contact—when, extremely frustratingly, he became the perfect gentleman.

He talked politely as they walked towards the pier, occasionally taking her elbow when the moon dipped behind a cloud. Millie couldn't decide if she was either totally misreading the signs and he didn't fancy her a jot, if he was literally giving her a guided tour of Melbourne, or he was an absolute master in seduction. But by the time they neared the pier every cell in her body was quivering, every nerve taut with arousal. The skin on her bare arms flared as he took her forearm and turned her around. Surely now, Millie begged to herself, her lips aching with want, surely now he would kiss her. Only his simmering tease wasn't quite over. Turning the burner down just a touch, even as Millie's want bubbled near the edge, he guided her back into a public place.

It was the strangest place to bring someone.

A seamy café in the red light district of Melbourne—a rather odd choice for a date. But Levander, Millie realised, truly seemed to fit in anywhere. Whether at an exclusive bar or an all-night café, he had that supreme confidence combined with something else that Millie couldn't quite define. The café's owner greeted him by name as Levander guided her to a table and then went over to order. As she sat, anxious and awkward amidst the tired sex workers who were taking a well-earned break, the street kids trying to make one coffee last for ever, Millie wondered why the hell he'd brought her here. How anyone could relax in a place like this was beyond her.

'The coffee is great here,' Levander said, as if in answer, placing two steaming mugs and two large cakes on the table. 'I come her sometimes when I cannot sleep—not for *that* reason.' He smiled at her disapproving expression. 'It actually reminds me of home. There was an all-night café opposite the…' He hesitated just a fraction and Millie frowned. 'There was a café like this opposite where I lived. Sometimes when I cannot sleep I come here and watch the sun rise; it is a good place for thinking.'

'But surely…?' Millie started, and then stopped herself. But Levander clearly guessed what was on her mind—surely this was the last place a person could relax.

'They are good people too, Millie. They have to work, like all of us. You should not be so quick to judge.'

'I wasn't,' Millie answered indignantly, and then felt guilty—because that was exactly what she had been doing. She had looked around her with less than an open mind.

'It is rare that anyone disturbs me—they value their time alone, and they seem to respect that I value mine. And, as I said, the coffee is good.'

'So are these,' Millie said, finally relaxing a bit now, biting into the pastry and closing her eyes as the cool sweet custard melted on her tongue. 'So, what do you sit here and think about?'

'At the moment—work.'

'Because you're so busy?'

'Because I am thinking of leaving.'

'Oh.' Pastry forgotten, it hovered in her hand as Millie's eyes widened. 'What do your family say?'

'I haven't told them yet.' He gave a small smile as her pastry dropped to the table when Millie realised she was actually the only person privy to this particular plan. 'And it is not a prospect I relish. They will tell me I have commitments—they won't want to lose me. I have saved the company from ruin and made them plenty of money since I came.'

'How?' Millie asked. 'How did you save it?'

He didn't answer at first—made no secret of the fact he was weighing her up, deciding whether or not he should answer. But after what seemed like a lifetime he nodded, inviting her a shade deeper into his magical circle, and Millie leant in gratefully—not so much for what she might hear, but because perhaps he had decided to reveal more of himself to her.

'That is for another time.'

'There can't be another time…' She almost wept with frustration at his tease, at the hand of fate that had granted her this unexpected encounter but with such a cruel timeline. 'You know I go home tomorrow.'

'Don't you want to stay?'

Oh, *how* she wanted to. So badly she wanted to say yes. The minutes they had were ticking away as loudly as a kitchen timer, and her heart was dreading the buzz that would signal the bitter end. But she had no choice.

He gave her a tiny glimpse of what she would be missing—his hand leaving the safety of the table, his fingers toying with a loose strand of her hair. His flesh was not even touching hers, but she could feel the heat from his palm and she wanted to rest her face in it, wanted contact so much it actually hurt.

'We all have commitments,' Millie breathed, faint now with longing. 'Even me.'

'Pity.'

He watched as she nervously licked her lips, his eyes squinting slightly just as they had when he'd looked at the paintings, and Millie wondered if she had what it took to hold his attention, or if afterwards he'd simply move on.

'You know,' he mused out loud, 'for an industry that is supposed to promote beauty, the fashion industry can be very ugly. To them, you would not be considered beautiful...' Only someone like him could make it a compliment—especially now that he was touching her, caressing her cheek with his finger, tracing it down her face and along her neck, almost as if he were drawing her, the pad of his fingers cool on her throat, resting a moment on her rapid, leaping pulse. 'The face, yes. But the body...' She gave a small nervous swallow as his fingers swept along her shoulder, dusting her bare arms; all the tiny hairs standing up to attention as their mistress shivered. 'You are too much woman.'

'Is that another word for fat?' Millie gave a slightly shrill giggle. 'I know I should go to the gym more— I mean, I pay my membership...' She was blabbering now, seriously so. Oh, she wasn't fat—not even particularly overweight—but maybe compared to the reed-thin beauties Levander was used to...

Her thought process halted there. Transfixed, nervous, she watched as he leant over and undid the top button of her blouse. No one turned, not a single person in the café gave a damn. She could feel the top of her cleavage exposed, feel his eyes burning into her pale flesh. If it had been anyone or anywhere else she'd have slapped him—would have got up and walked out. Only it wasn't anyone else...

...it was Levander.

Jerking her eyes to his, Millie couldn't read them—
was unsure of what to make of him. Unsure whether
his words demoted or promoted her. Unsure of what
Levander could possibly *need* from someone like her.
She knew for sure now that she was wanted—knew for
sure now where the night was leading…only an argument was brewing at the counter. Loud voices crudely
interrupted this sensual moment as a young man, clearly
the worse for wear, pulled out his pockets, trying to find
money he'd never had to pay for a two a.m. breakfast
that he'd already eaten. It was clearly the norm for this
place—no one bar Millie and Levander was even looking up at the distraction.

'I musssht have dropped it…' the guy was slurring.

'Hey,' Levander called, standing up, and not for the
first time during this crazy night Millie felt anxious—
here she was in the seamiest of cafés, with a virtual
stranger for company and a fight about to break out.
She held her breath as Levander stood up and headed
straight into the thick of things, blinking rapidly as he
pulled out his wallet.

'You did drop it…'

He pulled out his wallet and handed the owner a note
that would more than cover his breakfast. 'I found this
on the pavement outside—perhaps I should give it to
Jack to look after.'

'I want the change…' the guy slurred, but Levander
shook his head.

'Tomorrow you will be hungry again. It is better Jack
has it.' And without another word he headed back to

Millie—who didn't know whether to be touched by his kindness or furious at his stupidity for getting involved.

'Nice place,' Millie said darkly, and almost instantly regretted it—especially when she saw Levander's face.

'You prefer five-star?' Levander shrugged. 'Prefer pompous men drunk on malt whisky who have lost their gold credit card, perhaps, than some poor kid who probably hasn't eaten in two days?'

Though she bristled at his implication, she refused to back down. 'He could have had a knife—he could have…' She shook her head in exasperation. 'And what happens when the money you gave the owner runs out, Levander? What happens next week, when you're not here to fix it for him?'

'For the next few nights he eats.' Levander shrugged.

'But when the money runs out the same thing will happen, and you won't be here…' Millie insisted.

But Levander neither needed nor wanted her take on things. In fact it would seem Levander no longer wanted her. Because suddenly, not for the first time that night, he stood up to go, taking her hand and without a word hailing a taxi from the rank outside, giving his direction in a low, deep drawl. Levander stared fixedly ahead as the taxi slid through the night. So distracted, so far away.

Millie half expected him to drop her off where she lived and carry on, but as the taxi slid to a halt outside the fabulous five-star hotel that Levander called home Millie almost wept with relief. He offered her his hand to step out, and they stood outside the grand reception area. A doorman opened the door for them and they stood in the blazing lights, watching the busy theatre of the hotel even at this impossible hour—a gaggle of women spilling out of another taxi, clipping their way across the marble, an airline captain dressed smartly in his uniform on his way to the airport—the same airport Millie would be at in a few hours…

'I'm sorry.' This time his apology was as unexpected as it was unnecessary. 'What happened back there… well, it is something I am used to. For you, though, I can see it would have been upsetting. Clearly it was a bad idea—'

'It was a lovely idea,' Millie broke in. 'And I actually had a lovely time—in fact, I think it's me that owes you an apology. I completely overreacted.'

'No,' Levander disputed, 'you did not. Sometimes I forget that not everyone has…' He hesitated for just a fraction too long, those beautiful eyes clouding over, and Millie frowned in concern.

'Not everyone has what?' she pushed, but he shook his head and forced a smile.

'It does not matter.'

Millie was sure that it *did* matter, but clearly he didn't want to talk about it. To help, she changed the subject. 'I still can't believe you actually live in a hotel.'

'Why not?' Levander asked. 'A few of their suites are for permanent residents.'

'But surely if your family are nearby…?' She gave a slightly helpless shrug. She didn't really know what she was asking—he was thirty, hardly likely to be living at home with his father, but it just seemed so temporary, so impersonal, so soulless. 'Does it really feel like home?'

'Sorry?' He stared back at her, a slight frown forming between his eyes as if he completely and utterly didn't understand her question, and Millie wondered if she'd spoken too fast—if perhaps he'd misunderstood something she'd said.

She rephrased her question, and spoke just a touch more slowly this time. 'Can a hotel really feel like a home?'

'Of course it feels like home.' He was still frowning down at her, as if surprised she'd asked such a strange thing. 'It is, after all, where I live.'

'I meant…' She gave in then—gave in not only because he didn't seem to grasp what she was saying, because whatever magic they had captured between them seemed to have evaporated. At least for Levander. The silence in the taxi, the terse responses to her questions, his apparent distraction, all pointed to one reluctant conclusion.

He'd had enough of her.

'I should go.'

'I know.'

'I really do have things I should do…' She was gabbling now, the words that had come so easily before now strained and forced as this most wonderful night came to a bitter conclusion. Levander, clearly bored with her company, was staring somewhere over her shoulder as she attempted to say goodbye.

Dared he?

It was a strange question for him to consider—for

a man so used to women. It wasn't his seduction technique that was instilling such doubt—Levander knew she was ready. Despite the scene at the club, he'd felt her unfurl as he'd walked alongside her on the beach. What had happened between them in the café was what unsettled him. Hell, for a second there he'd lost all discretion—not just when he'd reached over and touched her, not just when he'd exposed her fragrant cleavage… She'd clouded his mind like a drug. He'd told her about the business, told her his thoughts. And for Levander that was unprecedented—so far removed from his usual reserve, at least where the family business was concerned, that it unsettled him. Disquiet seeped through his marrow at how this woman moved him so—how hard it was to field her questions. Because he actually wanted to tell her things, wanted to answer those perceptive questions…wanted her dizzy, happy perspective, wanted to lower his guard and laugh with her over and over again.

And if he kissed her he'd be lost.

'I have to go to the airport in…' She didn't have a watch, and as she looked at his and tried to read it upside down Levander relaxed.

She'd be gone soon.

Strange that it comforted him.

For a few hours he could hold her—concentrate solely on the one thing he did better than business, spend tonight with her, hush her questions with his mouth.

Indulge without consequence—safe in the knowledge that tomorrow she would be gone.

'...six hours.'

He was so tall she had to lift her head to look up at him, but it was worth the effort, because finally he was looking at her—finally the Levander who had disappeared for a while had returned. And he was so exquisitely beautiful it was surprisingly easy to be bold, to lift her hand and touch his cheek rather than keep it by her side. She knew he was going to kiss her goodbye—could almost taste the lips that were moving in on hers—and she wanted it over and done with almost. Wanted to move away from this breathtaking man so she could remember how to breathe again, could get on with her life after this strange but dizzying pause.

Only she'd never been kissed like this before.

His mouth was incredibly soft on hers; for someone so masculine, he was surprisingly tender. His lips brushed hers, faint-makingly erotic, and her hands that had been on his cheek moved around to the back of his head. If a minute ago she had been conscious of the bellboy, the cars, the lights, now it all faded into insignificance. It was like being kissed for the first time—actually, way better than being kissed for the first time. His tongue stroking hers, his chin scratching her smooth skin, the intoxicating scent of him as he pulled her in closer, the feel of his hard taut body against hers. Nothing—not a case to be packed, nor a plane to be caught—got a look-in. Her whole being honed in on this delicious moment, and there was no question of wanting it to be over—just the knowledge that tonight it couldn't be.

'Six hours leaves no time for sleeping...' He pulled

back just a fraction, his husky words not asking, but telling… Telling Millie what she already knew.

That the precious few hours she had left were for them.

It was as if all her rules had turned around—the inner compass that guided her running amok—north suddenly south—everything shifted.

This hadn't been a working holiday—it had been work, work, work. No sightseeing, no exploring this amazing country and no romance.

Why, Millie begged of herself, why shouldn't she allow this one indulgence—this one crazy, impulsive moment with a man she'd remember for ever?

Remember for ever because, gazing into his eyes, Millie knew she could never forget—when everything else had crumbled, when all she had left were her memories, this would surely be one. The most beautiful, sensual of men holding her in his arms and wanting her.

He kissed her all the way up in the lift—and all the way back down to the foyer when they missed their stop. Urgent, hot kisses that were as fabulous as they were indecent. His impatient hand barely missed a beat as he hit the twentieth floor again, then returned to her bottom, cupping it, pressing it against him as his tongue worked its magic. He was kissing her mouth, her eyes, her ears, making her shiver. His body was pressing hers against the cold mirror, and his want for her was not remotely overwhelming—because it exactly matched hers. Desire was lacing its way through her body, the pressure against the dam that had been building for hours unleashing inside her the second he touched her.

Nerves only caught up as she entered his vast suite— her glittering eyes widening as she took in the opulent surroundings. She'd known he was wealthy, but it hadn't really equated till now. She felt her heels sink into the carpet and suddenly it unnerved her—standing in her cheap waitress uniform, every scrap of make-up thoroughly kissed away. She knew she didn't belong in his world. She was frozen with the awareness that she should be bathed and scented and gorgeous, and she was feeling anything but.

Levander didn't seem to notice at first, taking her in his arms and proceeding from where they'd left off. But then he sensed her unease.

'I'm sorry…' She felt like a tease, seeing utterly and completely the error of her ways, but she just couldn't *not* tell him. 'I don't belong here—this just isn't me…'

'What isn't you?'

'Here…' Millie wailed, her arms flailing, her breath coming out fast as she rued the ridiculous situation she'd found herself in. 'This isn't me…' And it wasn't just the luxurious surrounds that were panicking her, but Levander. Even after she'd seen the tears from Carla she had kissed him so fully, pressed her groin against his in the lift—she had taken, utterly and completely, leave of her senses.

'Levander, I'm not like this…like that.' She gestured to the closed door and the lift behind it, her cheeks scorching at the inappropriateness of it all. Shame was sweeping through her at the thought that in a few seconds she would have to clip her miserable way through the hotel foyer. She knew he couldn't possibly understand, and at first tensed, flinching, when he came over and held her. But her panic subsided a touch when she found that, actually, he did…

'*That* was not you…' His voice was low and soft in her ear as he held her trembling body. Her face was burning as she leant it against his chest. 'And *that* was not me,' Levander said, lifting her chin with his hands and forcing her to look at him. Her eyes stared in wonder and recognition as he continued. '*That,* Millie, was *us.*'

It made sense—for the first time in this mad night something actually made sense. It wasn't just about her or about him. It wasn't just Millie acting wildly out of character. It was about them—about the instant chemistry that had ignited, the longing, the want that had flared.

Such longing.

She was shaking with arousal, literally trembling with want, and now that she understood it she could let it happen—could watch as his fingers opened the remaining buttons of her blouse, staring down at herself as if seeing her body for the first time, as if seeing it through his eyes, and actually feeling beautiful. He slid off her blouse, unhooked her bra, and all she felt was want—such want—as his tongue flicked her swollen nipple.

Such want as he slid the zipper down on her skirt

till all she wore were her shoes and panties. His tongue traced a line down her stomach as he knelt ever lower, her thighs twitching with anticipation as he slid his way down…

'I should…' She hadn't washed, had been working all night, then walking the streets with him. But she didn't have to say it. Those dark eyes were looking up, meeting hers.

'It is you I want to taste—not soap, not perfume—it is your scent that has driven me crazy all night—don't take it from me now.'

He made it sound like a gift, like a treasure, his fingers parting the flimsy fabric of her knickers, then growing impatient, sliding them down over her bottom, her thighs. He buried his face in her damp bush, and Millie's last stabs of embarrassment were quashed by moans of pleasure. His tongue was like a cool, insistent pulse, and her fingers laced through his hair as her body both willed him to go on but begged him to stop. She was sure her knees would buckle as he worked on. Her pleasure was his, and she knew it—knew from his moans, from his hot breath and the tense fingers digging into her buttocks that Levander was as lost in the moment as she.

At that second it was imperative he was as naked as her, and he sensed it, pulling at his shirt. As he stood her impatient fingers wrestled with the belt on his trousers, and even though his lavish attention might have abated for a few seconds just the sight of him naked had Millie gasping—that gorgeous body, toned and delicious, merely a breath away.

He asked her.

As she stood there, eyes wide with lust, staring at him, he actually asked her what she was thinking.

She toyed with the idea of telling him the truth, tried to work out how to say what was truly was on her mind: that she'd never been with anyone before, that even though it must surely seem otherwise this was actually her first time—the first time she'd ever been this intimate with anyone. But she knew, just knew, she couldn't—knew from the little that she *did* know that the night would cease if she told him that truth. So instead she told him another—her answer raw and honest...

'It's beautiful...'

'Then hold it.'

So she did, tentative at first, and horribly, horribly gauche. But, feeling him so silken yet so strong beneath her fingers, something trilled inside her. Feeling him grow in her hand, feeling him harden beneath her fingers, wanton, reckless, yet terribly shy, she sank to her knees as she held him, her hungry eyes begging to please be allowed just a taste.

'Careful...' His throaty word was more a threat than a warning—his explosive device was so charged to the hilt that Millie knew that with one false move, with one hasty, gratuitous shift, it would all be over.

He was divine.

Greedy now, she devoured him—just so, *so* much

pleasure in giving. She felt his fingers knotting in her hair, smelled the provocative scent of his most intimate place, felt black wiry curls kissing her eyes as she worked tenderly, boldly on…as he urged her deeper even while pulling her back.

'*Octahobka*,' Levander groaned, before repeating it in English. 'Cease now…'

There was no point trying to stand as he raised her up. Instead Millie fell on the vast bed with him—she so oiled and ready, and him so erect it was indecent. He was holding her—holding her so close she could hardly breathe—his lips kissing her eyes, his cheeks suffocating her with his desire. And it didn't matter about tomorrow; right now was enough. His tongue, hot and determined, pressed its weight on her, passion flaring as if they had been doused in petrol and set alight. His hands pushed her thighs apart more quickly than she could spread them. From his rapid breaths, from the rush of flesh swelling dangerously close, all she could do was guide him—guide him to her sweet, waiting entrance.

Her mouth was so full of his that she couldn't even call out as he thrust himself in, as her body adapted to the fabulous sensation of him inside her. It could have, should been over then. Only it wasn't. As if somehow just being there together was too good to end, his body sliding over and over hers, each measured stroke building towards a nearing target. Her throat, her stomach, her thighs contracted as still he bucked within, her fingers digging into his taut buttocks, her groin arching into his. She was weeping, frenzied, as he filled her, her orgasm so intense that she begged relief. But still he was bucking, still aroused when surely he should gladly wilt.

'I can't,' she wept in her exhaustion, 'Levander, I ca—'

Her sob was muffled by the muscle of his shoulder, and she bit into his salty flesh as she realised that, actually, she could.

'Millie.' He was pounding every one of her senses as he swelled further inside her, and though she had nothing to base it on, no touchstone to measure by, somehow as he eked the last dregs of restraint from her, as Levander spilled his full cup, taking her to the brink of insanity, she knew this was once in a lifetime. That this wasn't what she had been missing out on—this was what she must now forever miss.

And later, when exhausted, sated, she fell asleep beside him, instead of relaxing, instead of merely enjoying the precious time that remained, Levander wrestled with the impossible.

One heady taste had him hungry for more.

And not just for her body, but for her mind. He wanted those blue eyes to open on him—wanted to hear that voice—wanted more of the closeness they had shared tonight…

And that was what terrified him the most.

CHAPTER THREE

'You don't have to go.'

Waking to those words, Millie felt her heart still in her chest—her mind struggled to wake up, to assimilate all that had happened, and frantically she sat up, panic seizing her as she realised she'd fallen asleep.

Levander pushed her gently back down. 'It is only eight a.m. Relax.'

'Relax!' Millie let out an incredulous gurgle of laughter. 'I have to be at the airport to check in in two hours.'

'I say you don't.' He was propped on one elbow, leaning over her at the same time, his free hand stroking the outside of her thigh under the sheet, and for the second time in less than a minute Millie's heart stilled.

All the promise she hadn't dared glimpse dazzled her now, as she took in his raw naked beauty, that colourless face even more sensual somehow, his face pale in the stark morning sunlight, heavy-lidded eyes squinting slightly as he stared down at her—unshaven, untamed, and utterly unattainable, Millie decided with a reluctant sigh. Levander Kolovsky was so far out of her league it wasn't even worth considering the possibility. Last night had been amazing, undoubtedly the most romantic, sensual night of her life—and one she would never regret—but whatever magic had caused their stars to collide was one cosmic miracle that surely couldn't be sustained. They came from different worlds—and not just geographically. It had been too much, too soon, but completely unregrettable, and that gave her the courage to answer him honestly.

'Yes, Levander…' She watched as his eyes crinkled into a frown and then elaborated. 'I do.'

'If your visa is a problem then I can have my lawyer sort it out,' Levander said dismissively. 'Surely a few days won't make a difference? I can buy you another plane ticket if you have trouble cancelling at such short notice.'

His answer only strengthened her resolve—people like Levander gave no more thought to an international flight than Millie would to catching a bus, yet her airline ticket—the entire trip, in fact, had taken months of saving and planning. But, aside from that, a few more days wasn't going to change the ending to this dream. A few more days could only make the inevitable parting all the harder—at least for Millie.

'My family's expecting me.'

'Tell them you've been unexpectedly delayed…' His hand was moving to the inside of her thigh now, delivering long strokes, and though his touch was softer now the effect was heightened, making arguing her case all the more difficult. 'Tell them something came up…' His sensual mouth curled into a slow smile as he moved her hand to his morning erection. 'See—you would be telling the truth... You know it is too soon for this to end.'

He whispered the words to her left breast, taking the nipple in his mouth and sucking slowly, drawing sense from her mind with each decadent motion. His impact on her actually unnerved her, and if he touched her for even a second longer then Millie knew she was lost.

'No—I have to go, Levander...' Jerking her hand away, wriggling herself free from him, she stepped out of the warm bed, her words, her actions coming more harshly than intended.

She tried to read his expression, but it was as if bandit screens had come up at a bank—like looking at him, talking to him, through thick glass as he stood up and pulled on a robe. All the closeness, all they had shared last night, was gone now—and she couldn't blame him for what he must be thinking: that scenes like this for Millie must be the norm. They certainly were for *him,* she thought, remembering the beautiful teary Latina of the night before. Holding on to that thought, she squared her shoulders, grabbing her clothes and almost running for the bathroom, desperate for distance.

Closing the door, she sat naked and trembling on the edge of the vast bath. It *had* to be this way, Millie assured herself. For a dangerous moment she'd actually considered what he was offering—succumbing to his lovemaking, staying on for the golden few days he was offering. Peeling herself out of his embrace had taken a supreme effort, but the thought of ringing her family—

her family who, so excited at her return, were preparing a little welcome home party—telling them…

Telling them what?

Turning on the shower, Millie stepped in, closing her eyes as a blast of hot water brought her to her senses. That she'd met some rich guy a few hours ago who'd offered to buy her a new ticket? That she'd fallen into bed with a man she barely knew and was seriously considering letting everyone down just so she could get to know him a little better.

Millie barely looked at guys, was always so careful not to let anything interfere with her dream. And she had been, Millie realised. All her life she'd been careful—right up till this point. Her hand stilled on her body. In fact for a second everything stilled. And Millie wasn't sure if it was the water running or the blood gushing through her ears as an appalling truth hit.

Not only *hadn't* she been careful, last night she had been downright reckless. He was so intriguing, so intoxicating, so potently sexual she hadn't even considered contraception—hadn't thought of a single consequence.

Oh, God.

With a whimper of horror she almost doubled up in self-loathing.

Where had careful been when she'd needed it most?

Naïve, reckless, stupid… Brutal words slapped her ears as she quickly dressed.

'Would you like some breakfast?' His voice sounded incredibly forced as she came out of the bathroom, and

Millie couldn't really blame him. She was having trouble with her own words.

'I really ought to get moving.' She attempted a smile, but it faded when he didn't return it. 'Look, it really was terribly nice of you to offer to get me another ticket—'

'It probably is for the best that you go,' he interrupted abruptly. 'I am extremely busy over the next few days—I probably wouldn't be able to schedule much time with you.' Even allowing for his slightly limited English, his words were brutal. 'I'll make sure there is a driver available for you this morning—he can take you to your hotel, and when you are ready to the airport.'

And if it seemed like a kind offer, it only served to make her feel worse, if that were possible—as if somehow he were paying her back for her time. Perhaps the driver would stop *en route* and let her pick a bauble? She hated how he'd changed since she'd insisted that she was leaving—as if now he didn't even have to pretend to be nice to her any more. Tears glittered in her eyes as she declined his offer.

'I'd rather take a taxi.'

'As you prefer.'

She didn't bother with make-up. Rummaging through her bag, she just gave her hair a quick comb, wishing she could look more seductive, just a touch more fabulous as this amazing chapter of her life came to its sad close. But she couldn't. Couldn't just walk out on him as if last night didn't matter, and she couldn't tell him either just how much it *had*. So, awkward and horribly shy, but trying not show it, Millie tested the water.

'I can give you my phone number…perhaps you could give me a call?' It was a brave thing to offer, but incredibly stupid to lay herself so open to rejection, and it stung like hell when he shook his head.

'Perhaps not.'

Trying not to cry, trying to get out of his apartment with just a teensy shred of dignity, Millie didn't turn around. But she stilled for just a second as she walked out of the door and his beautiful rich voice delivered the strangest of farewells.

'You know where I am if you decide to come and get me.'

It took no time to get ready—three months of clothes thrown into a suitcase, her passport and tickets collected from the hotel safe and her bill paid. And as Millie took her second taxi ride of the morning, she stared at the streets she'd walked last night with Levander. She was filled with longing—almost homesick for a city she'd barely graced—and, passing the gallery, it was impossible not to stop for one last look. With the meter running she dashed out, blinking in amazement at the red dot on her painting. She raced inside and greeted an equally delighted Anton.

'You just had your first sale, honey.'

'Levander?' It was the only name on her mind, the only thing in her head. But the bubble of hope burst when Anton laughed and shook his head.

'I wish! No—some rather staid lady. You just missed her—the ink's barely dry on her cheque. Is there any way you can change your flight, Millie? Things could be turning around for you...'

She actually had a legitimate excuse to ring home with now—a real reason to stay on just a little bit longer. But Millie couldn't do it. She wanted home, wanted her mum—and, Millie realised with shame, needed to see a doctor. She could still see Levander shaking his head when she'd offered him not just her phone number but the chance to get to know her a little better—a chance to somehow build on the one night they had shared. A few days as his *scheduled* plaything was the last thing she either wanted or needed to be.

'I really need to get back.'

'Shame.' Anton smiled. 'You should be sipping champagne with your gorgeous date from last night, not fleeing the country, you know. How on earth did you land him, Millie? Have you any idea how many women would kill for a chance to date him?'

'Does he date lots...?' Mille gulped. 'I mean, I gather he's no angel, but...'

'He's incorrigible.' Anton giggled. 'He'd only just started working at his father's company when he dated some actress—not that anyone knew who he was then. She was over here from the States to promote a film, and the next thing she was crying her eyes out on live television mid-interview because she'd just been dumped by Levander Kolovsky. Well, from that moment on the press have been in love with him, and his little black book reads like a Who's Who. We all live in hope that soon enough he'll work his way through the women and cross to the other side. We call him Georgie!'

'Georgie?'

'He kisses the girls, then makes them cry. It's probably best that you are leaving, honey. He'd soon mess up that pretty little head of yours.'

He already had.

As she climbed back into the taxi to head towards the airport Millie tried to fathom how in so little time so much could have changed. Selling her paintings had been her sole focus—everything had been geared towards making that first sale—only right now it barely seemed to matter. Everything that she had once deemed vital had gone tumbling to the bottom of her priorities. She barely knew him—and yet she felt different. As if in the couple of hours or so that she'd slept in his arms every molecule, every cell of her being had been taken out and then put back, only in a slightly different order.

'Could you go down Collins Street?'

The taxi driver just nodded. He probably didn't care if it took the whole day to get to the airport as long as the meter was running. But it was the most dangerous diversion of her life. As they approached the hotel, Millie asked him to slow down. She scanned the foyer for a glimpse, then stared up and up at the vast building, craning her neck. To see what, she didn't know—the thick black hotel windows gave no indication of what was going on inside. Truth be known, she had no idea which one was his. Yet she was sure, more sure than she'd ever been in her life, that Levander was staring down at her—that Levander was staring out through the window at her.

Watching her leave and maybe—Millie gulped—just maybe, waiting to see if she decided to return.

CHAPTER FOUR

'How COULD YOU let this happen, Levander?' Nina Kolovsky's voice was pure venom as she flounced unin-
vited into his office at 7:00 a.m. and slammed down a
newspaper in front of him. 'All your father has done for
you over the years—and here he is practically on his
deathbed and you disgrace him this way.'

Usually it was Levander's favourite time of the day—
he was always the first into work and more often than
not the last to leave, and the couple of hours before everyone else invaded gave him a chance to focus without
interruption. The sight of Nina at this hour, made-up to
the hilt despite the supposed drama, was for Levander
most unwelcome. Anyway, his father had been on his
deathbed for four months now—and looking remark-
ably well on it. So well, in fact, that Levander didn't
even bother to pick up the newspaper his stepmother
was jabbing a well-manicured nail at. Couldn't be bothered to read about his supposed latest exploits, or read
that the company shares had slid a quarter of one per-
cent—just couldn't be bothered, full stop.

'Out, Nina,' he drawled, his disinterest only inflaming her further. 'And I would prefer you arrange it with my secretary when you want to talk to me.'

'This won't wait!' Nina screeched. 'How could you do this to us? There is the reputation of our family to consider, your father's health. A shock like this could mean the end of him.'

Reputation.

It was the word he hated most to hear—a word that had been bandied around since he'd first set foot in Australia.

"Kolovskys has a reputation to uphold.'

"You will keep quiet, Levander.'

'You will be grateful for all your father has done for you.'

Not once.

Never.

His father and everything he was disgusted him— that he was a Kolovsky did nothing to make Levander proud.

'Annika pleaded with you to marry a nice girl, have babies—me, I pleaded with you to give your father his last wish, to let him go to his grave having seen the future of our family and the business. Instead you spit in all our faces—get some *cyka* pregnant—how could you let this happen?'

'You really think I am that stupid?' Levander sneered. 'As if I would be so careless, Nina. As if I don't know how many women would love to trap a man in my position. So, forget this rubbish you read...' He picked up the paper, ready to toss it in to the bin, ready to tell

Nina to get the hell out of his office so that he could get on with his work. But his voice faded mid-sentence as he stared again at the eyes that had enchanted him, remembering the one time in his life he hadn't thought to be careful.

Because that night he hadn't thought—he'd felt.

'So you do know her, then?' Nina lit a cigarette and stood taking in his reaction, her face as hard as stone behind the make-up. 'You know this cheap, conniving tart—'

'Enough,' Levander roared, halting her filthy mouth momentarily. But the words hung in the air as he skim-read the article. Bile churned in his stomach as he read that not only was Millie pregnant, but that she'd deliberately withheld the information from him. Had chosen not to tell him—had even, Levander read, a great wave of nausea rolling over him as he did so, considered a termination.

'She would not do this.' It was a knee-jerk reaction, an absolute state of denial, because even though the paper screamed the words, the Millie he had met, *his* Millie, would never—could never say such things. 'She would not say these things…' Levander insisted, like a drowning man reaching for a safety rope—a man who would do anything to reach safe shores. He actually turned to Nina, sought comfort from the unlikeliest of sources, where he knew he would never receive the slightest of warmth. 'She would not do that.'

'Think with your head where this woman is concerned, Levander—because she has.'

'Meaning?'

'According to the paper your lady-friend's plane is due to land here in Australia in less than an hour.' Nina's grating voice jangled his every nerve. 'How convenient that this woman no one has ever heard of is suddenly in the news. She's made very sure there is no chance now of you paying her off quietly to get rid of her.'

'She's not like that.'

'Oh—and you know so much about her? Tell me, Levander—how did you meet this lovely girl?'

'That's none of your business.'

'It is *everyone's* business now,' Nina shouted. 'Read the rest, Levander. Read on and see that it says you met one night when you were out with your sister—she was waiting on your table. Given that you choose not to so-cialise often with your family—it narrows it down.'

'So?'

'You spoke in Russian or English?'

'What?' Levander frowned.

'That night—what language?'

'In English.' Levander frowned. 'Annika's Russian is not so good…'

'You fool…' Nina spat. 'Your little waitress tart heard every word—she knew you were upset, possibly that you were looking for a bride.'

'I wasn't upset,' Levander refuted. 'And if she had overheard she would have heard me tell Annika I most certainly am *not* looking for a bride.

'It is your father who is dying, Levander—even an insensitive brute like you would have felt something that night—and she knew it. That *suka* saw her chance and took it.'

'It wasn't like that,' Levander responded angrily. But Nina wasn't going to be silenced again.

'Tell me you were careful,' Nina demanded. 'Tell me you were careful that night and I will have PR straight on to it—Katina will have a retraction in tomorrow's paper and—'

'I'll deal with this,' Levander gritted.

'Tell me you were careful.' When Levander didn't answer, when he clearly couldn't tell her what she needed to hear, Nina sneered her disgust. 'You bloody fool!'

Levander closed his eyes, drew in his breath hard and held it, blocking out Nina's tirade and focusing only on Millie.

Pregnant.

Despite feeling as if a fist had been rammed into his stomach—despite his complete lack of preparation for the news—somehow it wasn't a complete surprise. Because a night like they'd shared couldn't ever just end, and for Levander it hadn't. Like trying to recall a dream, each morning he awoke to the fractured memory, chasing her image as it dispersed, trying to identify just what it was that had taken place that night, somehow assured that the energy they'd created couldn't just dissipate… No, it wasn't a complete surprise, Levander concluded.

That night had been too vast to amount to nothing.

'Where the hell's Katina?' As Nina grabbed for the phone, Levander caught her wrist.

'You already called her? You rang her before you spoke with me?'

'Of course.' Nina eyed him as if he were mad to think it an issue. 'She is our head of public relations...'

'Yours, perhaps, but she's not mine.' Picking up his briefcase, Levander marched to the door.

'Walk out, then,' Nina called. 'Walk out early on your contract while you're at it—walk out on your family when they need you most, when like it or not you need them too...'

'Need you?' Levander gave a mirthless laugh, didn't even look over his shoulder.

'How much time do you want to spend in your new job looking for a lawyer?'

'Take me to court,' Levander jeered. 'You think I've put up with you because I'm worried you'll sue, or because I don't think I can do better? I've put up with this because sadly you're family—because without me the House of Kolovsky would have been a joke by now.'

He was done.

Done with the lot of them. He couldn't even be bothered arguing the point with Nina—because he didn't care, hadn't for the longest time, and now it was time they got it. His only thought now was to get to Millie, to find out what the hell was going on.

'Why would we take you to court?' Nina's question went unanswered—striding across the office, Levander couldn't care less what she had to say. 'It's that little *cyka* who'll be taking you.' Keep walking, he told himself, don't even listen. 'To the family court, Levander...'

He hesitated for less than a second, but that was all that was required for Nina to swoop. 'There it all comes out—there we sit in the gallery and watch others deal with our business. Ivan Kolovsky is dying, and his first-born son…'

Levander ran for an hour every morning—pounded the streets till it hurt and barely broke a sweat. But he was breaking one now… a sickly, cold sweat that came in seconds; he could literally feel the blood leach from his skin, feel the trip of his heart as it struggled to adjust to impending crisis. Rapid, shallow breaths dizzied rather than nourished, the blood rushing through his ears blocking her hateful words…his mind clamouring to find his own truth.

'And after that…' Nina's voice seemed to be coming from a great distance, pungent words that had the bile churning in his stomach. 'After everything has been said, when she's pulled our family and business apart and she's sitting laughing in England—then, Levander, *then* you will have to pay her.'

'I don't need Katina to deal with this….' He dragged the words out through pale lips.

'You might.'

'If I need her, I'll ask.' The world was coming back into focus now, but everything looked different—everything *was* different. He was stuck here, stuck here whether he wanted to be or not. Nina's bloated, over made-up face repulsed him so much he was sorely tempted to slap it, but he wouldn't give her a single second of martyrdom. Finding his voice, Levander said, more firmly, 'I'll sort it.'

'Sort it, then, Levander…' Nina jabbed a long red nail in his chest. 'And I tell you now, so you can tell that *suka* when you see her, whatever shame she brings to the Kolovsky table I serve her and her family double in return!'

'Levander…' Pale and distraught, Annika ran into the office, staring wide-eyed at him when she realised he clearly already knew. 'I heard it on the radio. You have to do something; the phones are ringing off the hook out there—the press are going crazy… Her plane's due to land soon—'

'When?' Levander cut in. 'When does her plane get in?'

'Levander,' Nina roared to his parting back. 'First we sort out properly what we do—'

'Get this.' He was back, his face just inches from Nina's, his face black as thunder as he eyeballed the woman he hated most in the world. 'I stay now because I have no choice. But you understand this—you are the *last* person I take advice from, the *last* person to tell me how I will raise my child…'

'Levander, stop it,' Annika sobbed. 'What are you saying? What are you doing? You know how sorry Papa is for what happened when you were younger, but that is done now—it cannot be changed.'

'Listen to your sister, Levander. We are all sorry for the past—' Nina started.

But this morning he could take it no more. Pandora's

lid was lifting open and his rage bubbled to the surface. Because today—today Levander didn't want to hear those lies from Nina. Lies she repeated so often that sometimes Levander actually thought she must somehow believe them.

'You know it kills your father to think of what happened to you....'

'Don't even try, Nina,' Levander breathed, his voice low and menacing, speaking to her in Russian, watching as the colour seeped out of *her* face now. *'Min znatts.'*

I know the truth.

Finally—finally he was telling her the one thing she thought he didn't know, still speaking to her in Russian. Just in case she remained in any doubt, he spelt it out just a little bit more. *'I remember what you choose to forget.'*

'Why are you speaking in Russian?' Annika's nervous voice had Nina's eyes darting.

'Ask your mother,' Levander said without looking over, pinning Nina with his eyes, daring her to continue this conversation with Annika in the room, taking some small solace at the sheer horror on his stepmother's face. Now that she was finally silent, Levander had his say.

'Your mouth is filthy, Nina, and if I ever hear you speak of the mother of my child like that again then I will not be responsible for my actions. Oh—and I made a mistake before,' Levander said nastily, his accent heavy in his anger. 'It is my father who is the *last* person I take advice from—you, Nina, come a very poor second to last.'

CHAPTER FIVE

SELLING A PAINTING, Millie mused, lifting up her tray and raising her seat as the cabin crew prepared for the final descent into Melbourne, was rather like having chicken pox—without the awful itching, though. One little dot had appeared, followed in rather quick succession by another two, and then little crops of them. A mention in the local newspaper had been followed by an interview with a national, then a couple of interviews on the radio. As her life's work had started disappearing around her, galleries who once hadn't even returned her calls had begun ringing to invite her to showcase her work—and, even though it was early days, any teaching plans had been happily deferred. And now here she was, revisiting Melbourne to personally deliver more of her work and to appear at one of Anton's swanky 'meet the artist' nights.

Though a rather flimsy reason to head halfway around the globe, it had proved enough of an incentive to muster all her courage and do what was becoming more and more unavoidable as each day passed.

Tell Levander.

His name popped into her head more times in a day than she dared to count. Working, shopping, eating, even while sleeping, he was a constant companion to her thoughts. Countless times she'd wanted to call him, to write to him, to tell him her news—but how could she?

God, she hated landing…the lights dimming in the cabin, no movie for distraction, the false hush that seemed to descend as her ears tried to adjust to the change in pressure, nowhere to go except to her thoughts…

She'd looked him up on the internet.

The day she'd got home, before she'd checked her emails or waded through her post—almost as soon as politely able—she'd escaped to her computer and with a knot in her stomach she'd typed in his name. Expecting what, she didn't know. She had reeled as page after page, image after beautiful image, had mocked her a thousand times over. Masochistically almost she had forced herself to read interview after interview…though none directly with him. The occasional quote in the business papers was all she could find actually from Levander. Still, there were plenty of women happy to talk about him, and hardest of all for Millie to bear was that—unlike most women scorned—not a single one of them was vicious. Apparently Levander Kolovsky got a big red tick in every box. Their single pervasive complaint about Levander was merely that it was over.

How could she possibly tell him her news?

And how could she possibly not?

It was nearing winter in Melbourne now, and as the

plane descended through the low, grey clouds Millie
wondered for the millionth time what his reaction would
be when she landed on his hotel doorstep.

Maybe she would ring up to his room and ask him to
meet her in the bar. Maybe she should actually sit down
and write the letter that was permanently penned in her
head, give him a little time to digest the news before
they had to face each other.

It was all she'd thought about for the last weeks and
months, but especially now—walking through Arrivals—all Millie could think was that she was back in
Levander's world, that soon she would see him. The
thought was so consuming she had to ask the immigration officer to repeat his question as he flicked through
her passport.

'I asked what is the reason for your visit?'

'Business,' Millie answered, frowning at his scrutiny
and colouring just a touch as she realised she wasn't
being entirely honest. 'Well, there are personal reasons
too. But I am here for my work.'

'I'm more interested in those personal reasons.'

Immigration control was probably the only place on
the planet where they could say such a thing and not get
back a smart answer.

'I'm hoping to catch up with someone,' Millie
croaked.

'A boyfriend?'

'Not really,' Millie said, flustered. 'He's just someone I met last time I was here—I'm hoping to see him,
that's all.'

'Where will you be staying?'

'I've booked a hotel.' Millie tried to answer evenly, but her voice was growing more shrill. 'The same hotel I stayed in last time.'

'And you've no intention of staying longer than a month?'

'None…' Millie frowned, flummoxed by all the questions and for the first time worrying that she mightn't actually get in. 'Look, is there a problem?'

'That's what I'm trying to find out.' The officer gave a tight smile. 'Can I see your travel insurance documents?'

Blushing from her toenails to her roots, Millie handed them over, swallowing hard as he checked out the forms.

'I did check with my doctor that it was okay to fly while I was pregnant—I wasn't aware—'

'Have a nice stay!' Cutting her off mid-sentence, he stamped her passport, and Millie gave a tiny bemused shake of her head as she realised the mini-interrogation was over. It was almost as if he'd known she was pregnant and had been waiting for her to reveal it, Millie thought as she made her way over to baggage reclaim, and lugged her case and her carefully wrapped mountain of boxes onto her trolley. Oh, well, it was their job to be thorough.

Customs, in comparison to Immigration, was a breeze. Faithfully following the redline that meant she had 'something to declare,' Millie braced herself for a further barrage—but after a cursory look at her mountain of artwork and a brief look at her paperwork she was in.

'Welcome to Melbourne.'

'Thank you.'

'Would you like someone to escort you out, Miss Andrews?'

'I'll be fine.' Millie beamed, taken aback by the friendliness and steering her massively overloaded trolley along the red line and out through the sliding doors.

For a second the flash of lights dazzled her—twenty-four hours on a plane and she was a touch dazed, to say the least, because at the end of the walkway was a group of photographers, all shouting out. For a second Millie faltered. Clearly she was blocking the path of someone rather famous. It entered her head to turn her trolley around and go the other way, but it was just too big and too overloaded to attempt the manoeuvre. Instead she glanced over her shoulder, ready to let whoever it was past. Somewhat puzzled, she took in the elderly couple dragging along behind her, and the frazzled mother with the even more frazzled toddler who had cried non-stop from Singapore: they didn't look particularly famous.

'Over here, Miss Andrews.'

'This way, Millie.'

It was *her* they were calling to. Mid-step, Millie literally froze, completely taken aback that these photographers were calling out to *her*. On closer inspection there were a few microphones amongst the crowds and a television camera. That a couple of radio interviews and a few lines in a newspaper could generate such interest just didn't add up. This was surely more the type of reception afforded Princess Mary than a struggling, almost known artist. Aware that her lank hair, her un-made-up face and, worse, her rather scruffy leggings and T-shirt, though comfortable for a flight, were pathetic to face the cameras with, for the second time Millie considered turning and running. What they hell did they want? Why were the press here?

And in that split second her question was answered.

It had little to do with her and everything to do with *him*.

Stepping out of the sidelines and into her line of vision was the man who had invaded her thoughts for sixteen weeks now…or one hundred and twelve days…or two thousand, six hundred and eighty-eight minutes. She knew that because she'd done the maths on the plane—only she'd never factored in *this*.

Dressed in a charcoal suit, his shirt so white Millie was tempted to scrabble in her bag for sunglasses, Levander actually surpassed the generous realms of her memories. He was, quite literally, breathtaking. Like some delicious Mafiosi movie figure who had stepped off the movie screen and into real life—her life—with that unruly dark hair neatly brushed back now, his dark morning shadow a mere memory because he was utterly, utterly clean-shaven. What was more, he was walking towards her as if he'd been waiting for her—walking towards her so purposefully that every atom in her body told her to run to him. She was the iron ore shavings in a school experiment; he was her magnet.

But as she let go of the trolley and in a reflex action went to run, something stopped her—something in his stance, his expression, telling her that even though he was holding his arms out to her, even though he was calling her name, for Levander there was nothing tender about this reunion. The thought was confirmed as menacing eyes held hers, his generous mouth taut and strained...

'Levander!' It was too confusing—too much to take in. Cameras flashed over his shoulder as her fellow travellers bumped their way past, the noisy buzz of a busy airport small fry to the whirl of questions spinning in her mind. 'What's going on?'

He didn't answer, just confused her more with his actions—dragging her fiercely into his embrace, clamping his mouth on hers so firmly that even breathing was impossible, kissing her so thoroughly, so passionately, holding her so tightly, that all resistance was smothered. He tasted just as divine as she remembered, felt as taut and as terrific as memory had told her. His scent was so intrinsically masculine, so replicate of her dreams, that it should have had her keeling over—*this* was the reunion she had secretly hoped for. If only his eyes weren't so cold...two black chips of ice staring down at her, belying the warmth of his embrace. And the hands seemingly holding her close were actually restraining her, holding her, kissing her, confusing her—until finally he drew back just enough to whisper into her ear.

'You, Millie, will say nothing—I will do the talking.'

'I don't know what...' Her voice was lost in the ferocious crowd. A man, presumably one of Levander's sidekicks, took her trolley as Levander walked her towards the waiting journalists. For all the world it looked like a protective arm around her, but it was more of a vice grip. She could feel the tension in his fingers as they dug into her shoulder. She was still reeling with shock as a microphone was thrust into her face, the sea of faces blurring as question after question hit.

'When is the baby due?'

'Do you have plans to settle here in Australia?'

'How long have you known?'

'When were you planning to tell Levander?'

Helpless, aghast, she looked up at Levander. The news she had wondered over and over how best to deliver was already public property. And the blows just kept coming—each revelation, each turn of events tumbling her further into confusion. Until Levander took control. Somehow, despite the slight grey tinge to his complexion, he appeared utterly unruffled, even the tiniest bit bored with the whole circus as he authoritatively addressed the hungry crowd.

'You will understand that my fiancée is tired after such a long journey.'

She opened her mouth to protest, to correct him, but his fingers tightened their grip around her waist—and thank God they did, Millie thought. Because otherwise her legs might have crumpled beneath her.

'Contrary to the scurrilous reports in your paper this morning...' Levander eyeballed one particular journalist, and Millie noticed the colour drain out of the poor woman's face as Levander continued with his response. 'We are both thrilled at the news that we are expecting a baby.'

'So you two *are* engaged?' Remembering her training, the journalist thrust a small tape recorder under Levander's nose.

'I believe that is what the word fiancée indicates.'

His sarcasm was biting—not that it stopped them. Microphones jostled for space as another burst of rapid fire hit, and Millie wanted to duck for cover, actually leaning into Levander as somehow, despite his loathing, he shielded her.

'What about your family?' a voice boomed above the rest, and the babble hushed as they awaited his answer.

'Delighted—naturally—and looking forward to the event.'

'Which is when?'

'Enough questions. My fiancée is clearly exhausted.'

And without another word he marched Millie out of the airport to a sleek black car waiting on the no-standing zone outside. Her luggage and her precious paintings were being loaded into the boot. When the driver opened the back door, for a second Millie wanted to turn and run—the photographers and the chaos in the arrivals lounge were infinitely preferable to facing Levander. Getting on a plane and heading for home even after a twenty-four-hour trip was way more appealing than getting into the car and facing him now. His anger was palpable as he snapped his orders to her.

'Get in.' Levander's words were like two pistol shots,

and that once beautiful mouth was pale and taut as he spat the words out and took a seat. Only then did she realise how much she was shaking. While the driver finished loading her belongings into the boot they were alone for a few seconds, and she tried to regain control—tried to assert herself with this impossibly distant stranger.

'You had no right to say that I was your fiancée, Levander. No right at all.'

'No right?' He gave a low, mirthless laugh. 'You have no idea how many rights I have, Millie. And I intend to exercise each and every one of them.'

As the driver got into the car he leant closer towards her, and for a second she thought he was going to kiss her again, recoiling at the thought of another feigned show of affection. But the disgust in his eyes told her he felt the same, and his breath was hot with fury as his harsh whisper hit her ear.

'Some reading material for the journey,' he said, handing her a newspaper.

The bottom fell out of her world as she read the article, bile rising in her throat as she saw in print the hundred conversations that had taken place over the past few weeks with Janey, her friend. Private words, spoken in confidence as she'd struggled to come to terms with the fact she was pregnant, were all distilled into the most potent of poisons. Tiny fleeting thoughts that had entered her troubled head were neatly typed in black and white for the world to see, and worse—far worse—for Levander to read…

'Oh, God, Levander. I never—'

'Save it,' he hissed, calling for his driver to get going, then leaning back on the leather seat and reading over her shoulder as tears coursed down her cheeks. 'This bit's my personal favourite…' He jabbed his finger at a paragraph.

Millie couldn't have read it if she'd tried, her eyes were swimming with tears. But she knew without looking what he was referring to: that horrible night when she'd explored her options out loud, the fleeting moment when she'd examined the possibility of ending the pregnancy and getting on with the scattered fragments of her life. How cold, how emotionless it sounded as he read it aloud to her—how devoid of the desperation that had made her voice tremble as she'd sobbed the appalling thought to Janey. Though what trashy journalist worth his salt, what friend greedy for a quick dollar, would bother to add in the convulsive tears that had followed, to say that even before she'd finished talking she'd shaken her head in hopelessness, knowing for her it could never be an option?

But how could a man like Levander possibly understand?

'Maybe we should cut this out and save it for the first page of the baby album?' Back in his hotel room, still the onslaught continued, his contempt so palpable it was like being slapped.

'Don't say that,' Millie begged.

'Oh, but you were the one who *did*,' Levander threw back at her coldly.

'I know it must have been awful to find out like this—'

'You know nothing,' Levander sneered. 'Is this all true—what is written?'

'No...' Millie attempted, then gave a helpless shake of her head. 'Some if it. I did say some of it...'

'All of it, perhaps?' Levander interrupted. 'Don't lie to me here, Millie.'

'I'm not,' Millie gulped, still frantically looking for an out. 'Papers make up stuff—exaggerate things... Surely you of all people would know that?'

'They would not dare.' He halted her attempt, his voice curiously calm now. Only it did nothing to soothe her, each word he delivered backing her further into her miserable corner. 'This newspaper I have already sued—already forced to print a retraction when they were less than accurate with their reporting. Two years ago they accused me of sleeping with the wife of one of our rivals—the truth was we had met for lunch twice, as she was planning a surprise party for him. That surprise party nearly cost her her marriage. They have been waiting to get me ever since, and I know they would not go to print unless they could account for every word. So tell me, Millie, and I would appreciate the truth—did you or did you not consider withholding the news about the baby from me? Consider that you would just raise the baby without my knowing?'

She had—the night she had performed her pregnancy test, when her whole world had spun out of control, yes, she'd thought about it—about if she was actually pregnant never letting him know. But almost instantly she'd dismissed the idea, and now, sitting on his sofa, hearing the accusation in his voice was more than she could bear. 'I did—but I'm here, aren't I?'

Levander didn't respond, just hurled another question. 'And did you also consider terminating the pregnancy?'

Millie ran a dry tongue over her lips, a fresh batch of tears threatening. Her attempts to hold them back were rewarded with a running nose, and she gave a rather ungracious sniff before she finally answered, in the shakiest of voices, 'For about two minutes.'

The look of absolute disgust on his face told her exactly what he thought of her response.

'And while you were so—you will forgive me if I quote,' he checked nastily, picking up the hateful paper and reading loudly, each word like a hurtling knife aimed in her direction. 'While you were so "confused and vulnerable", it says that your friend Janey kindly pointed out to you that, given my extreme wealth, you and the baby would be well looked after, and that there were "plenty of women who would give their eye teeth for a regular maintenance cheque from a Kolovsky".'

'They were her words.' Millie shivered.

'But, "I'm here, aren't I?" were yours,' Levander cruelly pointed out. 'Here to arrange your regular cheque, Miss Andrews? Here to make sure that your future is secured?'

'I'm here to tell you that I don't know what to do…' The tears were coming now, and the fear, the misery, the utter bewilderment of the past sixteen weeks was nothing compared to the horror of facing Levander in this mood. 'I'm here to tell you that I've messed up our lives and that I'm having a baby.'

'Well, as you can see…' utterly unmoved, he stood there '…I already know.'

'I'm sorry.'

'Save it for later,' Levander sneered. 'Save it for our child when it learns how to read.'

'Stop it,' Millie sobbed, placing her hands over her ears, hysteria rising in her voice. 'Please, just stop it. I never meant for those things to be printed, and I never, *ever* want the baby to hear them.'

'Drop the drama, Millie, it does not move me.' His voice was eerily calm, but his face was menacing as he stepped in closer, his two hands removing hers from her ears and pushing them down by her sides, pinning her against the wall, not with his strength but his hatred. 'Tell me, have you cancelled your gym membership yet?'

'What?' She had no idea where he was going, her mind a blizzard of thoughts attempting to focus on his strange question.

'You told me that night you pay for your membership but you don't go…'

'So…?' Her eyes darted, looking for an out, looking at anything other than him—the wall preferable to the sheer loathing in his eyes.

'I find that lazy.'

'I don't understand…' Millie whimpered, feeling his

hot breath on the shell of her ear, feeling the bristling emotion emanating from him, shivering with misery at all they had become. 'I don't understand what you're saying.'

'Then allow me to explain better. When I sign for something, when I pay for something, when I set my mind to something, I make the most of it—every time.'

'What does my gym membership have to do with this?' Millie asked. But she knew what was coming, and wanted to slam her hands over her ears again as he spat out his demands.

'I am telling you that I am not lazy, Millie. Don't think for a minute you get a cheque from me and I make an occasional visit.'

'I wasn't th-thinking that at all...' Her teeth were chattering so violently she could barely get the words out.

'Don't think I pay my membership and then forget, or I am too busy to come. I am there every time.' He was there now, right in her face as he made himself beyond clear, his accent more pronounced in his anger. 'Making use of all facilities, making sure I get full use—'

'No!' Millie shook her head at what he was surely implying, but Levander just laughed in her face.

'You think I talk about *you?* You think I could want you after reading this filth? I am talking about our baby—I am in that child's life now, whether you like it or not. So get used to seeing me, Millie. Get used to it quickly—because I am in your life now, every day.'

Emotion and exhaustion, coupled with a good dose of

the morning sickness that had her feeling so wretched, so weak, washed over her. She couldn't even attempt to argue with him—to thrash out the details that she knew had to be sorted. She just wanted to close her eyes on the horror, to find somewhere safe where she could lick her wounds and regroup.

'We'll talk about this later…' Somehow she found her voice, somehow she managed to look at him, her red, bloodshot eyes trying and failing to recognise the man she'd thought she once knew. 'You do what you have to, Levander, and I'll do what I can. But right now I'm going to my hotel…'

'You're staying here.'

'After the way you've just spoken to me? You really think that I'm going to stand here and attempt to defend myself to you when you've clearly already made up your mind?'

'You have no choice,' Levander retorted. 'There are photographers, press down in the foyer. You really think they will just let this story go?'

'Why the hell are they so interested?' Millie flared. 'What does it have to do with them?'

'I am a *Kolovsky!*' Levander shouted at her for the first time—and it was almost a relief. Raw anger was easier to face than the simmering hatred that had greeted her at the airport. 'I am one of the wealthiest single men in Australia—my *life* is their interest. Do not pretend for a single moment longer that you didn't know that. Now, if you choose to go down there and make matters worse instead of better then I will not stop

you. I wish you luck getting past them and into a taxi.
I wish you luck checking into another hotel and trying
to get the sleep you clearly need…'

He had a point, Millie realised, recalling the frenzy
of the press at the airport. The thought of facing them
without Levander to control them wasn't particularly
appealing.

'Go to bed.' He must have sensed her hesitate and
he seized on it, his voice more reasonable now. 'Go to
bed and I will not disturb you. Rest, and then, when we
have both calmed down…'

'When did you find out?' For the first time she got
to ask a question—strange the details that mattered
when chaos reigned. 'Did they call you to confirm…?'

'I read it an hour ago.'

It took a moment for it to sink in, for her to realise
how low the press had really stooped, the shock tactics
they were prepared to use. She might have landed in
Melbourne to face that greedy crowd alone. And even
if Levander's greeting had been less than cordial, even
if his words had been reprehensible, she was grateful
that despite his own shock he'd been there for her.

'I was going to tell you.'

'Just go to bed, Millie.'

Only she couldn't now. The massive impact that had
hit was receding, but aftershocks were rippling in. 'I
really thought she was my friend…' Rubbing her fingers on her temples, Millie struggled to take it all in. 'I
trusted Janey. I can't believe—'

'It is done,' Levander interrupted. 'Now it is time to fix it.'

'Can we?'

'I will think of something,' Levander answered. 'When you go to bed I will speak with the public relations people and work something out. Tonight we will have dinner with my family. At least if we put on a united front for now...' His voice trailed off. Perhaps he was realising she was too dammed exhausted to take it all in, too bone-weary for out-loud musings. 'Get some sleep, Millie; just try not to think about it now.'

With a tired nod she headed to the bedroom, peeled off her clothes and sat on the edge of the bed in her bra and knickers, wondering just what the hell she should do—how on earth it had come to this, how she could possibly tell her parents what had happened since her arrival in Melbourne. She jolted as yet another aftershock hit.

'Oh, no...' A whimper of horror escaped her lips as the implications of the very public demise of her reputation became all too apparent—as the appalling realisation hit that her parents would probably already have read a similar article in the UK, would be reeling in horror at the thought of their daughter landing on the other side of the world to this nightmare.

They already knew.

Everyone knew.

That was why the immigration officer had given her such a hard time. He had known she was pregnant—had known because he'd read about it...

'I need to borrow your phone…' Her tear-streaked face appeared at the door. She didn't even notice he was standing where she had left him, talking on his mobile.

'Of course.' He gave a bemused nod. 'Is the one by your bed not working?'

'It's an international call…' Mille started, then understood the confusion behind his question. The richest, most eligible bachelor in Australia clearly didn't give two hoots about his phone bill.

Perhaps he heard her numerous attempts, understood that in her emotional state the international code to the UK might not come easily to mind, because after a few moments he came in, dialled in the number, and turned to go. He halted as she literally crumpled at the sound of her mother's hysterical voice.

Seeing her standing in just a bra and knickers, shivering in her own misery, hearing her shaking voice begging her mother to calm down, for the first time he wasn't thinking about the baby, nor was it the vile words in the article that consumed him. For that moment it was her. Her pain, her anguish, was so raw, so deep, even Levander couldn't remain unmoved. He placed a hand on her shoulders for support as she doubled up with the pain of it all.

'Mum, please,' she begged, over and over. 'It's not that bad. I'm fine—the baby's fine. I know—I can't believe what's happened… You have to calm down. I can hear Austin getting upset. Please, Mum, it really isn't as bad as it seems…' But clearly Mrs Andrews didn't believe her daughter; Levander could hear her cries as Millie attempted to reassure her.

'I don't know why Janey did it, either. She's been acting a bit strange recently—I thought she was a bit jealous about my paintings. But whatever her reasons, it's done now...'

Again his conviction wavered. The anger, shame, and humiliation at being the last to know, the sheer panic that had propelled him to the airport, dimmed a touch as he started to see things from Millie's side.

Her best friend had betrayed her. Her whole life was under the microscope. Though for him it was the wretched norm, for Millie it must be like awaking to a nightmare. Seeing her pale, shell-shocked face, listening to her try to sound upbeat for the sake of her mother, he felt something inside him shift—and not just towards her. Guilt flickered in for the way he had spoken to her, for the anger he had unleashed towards the mother of his child.

His child.

The realisation was starting to hit home. She was carrying a baby—his baby—and the thought literally paralysed him, terrified him more than Millie or anyone could ever know. Yet somewhere deep within there was a flicker of excitement—a flare of want for the tiny life they had created.

A strange defensiveness towards her.

'Do you want me to speak with your mother?' Levander offered. The sudden change in his manner obviously confused her, and he watched as Millie's stunned eyes jerked to his. Though she shook her head, and gripped the phone tighter to her, he could tell she was considering it. 'I will tell her that I am sorting things out.'

'I don't think speaking to you will help right now...' Mille covered the mouthpiece with her hand. 'But I don't know what else to say. She's really upsetting my brother. I just can't calm her down.'

'I will talk with her,' he said, and even though he had no idea what he should say, he *was* ready to step in. But as he held out his hand Millie shook her head, closing her eyes as she swallowed her bitter medicine—the united front she'd so vehemently opposed just a few moments earlier was the only viable option for now at least.

'Levander met me at the airport, Mum...' She blew her hair skywards as her mother's hysterics halted. 'He's dealing with the press. I promise you he's taking care of it, and that things will all seem better tomorrow. I'm at his home, he's standing next to me now...' She was trying to sound positive—happy, even.

But seeing the tears coursing down her cheeks as she spoke, as she tried to look out for her mother, made Levander feel like an utter heel.

'Honestly, Mum—Levander's not cross. He knows me better than to take what Janey said at face value. We're going out tonight with his family. Yes...' With her free hand she pushed his off her shoulder, gritting her teeth as she lied into the phone, her eyes blazing with loathing for Levander as she spoke. 'Please don't worry—tell Dad not to, either—everything's going to be fine.'

Finally, when nothing she could say would appease her mother, when she could hear Austin's mounting distress in the background, Millie gave in, handing the phone to Levander and dropping to the bed, hugging her knees and biting on her lip, wondering what reaction he would get.

'Mrs Andrews, I am sorry we have to first speak in these circumstances. I understand that you must be distraught, but let me assure you that your daughter is okay…'

He was so commanding, so perfectly polite and yet so effortlessly charming, that the tears, the panic that was engulfing her stilled. Millie jerked her head upwards as clearly Levander had the same effect on her mother. The buzz of anxious chatter spilling out of the phone hushed as Levander took control—but even as he said the right things, even as he soothed with his silken voice, still he unnerved her. Like a doctor walking in and giving a cancer diagnosis, his delivery was slick and effective, riddled with fact yet utterly devoid of compassion.

'I met her myself at the airport, and I will tell you now what I told the press, so you get no more surprises—I have asked that your daughter be my wife. Tonight we are going out with my family to make things official.' He handed the receiver back to her and Millie listened to her much calmer mother, twittering away, saying that Levander sounded nice, that it sounded as if he had things under control, was she sure she was really okay…?

'Honestly, Mum, I'm fine.'

Millie dropped the receiver into the cradle, and her voice was a monotone when next she spoke, her eyes dull when finally she managed to look at him. 'Well, you got what you wanted—you got your united front.'

'I always get what I want,' Levander said ominously. 'Always.'

She could go.

Sitting in semi-darkness, all phones turned off finally Levander could think. He had had to resort to calling hotel security and insisting someone be placed on his floor, to halt the endless banging on the door, telling them that under no circumstances, no matter how dire the emergency, was he to be disturbed.

This was the emergency he must deal with.

What the hell had he been thinking? Over and over he berated himself for even thinking of taking her out to dinner tonight—exposing her to the snake pit of his family and the chance of stumbling on the truth.

He managed a glimmer of a smile as he envisioned her happy, lively voice attempting conversation, asking questions that, when you were with a Kolovsky, were completely out of bounds.

They'd crush her.

He had to somehow warn her without telling her—but how?

How many times he'd headed to the bedroom door,

braced himself to enter, to wake her from her much needed slumber and tell her what was on his mind, Levander didn't know. A couple of times he had even got as far as opening the door, standing for a breathless second or two and watching her sleep—her tumble of curls sprawled across the pillow, the steady rise and fall of her chest, long eyelashes fanning her cheeks and the flicker of her eyelids that told him she was dreaming…

How could he wake her to tell her his nightmare?

And if he did, then what?

How could Millie, how could anyone, fathom what he was feeling? And anyway, if he told her his truth—if he exposed his family secret—she could use it against him. Closing his eyes, Levander dragged in air, his mind racing faster—wincing at the prospect of the Kolovskys undertaking damage control. Like a flawed piece of silk, she'd be relegated as seconds, her name muddied and soiled till there was nothing of her left— anything was permissible if it meant preserving the family's reputation.

He stared at the passport sticking out of her handbag, sitting beside the suitcase half opened on the floor beside the bed. He figured at most it would take her five seconds to pack and walk out the door.

And who could blame her?

He couldn't keep her a prisoner here. And no matter how loudly he might have insisted today that he would fight her all the way, a woman like Millie wouldn't take long to regroup—in a day or two the wind would be back in those glorious sails and she'd be gone.

They'd be gone.

On the next flight to London, with all the ammunition she needed to fight her case. What court in what land would rule in his favour?

Nina's jeers were coming back to haunt him now... making him imagine the vile outcome if Millie ever had her day in court.

It wasn't the fear of losing money or reputation that had stopped him in his tracks with Nina—it was fear of the court's inevitable decision that had chilled him to the bone.

How could she *not* be the better parent?

Closing the door behind him, Levander knew what he had to do.

Stepping into his lounge, he pulled back the curtains and stared out at the wintry morning, at the heavy grey clouds that smothered the skies Millie had been in so recently—the skies that would surely claim her if somehow he didn't get in first.

She had to marry him.

His breath whistled through his teeth as he let it out.

He couldn't let his guard down for a second—couldn't let her even a tiny bit close till that ring was safely on her finger.

Whether she wanted to or not, Millie had to marry him so he could protect them all.

CHAPTER SIX

'MILLIE?' JUMPING AT his rather brusque greeting, blinking as the bedroom door opened, Millie could only compare this awakening to her father coming in a decade earlier, when she'd stayed out too late and partied just a little harder than she'd promised her parents she would.

'Am I grounded?'

'What?' Cruelly turning on the lights, he frowned down at her and placed a heavy glass of water on the bedside table. Despite not wanting to accept anything from him, the chink of ice against the glass, combined with a very dry mouth, had Millie reaching over and gulping thirstily as Levander continued. 'It is time for you to get ready. I tried to let you sleep as long as possible, but our dinner reservation is for eight.'

'Oooh…' Millie closed her eyes and leant back on the pillow. 'How could I forget that little gem?'

'You should start to get ready.'

'Do we really have to go?'

'We agreed on it.'

'Actually, no, *we* didn't.' Sitting up, Millie wrapped the sheet around her, her woolly jet-lagged brain functioning a lot better after a decent sleep. 'I was told there were a lot of things I ought to do, but I can't actually remember agreeing to any of them. And for your information I don't want to go—so I'm not.'

There. With a little nod at the end, she said it and, closing her eyes, rested back on the pillow.

'Are you always this selfish?' She'd expected him to stalk out—had prepared herself for a rather loud slam of the door—but instead he stood over her. Not that she could see him—her eyes were still firmly closed—rather she could feel his brooding presence, hear the contempt in his voice as he stared down at her. 'You really think *I* want to do this tonight? You really think *I* want to be out with my family, posing for happy-family shots after all that has happened?'

'Then don't,' Millie attempted, only her voice wasn't quite so brave. Peeking one eye open, she remained insistent.

'We have to make things better.'

'How?' Millie demanded. 'How could it possibly make things better? Frankly, from where I'm standing—or rather lying—going out tonight hand in hand, and pretending everything is okay between us, can only make things a whole lot worse.'

'Ring your mother and tell her that, then.'

'Fine.'

'And then you can ring the restaurant and tell them to cancel the booking, and let our guests know when they arrive.'

'They're *your* family,' Millie said, huffing onto her

side—hating what they had become, refusing to be forced into a corner.

But the sight of her back didn't halt him. In fact it inflamed him. 'And they are the very last people I want to dine with—who, despite what you read, I do not get on with.'

'So why—?'

'Why?' His voice was incredulous. 'You have the temerity to ask *why?* Do you ever stop to think of consequences, Millie? Do you ever think more than five minutes ahead in your life?'

'Of course...' she attempted.

'You know...' He shook his head in disbelief at her response, and with each passing word his accent was more pronounced. 'My family think you trapped me—they try to tell me you *knew* what you were doing that night—'

'I didn't.'

'I know that,' he roared. 'Despite what everyone says, I *know* that—because I think you're too dizzy to even come up with it...because you just don't think, do you? You meet a stranger, forget your pill...'

'It takes two...' Millie shivered.

'One night, *trajat'sya,* of sex, and now we pay the price—now we do as countless other couples have done when their one night of lust comes back to haunt them.'

'Haunt them!' Millie gasped. 'Levander. How could you say such a thing...?'

'How could I not?' Levander barked. 'What did you think would happen here? Did you expect me to start crying? To take you in my arms and say this is the best news I could imagine?'

'Of course not.' Unwanted tears welled in her eyes. His choice of words was so appalling, she simply couldn't help herself—the fact that he saw this baby like some dark ghost coming to haunt him was almost more than she could stand.

'So what did you think, Millie? Come on—tell me— what-did-you-think-was-going-to-happen?' Her threatened tears didn't move him. 'You don't *think* when you walk out on me, when you don't bother to tell me about our baby, of the consequences. Instead you open your mouth to your so-called friend. Well, unlike you, I *do* stop to think—I think of ten, fifteen years from now, when our child can read, when it stumbles on the filth that you spouted.'

'It won't be like that—'

She didn't get a chance to finish. Two strong hands were ripping at the sheet, pulling at it like a magician with a tablecloth—only instead of plates and cutlery left intact on the table it was a thoroughly shaken Millie left lying on the bed as Levander stood over her.

'This is not about what *you* want and it is not about me. It is about our child.' He didn't point, he didn't even look, but exposing her, letting her glimpse the full horror of a future without first making amends somehow made his words sink into her core. 'That newspaper article will always be there, the slur getting bigger with each passing day unless we halt it right now. Tonight we can make it right—make sure that when our child is old enough to stumble on it, be horrified by it, he or she will find out that the next day it was all discounted. So get up, get dressed, and get smiling—tonight we do our best for our child's future.'

Which didn't exactly give her much choice.

Pale, shaking, and feeling utterly wretched, she climbed out of bed. Though he was loathsome, he was also right—and she could actually glimpse an exit from the impossible, unsalvageable situation Janey had dumped them in. She even managed a wry smile as she glanced down at her suitcase. Which reminded her of her next problem.

'I know in theory it shouldn't matter a jot…' Jet-lagged, and as dizzy as if she'd drunk half a bottle of champagne, Millie raked a hand through very messy hair as she rummaged through the case. She was talking to herself more than him, delivering a swift pep talk and pulling funny little faces as she did so. 'I should just be myself, and not care about the cameras or the fact I'm dining with the *Kolovskys*…'

She pulled out the faithful red dress that had seen her through a couple of weddings, many first and last dates, and hopefully—if she didn't put on another ounce between now and next Friday—would see her through the 'meet the artist' night. Millie groaned at the blob of dessert she'd meant to dry-clean to oblivion, and closed her eyes in hopelessness. Resting back on her heels to look up at Levander, she missed the glimmer of a smile that briefly dusted his lips.

'Levander—what the hell am I going to wear?'

She sighed in utter relief when he delivered his answer. 'It is all taken care of.'

It was.

He must have had the entire Kolovsky range transported to his suite, and a hairdresser and a make-up artist were awaiting summons. Weary, utterly drained, and still stinging from his words, for now she played along with Levander's spin doctors, hoping and praying that even if Janey's words couldn't be erased, somehow they might manage to dilute them.

Choosing from such a dazzling selection of evening wear was a feat in itself, though. The stunning colours and heavy silks that were such a trademark of the Kolovsky line, though undoubtedly fabulous, were just a touch too vibrant for five feet three of drooping exhaustion. Even the basic black seemed just a touch too opulent. But there, amidst them, was the palest grey dress, its silk so thick it felt like wool, and as she slid it over her head for the first time Millie could see why people spent thousands to own a dress as fabulous as this. The cut of the fabric was to die for, tapering over her ribs, and there was soft ruching over her stomach which took away any attention from there and diverted it to her bust—the empress neck somehow giving Millie's rapidly expanding cleavage absolute centre stage.

With a cape draped around her she closed her eyes as the hairdresser transformed her strawberry-blonde curls into a thick glossy mass while the make-up artist, with as much skill with a brush as Millie herself possessed, accentuated her blue eyes with grey eyeshadow, lashings of mascara, and made her lips so full and sexy it was a shame she didn't feel like smiling.

'That's better.' Levander barely even glanced in her direction as he lifted his collar and fed in a tie. 'We'd better get moving.'

'Am I allowed to ask who's going to be there?'

'My father Ivan, his wife—my stepmother—Nina, and no doubt her ugly sisters and their hangers-on. And my half-sister Annika will be there, too.'

'The one I saw you with at the restaurant?' Millie asked, and Levander nodded. 'What's she like?'

'Sweet.' Levander shrugged, then cursed as his tie refused to knot. *'Govno.'*

Watching him heading to the mirror, muttering under his breath and knotting his tie there, for the first time Millie actually registered that he was nervous.

'And that's it?'

'That is enough for tonight. I have two half-brothers—twins, Aleksi and Iosef—but they are overseas. Aleksi is in London, working for the company.'

'And the other twin?' Millie asked, overwhelmed and wretched at the impossibility of them all.

'Iosef is a doctor—a trauma specialist,' Levander clipped. 'He has been working in Russia for the last five years.'

Which sounded rather more safe and normal—strange how the most esteemed profession could sound positively bland when you were a Kolovsky.

Tie still nowhere near knotted, he glanced over to her. 'Here.' Digging in his pocket, he pulled out a ring—

with no box or bow, and absolutely no ceremony. 'You'd better put this on.'

'Dig myself in deeper, you mean?' Millie retorted.

'Don't play the innocent. I told your family and mine that tonight we will make things official—we can hardly do that without a ring.'

Pushing the ring on the suitable finger, Millie gave it less than one glance and certainly not a second. She wouldn't give him the bloody satisfaction. 'Well, so long as you know I'm a firm believer in long engagements. I'm not going to be pushed into anything.'

'And as long as *you* know that I'm not to be pushed *out* of anything either—then at least we'll understand each other. You'd better help me with this. I can't get it to sit right.'

He *was* nervous, Millie thought again, fiddling with his tie knot. And so was she—and not only about tonight. Standing less than a few inches away from him, trying to sort out the mess he'd made of his tie, she could feel his body was rigid with tension. His eyes stared fixedly ahead, and he was so tall her face was at his chest—so close it was impossible not to breathe him in, not to notice the strong angle of his fresh-shaven jaw, the thick set of his neck, impossible not to think of the last time they'd been this close.

What did this man do to her?

Her hands were shaking like an addict, her body craving the next dangerous fix. She focused on the ring she'd sworn not to pay any attention to—but a generous carat of diamond was a poor diversion when it was attached to a hand that was touching him.

'That's better…' She had to clear her throat to speak, and stepped back a bit, admiring a little more than her handiwork. 'Should we go?'

'We're supposed to wait for Katina.' Levander glanced at his watch. 'She is our head of PR—she should be here by now to brief us.'

'Brief us?' Millie gave a nervous giggle. 'We're going for dinner with your family. How bad can it possibly be?'

'No worse than today…' He gave her the coldest of smiles. 'Unless, of course, we find out tomorrow that you chatted to someone else—got bored on the plane, perhaps, and discussed—'

'That's uncalled for—Janey was my friend…I trusted her.'

'So who's the fool?' Levander sneered. 'Who has to clean up the mess now? You know…' he actually deigned to look at her '…I cannot make out if you just pretend to be stupid or if you really are.'

'You bastard.'

'Correct.' Livid, he faced her. 'I *am* a bastard. I grew up a bastard. And if you think for a second I will allow my child the same fate—then you really are beyond stupid. I'm tired of waiting for Katina. Let's get this over with.'

He had the nerve to offer her his hand as they went out through the door, but reeling, stunned and terribly close to tears, she shook her head, pulling her bag tight over her shoulder. And even though he was beside her as she stepped in the lift, as she remembered their first night in there, all the love and emotion that had somehow jetted them to this bitter point, she could hardly bear it—she couldn't keep the truth from him for even a second longer.

'What you said…' Millie attempted. He was pushing the button, the lift doors were sliding downwards. Soon they'd be hurtled out into the public, to his family, and suddenly it was imperative that he knew the truth. 'I didn't forget.'

'Leave it now.' As the lift plummeted Levander frowned over, but she couldn't.

'I didn't forget to take my pill.' She watched his face tauten. 'I didn't forget because I wasn't even on the pill.'

'Are you telling me that Nina was right? That you knew exactly what you were doing?'

The lift stopping on the twelfth floor prevented further discussion. An elderly couple stepped in—dressed to the hilt and utterly gorgeous, they made polite greetings, then held hands as the lift plummeted again. Their obvious love and affection for each other was a bitter contrast to Levander and Millie. When they finally arrived at the ground floor they were greeted by a pretty little thing, no doubt hand-picked by Levander, stepping forward and smiling brightly, introducing herself as the Kolovsky head of PR.

'You were supposed to wait for me, Levander.'

'You were late,' he answered tartly.

'Nina took a little longer than expected. Now—no

interviews, no comments, no matter how provoked, and above all else make sure they can see the ring.'

Pretty and smiling she might be, but she was as sharp as a tack, her shrewd eyes taking in the pair of them.

'Get over it now, guys,' she hissed through her glossy red lipstick. 'The photographers are mainly at the restaurant, but there's no doubt still a couple outside. So unless you want this mess still staring at you from the papers at breakfast tomorrow, I suggest you start smiling. I'll take the car in front and field any questions. And, Millie...' she was walking swiftly beside them to the waiting car '...at least *try* and look as if you've missed him. Levander, hold her hand...the right one...' she directed. 'When you get to the restaurant make sure it's her right hand you're holding.'

He held it, all right—held it so hard it hurt. And despite his insistence that they attend, it was Levander who was flouting the strange rules—marching her to the car just as her father had done at that long-ago party, bundling her into it in a similar fashion, too, not even attempting a smile for the cameras.

'You *knew*...' he gritted as the car sped off towards the restaurant. It was a trip of less than half a kilometre, but there had been no question of walking. 'You deliberately forgot to take it. Well, enjoy the pantomime you've created tonight, Millie. You've clearly worked hard to be here.'

'You're so ready to think the worst of me,' Millie snarled, not caring that they were already pulling into the restaurant, and barely even registering the crowd on the pavement outside. 'Maybe I am thick and stupid, but the fact is I wasn't *on* the pill—and, unlike your usual sophisticates, I don't happen to carry condoms in my purse just in case some bloody six-foot-three Russian decides to come and take my virginity.'

'What?' His voice was hoarse, his eyes darting to Millie's as she tried to look away—anywhere but at him. 'You're telling me—?'

The door was opening on their heated exchange, cameras flashing as their names were called—and she could actually see him hesitate, caught in the desire to shout something rather impolite in Russian, slam the door closed again and carry on what they'd started. But Millie had no intention of continuing this conversation now—or ever, if she could help it.

'That's exactly what I'm telling you,' Millie snapped, before propriety took over and they stepped out of the car. But she delivered one tiny little parting shot for him to chew on over dinner. 'So tell me, Levander, what's *your* excuse?'

CHAPTER SEVEN

'MILLIE!'

'Levander!'

'Over here, Millie!'

As they stepped out of the car and towards the restaurant their names were being called from every angle, and despite the arguments, despite her fury, she clung tightly to his hand—because otherwise she'd surely have turned and run. Though with Katina answering on their behalf, the horror of the press with their blood up was perhaps the lesser of two evils when Levander's family were on the other side of the door, surely furious with this naïve little thing who had got them all into this impossible mess.

The flash of the cameras barely made Levander blink; rather it was her revelation causing shards of glass to explode in front of his eyes. His first instinct was to pull her away from the maddening crowd, to refute her claim, to tell her that the hot, sensual woman he had held that night had known exactly what she was doing, had known exactly how to please a man...

...or how to please *him*.

As they walked the short distance, continuing to be bombarded with questions, he willed himself not to think about her warm body entwined around his, the places they had taken each other that night. Her sweet, tentative, but oh, so tender tongue exploring him, eyes like jewels staring up at him, laced with questions, searching for approval as he'd implored her to go on.

He barely registered the questions that were hurled at them, retracing instead that delicious night—but with guilty feet now, because he *had* thought about a condom.

For the first time Levander admitted that to himself. For that split second as he'd hovered at her entrance, as he'd felt her silky and warm beneath his skilful fingers, it had crossed his mind to reach over as he always did to his bedside table…only he'd *chosen* not to.

Chosen, if not rationally, to allow himself the feel of her. He had given in to want, hollow with a lust that only she could make him feel—the heady release he'd encountered so intense, so vivid, he'd chosen that pleasure.

'Do you or Millie have anything to say about the allegations in the paper this morning regarding a termination?'

It was the one question that stopped him in his tracks—the one question he chose not to ignore.

'Nothing.' Levander disobeyed Katina's orders, not just in his surly response, but by wrapping his left arm around Millie's shoulder and gripping her hand with the other. There wasn't a hope in hell of them getting a shot of the ring—not that Levander seemed to give a damn. His face a picture of contempt as he stared boldly into the crowd. 'There is nothing I want to say to any of you—you all disgust me.'

It would have been a relief to step inside if his family hadn't been waiting.

And, despite Levander's 'ugly sisters' comment, each was more beautiful than the next. They swooped on her like humming birds—tiny, exquisite women, wrapped in vibrant colours, pecking at her cheek. Though there was nothing fragile in their voices. Despite her complete lack of Russian, Millie knew they were discussing her— thick, rich voices shouted for space as she attempted to centre herself, and she was grateful for the strong hand on her arm as Levander guided her through the maze of the restaurant, led her to the table, where she hoped to draw breath.

'This is my father.'

Millie stared at the most powerful man at the table. Even the best tailor couldn't disguise his emaciated body and gaunt face. Silver hair brushed backwards revealed a face that was almost skeletal; shaking hands reached for the glass in front of him.

'My son inherits my love for beautiful women...' He raised a glass in her direction and Millie, unsure of what to do, turned to Levander. But there was no guidance on offer there. Her heart stilled as the anger she had been on the receiving end of paled into insignificance. Like opals on fire, she witnessed the darkness of his eyes turn black as he stared across the table.

'If that is what I am to inherit from you I ask you to strike me off your will,' Levander said coolly, as Millie tried to contain a shocked gasp. 'Your treatment of women is something I hope to avoid.'

'Levander…' Millie couldn't help the scold. The hatred, the vileness in his voice, was toxic, and to aim it at someone so frail, so publicly, was more than she could comprehend.

'Why do you complain, Levander—I have given you everything—cars, money, yachts…'

'I have worked for them all,' Levander pounced. 'With or without you I would have made it—*vrubatsa?*'

'This much I understand,' Ivan answered. 'Whether or not I live to hear it—one day you will thank me for the opportunities I give you. Without me you are nothing.'

'Without you…' Levander stared across the table, and Millie realised no one was talking; every eye was turned to Levander. 'Is how I have lived my life. Don't ask me to cry for you now. I mourn my mother instead.'

'Levander.' The same throaty voice that had begged him for reason the night they had met was pleading again. 'Papa is sick, but he is here tonight for you. What is wrong with you, Levander? First you shout at Mama this morning…now this.'

What the hell *was* wrong with him? He never referred to the past with his family—with anyone—never let them close enough for that. Yet Annika was right. This was the second time today he had flown at the slightest provocation. Usually he prided himself on the charming yet distant mask he presented to the world, but today he was wearing every emotion on the outside of his skin. Every comment from his family ripped into the wounds he kept carefully hidden; every exchange with Millie delivered an anger he hadn't known since he was a boy.

Downing his drink in one gulp, he had barely hit the glass on the table before the waiter refilled it.

What the hell was he doing?

Tonight was about backing Millie one step further into his corner—to find a way to hold on to her, to ensure she became his bride before she found out about his murky past—and yet here he was, goading his family to reveal the truth they never acknowledged.

His truth.

'Leave it, Annika.' It was Nina who interrupted her daughter. 'This is not the place.'

As a waiter approached and placed a sumptuous seafood platter in front of them, the spitting insults melted into polite chatter, as if nothing had taken place.

'So, when is the wedding?' Nina asked, as Millie took a huge gulp of water.

'We are here, Nina,' Levander answered. 'That is enough.'

'For now.' Nina shrugged. 'You were the one who said to the press she was to be your wife—so now you must decide on a date. We fly to Milan in two weeks— and then on to Paris. Your father needs warm weather now. I think we will see out the European summer there…'

'I really don't need to hear your flight schedule, Nina,' Levander drawled, deliberately missing the point. But Nina was determined to ram it home.

'Sooner is better, Levander—if she is to have a hope of getting into the dress, then you need to get things going.'

The dress.

Nerves catching up, Millie almost giggled, but quickly she swallowed it, knowing not a single one of the Kolovskys would get her humour. Oh, she knew it was Nina's rather limited English that had caused the slip, but Millie had a sudden vision of a wedding dress hanging in a wardrobe somewhere, waiting for any woman with a semblance of a waist to step into it.

'Our wedding is our concern,' Levander said darkly, stopping Nina in her tracks—temporarily at least. But the night just continued in the same bitter vein, and for an already wilting Millie it was beyond confusing.

It was as if she wasn't even there—the charade for the cameras had nothing on this. It was hideous, sitting there while the whole family discussed their relationship as if it were for *them* to decide the outcome. Her cheeks burnt with embarrassment and anger as Nina started talking in Russian—clearly about Millie—rudely gesturing towards her.

The whole table joined in the loud conversation until Levander halted them. 'Millie speaks no Russian—you will speak only in English when she is present.'

'She might not want to hear what we have to say—' one of Nina's sisters attempted.

'All the more reason you should keep quiet,' Levander retorted, and even though his voice was even there was a warning glint in his eye that told all present he wasn't joking—a warning glint in his eye that stayed trained on his stepmother. Millie watched as she flushed, watched as a cruel smile twisted his mouth as Nina finally turned and, with a nervous croak in her voice, addressed her sister.

'We speak English.'

It was awful—the worst meal of her life—and even though she'd only seen them a couple of days ago, Millie was gripped with longing for her own family. The gentle bickering that flared at their dinner table was a million miles from the poisonous atmosphere that shrouded this table. Even more bewildering was the fact that, though Millie spent the meal reeling, Levander seemed completely unfazed, sitting as brooding and as unmoved as he had with his sister on the night they had met, unperturbed by the toxic company...

When the waiter came to take their orders for coffee, she made a last-ditch effort to talk to the reticent Annika.

'You're a designer...?' Millie struggled to make conversation with Levander's stunning half-sister. 'Levander said you mainly do jewellery.'

'I do both jewellery and clothing,' Annika said warily, her eyes darting to her mother.

Levander watched Millie try so hard to fit in with them, and watched as they stonewalled her—just as they had him. He watched them retreat into their diamond-crusted shells when a question might actually demand an answer, watched until it actually hurt to look—till he simply couldn't watch any more.

'Which do you prefer?' Millie went on, and it seemed a perfectly reasonable question—especially from one artist to another—like Nina asking if she preferred to paint with water or oil. But, as Millie was quickly realising, nothing was normal in this family.

'I'm equally good at both.'

'Oh.' Millie floundered, utterly bemused by her response, but accepting it, and steered the conversation to something hopefully more sustainable. 'You were born here? In Australia, I mean?'

'Yes.'

'And do you ever get back…?' Taking a slug of water, and praying they'd hurry with the coffee, Millie glanced over to Levander, who wasn't even attempting to be nice. He appeared thoroughly bored with the night's proceedings. He was glancing at his watch, drumming his fingers on the table as if at any second he might just get up and walk out. Hopefully he'd remember to take her with him, Millie thought darkly, as she attempted to get this wary woman to at least make small talk.

'To Russia?' Millie's wide smile was so strained, so forced, she could almost feel her lips splitting under the strain. 'To…' She gave a tiny frown as she tried to recall the name Levander had cited. 'To Detsky Dom?'

If she'd stood up and danced naked on the table, if she'd passed wind and laughed, the response couldn't have been worse. Annika knocked over her wine glass as she let out a shocked gasp, Nina just gaped at her for her boldness, and Ivan spluttered into a noisy fit of coughing. But most curious of all, as she turned anguished eyes to Levander for support, as she tried and failed to understand what on earth she had said that was so awful, she was stunned to see him put back his head and laugh.

'I'm sorry,' Millie floundered helplessly. 'What did I say?'

'Don't be sorry.' Still Levander laughed, but his eyes when he stood were as black as coal. 'You see—Annika is too good for Detsky Dom—is that not right, Nina? Come…' As the waiter placed a shot of espresso in front of him, Levander didn't even give it a glance. 'We go now.'

'It is too soon—' Nina started, but Levander was adamant.

'Why?' Levander challenged. 'You have your pictures for the paper.'

And so it started again—scarlet lips air-kissing her cheeks, perfume wafting in her nostrils as the table noisily farewelled them. And if she'd been confused before, Mille was perturbed now, her head whirring with questions as they stepped out of the restaurant and into a waiting car—sped the few hundred metres to the hotel and in a matter of moments were back in Levander's sumptuous suite.

'What did I say wrong?' She was shaken to the core, but her voice was somehow strong. 'I don't understand.'

'You never will with my family.'

'They were so rude…' If the rules stated that no matter how much your partner did, one should never criticise his family, then it was way too late. 'And yet when we stood up to go…'

'Others were watching,' Levander elucidated, and for Millie it was just too much. She shook her head in astonishment as Levander continued darkly, 'What you just witnessed was a first-class production Kolovsky-style. All they care about is reputation—and how we appear to others. The truth matters nothing to any of them.'

'You were rude, too…' Millie said accusingly. 'From the second we got in there you were poisonous. Why don't you like him? Because he left your mother?'

'Leave it, Millie.'

'And Nina,' Millie insisted, recalling the hate in his eyes, the cruel smile on his lips. 'You don't just dislike her, do you? You actually *hate* her.'

How, Levander asked himself, did she do it? How did she know to ask the one thing he couldn't answer? He could deal with a boardroom full of questions, deal with his family with his eyes closed, fob them off with half-answers, yet with her he wanted more than anything to confide in her, to give her the answers she sought. He had to crunch his hands into fists, so tempted was he to take hers, to finally share his hell.

But how could he?

'It is complicated.' Levander closed his eyes as he tried to come up with a suitable answer, trying to buy himself just a little more time till she was his to tell. 'It is family business—my father's story as much as mine.'

'Well, given I'm carrying his grandchild, when *am* I allowed to know?' She watched his face quilt with tension. She didn't want another row, but she wanted to know what the hell was going on. 'He's not just sick, is he…?'

'No, he's not just sick; he's dying—happy now?'

'Happy?' She shook her head in disbelief at his coldness, reeling at the impossibility of him—the memory of the tenderness that she had surely once seen in him was dimming further with every bitter twist of his tongue. 'Your father's dying and you talk to him like that…'

'I said leave it, Millie.'

'I wanted to leave it.' Millie was shouting now. 'I *wanted* to leave it, but you were the one who sent me into that minefield—I want to know—'

'Men'she znayesh'-krepche spish'.' He shouted his answer in Russian, which really was no answer at all, but his voice was so hoarse, so angry, so full of pain it scared her—only not for herself, for him. 'You need to go to bed.'

'You're really good at telling me what I need to do—especially when I ask a question that you don't want to answer.'

She scared him—not the little five-foot-three ball of anger who stood angry and defiant before him now, but the woman she was, the questions she asked. And more than that it was the feelings she triggered—dangerous feelings that confused him, made him think he must somehow be losing his mind…

'Go to bed…' His voice was a croak, but his actions were insistent and he guided her to the bedroom.

It should have been familiar, but in the few hours they'd been away the bed had been re-made and turned down—strangers had crept in and changed the landscape again. That Levander wanted her gone rather than try to talk things through, explain his family to her, was for Millie the worst. With a sob of frustration she headed to the bathroom, ripping the beastly clips out of her hair, pulling off the Kolovsky silk dress and leaving it in a crumpled heap on the floor.

Not even bothering to take off her make-up, too angry to even tie up her robe, she wrapped a towel around her and stormed back into the bedroom as he was heading out of the door. 'You know…jealousy really doesn't suit you, Levander.'

'You don't know what you're talking about.'

'Oh, but I think I do—you're jealous of them, aren't you?' She watched his face whiten, watched a muscle leaping in his cheek as she taunted him with vicious words—furious, hurt-fuelled words for the way he had treated her. She was missing the man she had met oh, so briefly, and hating what he had become. 'You're jealous that while you had to struggle on the other side of the world the rest of your family was living in luxury.'

'You think I am *jealous?*' He spat out a mirthless laugh. 'You think *that* is what makes me like this? Well, then—you don't know me at all.'

'I'm trying to,' Millie shouted. 'But at every turn you silence me with your mouth. Kissing me, sending me to bed, answering me in Russian… What does it *mean?*' she jeered. 'Come on—what you said before; what does it mean?'

'I can't even remember what I said…'

'Men'she znayesh'—krepche spish.' She watched his hand tighten around the door handle as she said it—his back stiffened, the muscles across his shoulders so taut she could have bounced a ball off them. His expression was unreadable when finally he turned around. He must have thought she'd have forgotten, but the words, even if they hadn't been understood, had been so hollow, so full of hurt, they'd stay with her for ever.

'Okay, then—it is a Russian saying—a proverb…' He couldn't even look at her as he spoke, and perhaps she'd misread him—because he looked more jaded than bitter, more resigned now than angry. And somehow, even though she was standing there, even though they had been with his family tonight, never had she seen someone look more alone. 'It means—*the less you know, the more soundly you sleep.'*

'But what if I *want* to know?' Before she had even finished speaking he had left, closing the door behind him. And even though there was no turn of a key Millie knew, *knew* Levander was locking her out.

Over and over she replayed the night—reviewed his short but brutal history. Simultaneously she recalled the tiny snippets she'd gleaned, like ominous thick drops of rain pelting on a windscreen, warning her of an impending storm: Annika's horrified reaction when she'd spoken of his home town, his sudden arrival in Australia, his odd relationship with his father and his family, and his clear bemusement when she'd questioned his choice of home.

The truth she had so desperately sought was less than appealing now as realisation hit that in her search for answers she'd missed out on a question—had taken for granted the misinformation she'd been fed. She had never actually asked Levander *when* his mother had died.

Dressed in nothing more than a silk wrap, Millie pushed open the bedroom door and saw him standing, staring unseeing out of the window, more beautiful than any model in art class, so still, so tense, so loaded with pain it made her want to weep.

He didn't even turn his head—didn't move a muscle as she approached.

'How old were you?' She didn't need to elaborate, knew when he closed his eyes that he understood the question. But she waited an age before finally he gave his hollow answer.

'Three.'

'So, when she died, did her family...?' She couldn't go on for a moment. She wanted so much for him to interrupt her, to tell her that whatever she was thinking surely she was wrong. 'Did they raise you?'

'They would have had to take food out of their own child's mouth to do that... You do not understand poor...' He wasn't being derisive or scathing, Millie realised. Quite simply he was stating a fact. Her lips trembled in horror. She was trying not to cry, and somehow to absorb the information he was giving her—because even if she didn't know Russian...no guessing was needed now.

'Detsky Dom isn't a town, is it...?' Her hand reached for him, fingers gentle on his taut shoulders. 'When she died you were put in a children's home.'

'No.'

For the first time since she'd come into the room he looked at her, or rather towards her. His eyes were fixed on her, perhaps, but somehow not focusing. His voice was detached and formal, and listening to him, watching his tense mouth form the most vile of words, was like being plunged into boiling water—like blistering pain on every cell of her skin as she tried and failed to fathom all he must have been through.

'Before she died, when she was too sick to look after me, I was put in *dom rebyonka*—the baby house. Later, when I was four, I went to *detsky dom*.'

There was nothing she could say.

A million questions for later, maybe, but there was nothing she could say now...

'And, no—before you suggest it again—I am *not* jealous. I accept the past, and the impossible choices that were made. I accept what they cannot.'

'I don't understand.'

'How could you?' His voice was hollow. 'Now your curiosity is satisfied—perhaps it is better you go...'

'Go?' Her hand was on his arm and she could feel him now—could *feel* him. For a second or two she hadn't been able to, hadn't been able to feel anything at all. Shock was a kind of anaesthetic at times, blocking the pain that consumed her, numbing everything in its wake. Only feelings were creeping in now. The two of them were still there, still standing after his revelation. That he would push her away after she'd forced her way in was almost more than she could bear. 'Why do you want me to go…?'

Because you will.

He didn't say it, just stared—stared at eyes swollen from the tears he'd provoked at the once happy face, now devoid of her ever-ready smile—and hated himself for tainting her, for soiling what had once been perfect.

'It is better if you go to bed.'

It really wasn't her place to argue, Millie realised, pulling her hand back. She respected his decision and turned to go, because it wasn't her place to tell him how he should feel, to say that whatever he privately thought of her surely at this moment he shouldn't be alone.

'I'm sorry.' Those two words had surely never sounded so paltry, but they came from the bottom of her heart. 'I'm sorry for all you must have been through.'

She turned to go, then changed her mind—and leant forward to kiss him. It was with the least provocative of intentions—a kiss goodnight she would give to any mortal in agony, any friend who had bared a piece of their soul.

Only he wasn't a friend.

Leaning over him and dusting his lips with comfort had been the intention. But when she felt his lips beneath hers, that quick kiss goodnight lingered just a fraction too long. So easy to kiss, so easy to close her eyes as she did and chase away the atrocities... A sweeter feeling was rushing in, replacing the horror, but after a moment of indulgence she felt his hands on her shoulders, felt him pushing her back.

'This time...' His voice wasn't quite so detached now, and his breath was hard and ragged between each reluctant word. 'When I suggest you go to bed I trust you understand I am not angry...'

'I do.'

She did.

Absolutely she understood what he was saying.

And absolutely she understood the balmy sedative she was offering.

'If you want me to stay then I will.' Her voice was different, unfamiliar even to Millie. Wanton words from very deliberate lips as she offered him this—and it wasn't just for Levander, but for her.

She didn't want to visit his nightmare, yet—didn't want to lie alone in her bed and weep for his past. She wanted him *now*—wanted the escape she was offering, too. She could feel the rise and fall of his chest against hers. Her hands were filled with a shameful longing to move down, to feel what she knew was surely there—surely, because he was struggling to look at her, struggling to push her away as their bodies screamed otherwise.

It would be impossible to walk with legs that felt like jelly, but somehow she'd manage it. The bedroom door was a blur in the distance, the room so thick with

tension she'd need a scythe to get there—but if he told
her to go again then she would.

He didn't.

Didn't say anything at all. Instead his mouth crushed
hers in response, in a fierce, desperate kiss that slammed
the breath out of her, that exactly matched her need.
A kiss that hurt with its intensity—a delicious hurt,
though. His skin rough on hers, his tongue probing, his
arms dragging her tightly to him, but not close enough
for Millie. Her silk wrap slipping off her shoulders,
she grabbed at his shirt, ripping away the material so
that naked she could press against him—feel his hard
arousal beneath his trousers as his hands cupped her
bottom, the metal of his zipper digging into her.

'All-day-since-I-saw-you…' Between kisses he spoke,
with his mouth full sometimes…full of her mouth, her
shoulder, her breast. His tongue explored the changes
since last he'd visited, each stroke a fever on her ripe,
needy flesh, each husky word from his lips refuting
his earlier contempt, giddying her, yet propelling her
towards a rapidly approaching destination. 'All-day-I-
am-hard-for-you.'

So hard.

Desperate fingers pulled at his zipper, needy hands
freeing his heated length. She wanted to linger just a
second, but Levander wasn't having any of it. Strong
hands around her waist lifted her those necessary decadent inches and her legs coiled around his back. She
bit into his shoulder as he plunged inside her, gasped
as he filled her, not knowing what to do. But again he

showed her, his hands guiding her bottom into a delicious rhythm, thrusting till she found her own. And it was so much more than sex for the sake of it—because if ever comfort was needed it was tonight—and if all they had was this, then surely they must build on it.

'I cannot last…'

His apology was a second overdue. Millie was the first to arrive—and in fabulous style, with a flash of heat searing up her spine so intense and so unexpected it startled her. Her new-found boldness utterly gone, she locked shocked eyes with his, feeling a flash of fear as she faced the unknown. But it was Levander holding her, telling her with his eyes that it was all okay, just different. With a squeal of delighted terror she let herself go with it…gave the little piece of her heart that was left to him.

CHAPTER EIGHT

IF MILLIE HAD thought that his revelations, the fabulous sex, or even the fact that Levander was now firmly instated in the bedroom would mean they were closer, she was wrong on each count.

It was as if he'd never touched her—and certainly as if he'd never told her anything. The topic of his past was once again completely out of bounds. Brooding, impossible and utterly unreachable, he rumbled like a prolonged peal of thunder through his inhuman schedule. Up at the crack of dawn to go running, then out to face his brutal day. And rather than talking, or spending their time getting closer, instead she was paraded to endless business dinners followed by even more endless parties. Yes, he slept beside her—and sometimes in sleep he even reached out and held her—but he never actually laid a finger on her, and night after night she lay miserable in her own desire, staring at the man who said he wanted to marry her, yet didn't seem to like her very much at all.

'I rather like this one.'

At the end of the week, as Katina handed them both

individual copies of the same newspaper, Millie winced again as she re-read the headline that had hit the stands on her second day in town: *From London with Love*.

'In fact, all the newspaper reports have been favourable. I've also managed a sneak peek at some of the magazines out next week and, though I'm loath to say it, Levander, your rather surly interaction with the press seems to have them eating out of your hands... Paragraph two,' she clipped, like a schoolteacher, as she handed them yet another article. '*"Kolovsky appeared defensive of his young fiancée, shielding her from the press and clearly eager to get inside to share the moment with his family."* The two of you have done very well, and as a surprising bonus it's taken the attention away from your father's illness. I'd say they're all pretty much scrambling to break the happy news of your wedding date—so when can I tell them it is?'

'When I find out—' Levander gave a tight smile '—you'll be the first to hear.'

'Well?' Katina's very trim rear had hardly wiggled out of the room when Levander tossed the question at her.

'Gosh, you can be so romantic at times, Levander. I told you I wasn't going to be pushed into anything.' She ran a worried hand over her forehead. 'Look, I've got this "meet the artist" thing with Anton, and after that...' Biting her bottom lip, she forced herself to look at him. 'After that, I think I ought to go home for a bit—you know, talk to my family...' He didn't say anything. She'd braced herself for the rip of his words, or the crack of his temper, but he just sat there, staring at her coolly, making her squirm with discomfort. If anything, it was far worse. 'I need to go home and decide what I should do.'

'You *know* what you should do.'

She gave a tiny helpless laugh. 'Sign my life away to a loveless marriage…'

'It does not mean it would not be a good marriage.'

'We don't talk.'

'We're talking now,' came his flip response.

'You don't tell me how you feel…'

'Why would I?' He looked at her as if it were so bloody obvious he couldn't believe she had a problem with it. 'Why-would-I-tell-you?'

'So we can get closer…' Millie shivered. 'So we can…' She had to be brave, had to ask him, *had* to know. 'Do you think…I don't know…in time…?' She was trying not to cry, trying not to sound needy, but the memory of his cast-off lover came to mind as she heard shades of the Latina's pleading creeping into her voice. But, hell, there was a baby to think of—so she squared herself to ask the most difficult question of all. Difficult, Millie realised, because if you actually had to ask, you probably weren't going to like the answer. 'Do you think you could ever love me?'

'My God…' he muttered under his breath, as if she were some stupid little girl who bored him with senseless questions, each incredulous shake of his head humiliating her right to her core. 'Always this question comes— "Levander, do you love me?" "Levander, if I

change this maybe then you will love me?" "Levander…
why can't you just *say* you love me…?" I am not going
to lie to you and tell you I think I will be in love with
you. I cannot say that.'

'I get the message.' She halted him with a shaking
hand, her tense face splitting into a rueful smile, tears
stinging at the back of her nose, wishing he would stop.
But Levander hadn't even started.

'You know, I don't think you do—so I make this
clear. You are not a prisoner—your passport is in the
safe and you know the combination. Walk out through
that door—go back to England—the choice is yours.'

'I just need to think,' Millie said helplessly. 'I'm not
saying no to marriage…'

She was going. It was all he could hear—all that
consumed him. All week he'd been waiting, knowing
that now she knew the truth of what he was she would
leave him. She was going and taking his baby, and as
sure as night followed day Levander knew she wouldn't
be coming back. The second she got home, back to her
family, they'd claim her, talk to her, tell her just how
much she didn't need him.

She was going—and he'd move heaven and earth to
stop her walking through that door. He didn't deserve
her, but he couldn't let her go.

'You try to keep me from this baby—I warn you how
it will be.' Once again his deepening accent signalled
his inner emotional turmoil. His eyes were as black as
the darkest night as he fought with the gloves off. 'It is
your shame that was smeared over the newspapers—

your talk of ending the pregnancy that is documented. You are the one walking out on a chance of giving our child a stable home—you deny my child a chance to properly get to know its father. See how far you get.'

'I don't understand…'

'Then I will explain better,' Levander sneered. 'You are some two-bit artist who when we met hadn't sold so much as a painting. There is one advantage to being a Kolovsky—money—and if I have to work in the family business for ever I will do it—if I have to spend every last cent ensuring my child is brought up beside his father, I will.'

'Levander…' Fear was licking at the edges—real fear. His demands were so unreasonable it was almost impossible to fathom that he was serious. But he was. If she went back to England then she'd be plunged into hell: her private life spewed across the papers, endless lawyers and bills and fighting… But how, after issuing such threats, could he possibly expect her to stay?

'We'll go away.'

His voice was hoarse. As quickly as that he had changed. He had been a ball of lightning, rolling towards her, hissing anger and singeing all in its wake, but suddenly his anger had dispersed, replaced with an urgency that scared her on a different level—it scared her for *him*. For just a split second she glimpsed the little boy he must have been—the scared child whose life had been ripped away from him by the untimely death of his mother. Then the shutters came down, but he continued softly, urgently.

'Right now. We'll go somewhere we can talk. I will arrange it now—we will go this afternoon. I will try...' His eyes were imploring her to listen, to just please hear him out, two black holes of dark emotion as he offered her the impossible. 'I will try to let you know me.'

CHAPTER NINE

'NEARLY THERE NOW.'

They'd barely spoken the whole journey, but Millie didn't mind. As they'd headed for the fabulous tropical north, leaving the cool southern winter behind, the silence had at first been strained, then mutual. Both were lost in their thoughts, both trying to comprehend the magnitude of whatever lay ahead. Slowly, as the plane had gobbled up the miles, the tension had seeped out of them, and by the time they arrived at Great Barrier Reef Airport, where they boarded a seaplane to take them for the final leg of their journey, they were actually managing to string together a few words.

Millie's face was pressed to the window. She was taking in the azure of the water, so clear she could see the fish, and occasionally lush green islands rushing beneath them like some fabulous holiday brochure.

'Are you okay?'

'Fine,' Millie breathed. 'But cross with myself.'

'Cross?'

'I should have made the effort to get up here the

first time. I can't believe I might have missed out on seeing this.'

'You haven't seen anything yet.'

He wasn't exaggerating.

A small speedboat greeted them, taking them on their last journey, sweeping them up to the beach—and it was like stepping into paradise as Levander helped her out. Cool water lapped around her ankles, and a gentle breeze skimmed over the Pacific Ocean, heralding the arrival of dusk. The endless white sand was so soft and powdery it was as inviting as a bed, and beyond low wooden huts blended so carefully with the forest of trees that at first glance they were missed entirely.

'This whole island belongs to your family?'

'It does. This was one of my father's wiser decisions—he bought it for a song when mortgage rates soared and everyone was going under. At the time he couldn't afford it, of course, but now...'

'It's amazing,' Millie breathed.

'I come here a lot.' She heard the full stop, and watched as he faltered, as he visibly attempted to do what he had promised to do—let her in to his thoughts. 'Mainly I come alone—here I seem to relax.'

'I can see why.' Millie smiled. 'It's just stunning.'

'It is,' Levander said simply, taking her elbow and leading her along the beach to a vast hut, along its decking and through a vast marabou door.

Though it was simply furnished it too was stunning—massive white sofas, beneath a whirring ceiling fan, the focal point of the lounge. All the shutters on the windows were open and the setting sun streamed hues of orange against the white walls. Endless white sofas were littered with cushions, family photos adorned surfaces and walls—it was way more intimate than the lavish hotel Levander called home.

Millie took her time looking at the photos, smiling at a younger Levander, serious and scowling at a family wedding—but even as she smiled it tore at her heart. His undocumented childhood had never been more evident as she stared at dark-haired, dark-eyed twins racing around on tricycles, and Annika too, blonde and gorgeous, beaming out of her pram.

'Is that you?' Millie jumped at the prospect, picking up a black-and-white baby photo and staring at the solemn eyes and the thatch of dark hair.

'That is my father.' Levander glanced over. 'I am not so old that I wore a dress as a baby.'

'He looks like you.' Millie laughed. 'Or rather, you look like *him*. I wonder…' A shiver of the most unexpected excitement rippled through her. The fleeting maternal impulses that had seen her through to date were beating more strongly now, coursing through her and settling to a rhythm, thrumming into a beat, as she surveyed this magnificent gene pool—as the baby deep inside her was fashioned into more than a possibility. An almost tangible image was teasing her mind's eye as she merged their features.

'I wonder too.' Levander finished her sentence for her. 'Since I found out I have wondered if he will be blond…' She opened her mouth to correct him, but Levander spoke over her. 'Or if she will be dark.'

'What would you like?' Millie asked. 'I mean, I know it doesn't matter, but if you could choose, what would you like our baby to be…?'

He really seemed to think about it—frowning at her question, then shaking his head.

'I'll think about it and let you know.'

Which was rather a strange answer, but she didn't dwell on it. Her mouth had dropped open as for the first time she saw her picture—the one she herself had painted.

'You shouldn't have done that…' Even if he'd meant well, even if he'd done it for all the right reasons, still it was wrong. Her hard-fought-for success seemed not so worthy now. 'We both agreed that that would be cheating.'

'There was no cheating. I followed up with the lady who bought it. She was happy with my price.'

'Oh.'

He heard her little thud of disappointment and smiled. 'She is an art dealer, Millie—she bought it to sell it on. You are going to have to get used to that. People will not always buy your work for sentimental reasons.'

'So why did you?' Her cheeks flushed as she asked, a tiny glow flickering inside as she awaited his answer. But it was soon doused when Levander shrugged and then stared at the picture.

'It interests me, I suppose…' He peered a bit more

closely. 'Really I have never invested in art. But perhaps I will think about it now…'

'So it's just us here?' Millie checked, changing the subject, trying to hide her disappointment, kicking herself for expecting anything more and staring beyond to the vast view outside. 'Well, apart from the staff.'

She could see them on the beach—setting up a table, lighting a fire—but Levander had promised seclusion and he really meant it.

'They will leave soon—they come twice a day while there are guests.'

'Do they live here on the island?'

'No—there…' He headed to a window and pointed at some glittering lights, seemingly miles away. 'That is a luxury hotel, some ten kilometres away. The staff are from there.'

'So, no room service at night?' Millie said, blowing her fringe skywards as she let out a breath and reeled at the opulence of the Kolovskys' existence, trying and failing to see how she could ever even begin to belong.

'If you want something, then I'm sure it can be arranged.' There was a distinctive edge to his voice. 'I'll go and tell them we're ready to eat. Would you like to shower before dinner?'

Even in the middle of nowhere—even in the most romantic setting on God's earth—it would seem there were still formalities to be observed. Still there was protocol to follow if you were dining with a Kolovsky.

'Of course.' Mille gave a tight smile. 'I shan't be long.'

* * *

She'd spent that morning in a spending frenzy. Utterly unable to stomach another Kolovsky freebie, she'd taken a thoroughly excited Anton on a shopping spree—though he'd been initially less than delighted to learn she would have to postpone her 'meet the artist' night—and had spent half her earnings to date on what she hoped was a suitably fantastic holiday wardrobe. It seemed to have helped him get over his disappointment. Now making her way into the bedroom, ready to pull out the few inches of gold fabric Anton had selected from her suitcase, Millie blinked at the impeccable room. After a moment she realised there would be no unpacking. It had all been taken care of—her new clothes were hanging neatly in the wardrobe, her new shoes were neatly arranged on the floor, her perfume, make-up, even her hair straighteners were all neatly arranged in the fabulous bathroom.

The Kolovskys' attempt at low key made her swoon in wonder. Everything was cool white, from the floor-to-ceiling marble to the fluffy white robe and towels, and one wall entirely taken up with the biggest mirror Millie had ever seen—it was like stepping into a movie set. She wanted to fill the bath with bubbles and sink into it. But worried her hair would frizz, she pulled on a cap and settled for a quick shower instead. After that she pulled on her very new, very expensive, not particularly comfortable underwear—but the effect was surely worth it, Millie thought. She picked up her dress and pulled the raw silk over her head, the luxurious mate-

rial hugging the curves of her body as she stepped back
to check herself in the mirror.

Pregnancy was certainly starting to wreak its
changes on her body. Her breasts, which had always
bordered on generous, were like two ripe peaches
now—and just as bruisable. The tender nipples were
like two thistles sticking out under her dress, and nothing was going to slim down the curve of her buttocks
to the supermodel proportions he was no doubt used to.

And yet...

...she felt beautiful.

The strange, slightly angular jut of her stomach as
she stood side on fascinated her.

Pressing her hand against the dress, Millie closed
her eyes. Instead of a soft, doughy mound of tummy,
she was greeted instead with a hard wedge of flesh.

'Does it move?'

He made her jump, but Millie gave a resigned sigh—
since when would a closed bathroom door stop a man
like Levander?

'The baby, I mean,' Levander elaborated when Millie failed to answer, a touch embarrassed that he had
caught her staring at herself.

'It was jumping around like anything on the scan.'
Millie smiled at the memory. 'But I don't think I can
feel it yet. The doctor said not for a few more weeks.'

'You don't *think* you can feel it?'

'Sometimes...' Millie gave a rueful smile at her own
imagination. 'Sometimes I think I feel a little flutter,
but the doctor said it was probably just—' She chose not

to go on. She didn't really want to discuss her digestive system with him. But it was nice that he was so interested—nice that he wasn't angry, or mocking, or any of the other hateful things he could so often be. 'Do you want to feel?' Beneath her foundation she was blushing to her roots, but comfortable with her decision all the same. Sex was utterly off her agenda till this entire mess was sorted, but *this* wasn't about *that*. 'I mean, there's nothing to actually feel, but…'

'I would love to.'

His hand through her dress was thankfully more intimate than sexy. Even if her bump wasn't exactly spectacular, he ran a fascinated hand over her and it was his moment to keep. His hand moved up and cupped the soft jut of her stomach so tentatively that Millie gave a soft laugh.

'You won't feel anything like that; here—' She pressed his hand in harder, pushing his index finger in between her pubic bone and her tummy button, just enough so that he could feel the firm ridge of her uterus, and she stared down at their entwined hands. The glitter of the diamond on her finger caught her eye. It was a diamond given for the wrong reasons, but somehow it felt right that it was there. And she knew from the way he held her, from the intent concentration and wonder on his face, that come what may her baby would always have a father, that whatever transpired between them Levander would be in this child's life for ever.

'I would like our baby to be happy.' Levander smiled at her confusion at his unexpected statement. 'I was thinking about what you asked, and I guess if our baby is happy we will have done a good job.'

She'd meant would he want a boy or a girl—had thought surely he had understood that—yet the answer he gave was exactly the right one. Strange that it brought tears to her eyes…

'Everything is local produce.'

A waiter was ladling barramundi onto her plate. The tangy citrus of lime reached her nostrils, and tiny, heavily buttered baby potatoes tossed through caramelised shallots soaked up the fragrant juices. She felt the strategically lit fire warming her bare shoulders as the smoke drifted down-wind.

'It looks fabulous.'

It tasted it too, and under any other circumstances Millie would have closed her eyes and relished the cocktail of taste on her tongue. Under any other circumstances perhaps she would then have opened them and gazed in awe at her dining partner…

…just not this one.

As the waiter melted into the shadows Millie chanced a peek from under her curled and blackened eyelashes and rued the promise of make-up.

Truly impeccable features could only ever be enhanced by nature—and the low half-moon hanging like a strategic lantern in the navy sky did the job perfectly, shadowing his jawline, the jut of his exquisite cheekbones slicing through his face, over the dark, suspicious eyes that watched her.

'Do they have to be here?'

'Who?' Levander frowned.

'The staff,' Millie attempted, leaning forward, speaking in a low whisper, afraid that the waiter might hear what she was saying. 'I just don't feel we can really talk...'

'They are not listening to us.'

'Rubbish,' Millie retorted. 'I've been a waitress, remember—your waitress—and look where we ended up.'

'I can dismiss them for tonight, if it makes you more comfortable. If you are not happy with the service, I will tell them to be more discreet, to—'

'The service is fabulous...fabulous,' Millie said, her urgent whisper drifting across the table. 'But we might as well be sitting in a restaurant in Melbourne, or London, or anywhere on the globe...'

'I don't get you, Millie—I tell you I am taking you away, somewhere we will not be disturbed, you disappear for three hours, come back with your hair done and a whole new wardrobe. You are no sooner here than you moan there will be no room service...'

'I was being—' Millie attempted, but Levander spoke over her.

'You put on a gold dress for dinner, and use a trowel for your make-up, and now you complain that you want low-key.'

God, he could be so brutal at times!

'I don't know how I'm supposed to be with you, Levander,' she returned, salty, glitter-filled tears spilling down her cheeks. 'I know *myself* is the obvious answer, but since you came along I don't know who I am any more. I just hoped it would be the two of us.'

He didn't say anything. Just stood up from the table and headed over to the waiter, speaking in low tones Millie couldn't hear before rejoining her.

'They are leaving. There are enough provisions in the cupboards and freezers; I do not have staff when I am here by myself. I just wasn't sure what you would want.'

'Touché.' Millie sniffed, then managed a watery smile. 'You could have at least waited till they'd cleared up after dinner. I'm joking,' she added, in case he thought she was being precious.

'We met when you were clearing tables—and if you had any idea of the effect you have on me, you'd know how delighted I am to farewell the staff.'

It was dark enough that he couldn't see her blush, but it was a dangerous hint of a flirt and it worried her. Till they'd sorted out this mess, he'd jolly well better forget about any of *that*.

As the staff packed up and headed to the speedboat, as its engine faded into the distance, Millie felt a shiver—not of excitement, but of nervousness. Nowhere on earth could they be more isolated—now it really was just the two of them, with no distractions or duties to cloud the issue, no background chatter or waiters hovering.

Stuck on a desert island with the man she loved— the same man who'd told her outright that he'd never love *her*.

CHAPTER TEN

EVEN WITHOUT THE intrusion of staff—even though they were quite literally, quite unbelievably, on a desert island and the purpose of their trip here was to talk—it couldn't just happen on demand.

Despite all her best efforts to relax, on the first morning Millie was impossibly awkward—up early, she slathered herself in sunblock, then dressed in a bikini, shorts, T-shirt and sandals. She banged into Levander at every turn in the vast kitchen as she fixed breakfast, trying to avert her eyes as he wandered around in a very low-slung towel, even more impossibly gorgeous than usual, yawning and stretching and drinking milk straight from the carton as she rigidly chopped fruit.

'Do you want fruit salad?'

'No.' He leant over and took a slab of watermelon, his lazy eyes taking in her clothes, before smiling at her pursed lips. 'Can you get a newspaper from the shop when you go?'

'What shop?' Millie asked, then instantly regretted it. She realised he was teasing her for being so over-dressed and gritted her teeth, slicing faster.

'I'm going for a swim—coming?'

'No.' He was walking out through the door...the door that led to the beach, not the bedroom...and yet she was just so appalled at the prospect that she couldn't stand it, couldn't stand it a second longer. She was terrified he'd expect them to run around naked, like in some awful nudist colony...

'Levander—'

'Whoops—'

The two words were said at the same time.

Levander turned slow and lazy towards her, giving her a very nice smile. 'I nearly forgot to get my bathers.'

'Pig,' Millie mouthed at the gorgeous sight of his departing back, reeling at the change in him. Without his family, without the press, he was like the man she had fallen head over heels for on their very first night—*better* even than the man she had met on their very first night. But she was still furious with him for his hateful manner in Melbourne. Furious with him for the game he was playing. Furious with him for teasing. Furious with herself for still wanting him so.

Sitting scowling and burning on the beach, watching Levander churning the surf with impossibly strong strokes, wasn't going to help matters. When he was far enough out she took off her T-shirt and sandals, telling herself it was silly to be so shy. But she couldn't even contemplate taking the top of her bikini off and going for an even tan. After all they'd done he'd already seen everything, but she'd never felt fatter or paler or more exposed, sitting on a vast beach in a tiny red bikini and watching him rise like some sexy Greek god from the water. And he was definitely sexy when wet, Millie thought, watching from behind her sunglasses as he walked over and proceeded to shake himself like a shaggy dog, dripping water all over her.

'The water is nice.'

'Good.'

'You should go in.'

'I might mess up my make up,' she spat back—even though she wasn't wearing any.

'I'm sorry for what I said…' He smiled at her petulance. 'You actually looked very beautiful last night.'

'Thanks for telling me *now!*'

'I have learnt to fight dirty…' His admission halted her a fraction. 'I had to in order to survive—not just with my family, but before. I will try not to do it to you again.' He lowered himself down beside her. He didn't bother with a towel or anything, just laid his wet body on the sand and stared, squinting, up at the sun. 'You don't fight dirty—do you?'

She stared down at him as he asked, and it was easier somehow to look at him, to answer him, with her sunglasses on. 'I've never had to.'

'I've spent all this time thinking you are like them— like the others—but I realise now that you're nothing like them at all…'

'Why does this have to be a fight, Levander?' She frowned in bemusement, working hard to understand him. 'Why—when surely we both want the same thing for our child.'

'A family?' he asked, and behind her glasses she screwed her eyes closed, unable to answer his impassioned plea. 'That is what I want.'

It was Levander who broke the impossible silence. 'How did *your* family take the news?'

'They were shocked.' Millie gulped. 'Stunned, really. It was just the last thing they expected. I've always been so...'

'Cautious?' Levander offered, thinking of his own family's perpetual warnings.

'Not cautious.' Millie frowned. 'More—driven, I guess. Since high school, art's been my passion. My trip to Australia took months to arrange. The only dream I've ever really had is painting. Unlike most parents, when they waved me off the possibility of their daughter coming home pregnant was the furthest thing from their minds.'

'When did you tell them?'

'About a month ago.' Millie let out a long, shaky breath, then opened her mouth to carry on, and found that she couldn't just yet. But Levander didn't push. Instead, in his most surprising move since he'd grabbed her into that first fierce embrace at the airport, he wrapped his hand around hers, held it gently for a moment or two. It helped—really helped. Drawing from his quiet support, she was ready to continue.

'When I got back from Australia, after a couple of

weeks I plucked up the courage and went to a clinic—you know, to get checked…'

'There was no need,' Levander said. 'It was a first for me too, without…'

She couldn't really tell with her glasses on, but Millie could have sworn he was blushing a touch—and she was too, just recalling the mortification she'd felt, sitting waiting for her unlucky number to be called.

'Well, I didn't know that at the time,' Millie said with a tight smile. 'But, yes, the only test I failed was the pregnancy one. I didn't know how to tell them at first, and even when I did I didn't tell them it was a…' She swallowed hard before saying it. 'A one-night stand. I sort of let them think—well, that we cared.'

'We do.' It was perhaps the single nicest thing he'd said to her. 'What else did you tell them?'

'I said that…' Blushing, cringing, she could hardly bring herself to say it.

'You'd better tell me.' He smiled over at her embarrassment. 'If I am going to meet them, perhaps I should know.'

'I said that your family owned a shop near Anton's gallery.'

'A shop?'

'A little shop.' Millie cringed again.

'So they think I am the local greengrocer's son?' He was joking, but seeing her anguished expression he realised *she* wasn't. 'You're not serious?'

'Well, not a greengrocer's. I said that they ran a clothes shop. Obviously they know the truth now.'

'But why would you not tell them in the first place? Surely it could only have made things easier...'

'Or scarier for them.'

He stilled beside her.

'This is their grandchild, Levander. Knowing who you are, how powerful you could be...well, I guess they'll be scared for the same reasons I am.'

'I don't want to fight you, Millie.'

'Then don't.' Regretting the warning note in her voice, she sought diversion. She didn't want to push things to another ugly head—here was their chance to find each other. 'Let's paddle.'

'Paddle?' Levander frowned. 'The boats are...'

'Paddle.' Millie laughed. 'With our feet.'

He had no idea what she was talking about, Millie realised, taking him by the hand towards the lapping foreshore—had no idea what it was to stand in the surf and just enjoy the heavy pull of salt water as it gushed around your ankles.

A playboy who didn't know how to play.

But he learnt quickly.

She'd braved Brighton in an English summer, so it was really nothing to throw off her inhibitions, take his hand and run screaming into the warm Pacific Ocean. Just one bemused frown from Levander, as she skidded a fistful of water in his direction, then he quickly caught on and skidded one back. They played in the water like carefree children, Levander spluttering with laughter as she dived underneath and caught his ankles. She held her breath as he had his revenge, ducking her under, and then his strong thighs caught around her and pulled her up to the surface. She gulped in air—until his mouth caught hers, kissing her so hard, so fiercely her head swam. Not from lack of oxygen but from the sheer intensity of his kiss.

'This we do well...'

'We do...' She hated that she was so weak, so lily-livered with him—hated how her body screamed for him. And yet somehow she revelled in it, revelled in the new dimension he had brought to her existence.

'And it is better than fighting...' He was kissing her neck, kissing it so deeply surely he was bruising her, and bruising her mind as well... His voice was a plea as he tried so hard just to talk to her. 'Millie, I can't do *that* without this...'

He carried her to the water's edge and laid her down. It had been pointless her wearing a bikini top, because it was now halfway around her neck. Then it was completely tossed aside, and Millie watched with a fleeting smile as the ocean claimed an hour of shopping.

She could feel the wet sand on her back as her body curved in—could feel the cool weightlessness of the water contrasting with his warm, heavy body as he lay on top of her. Hands that had once been tentative were brave now as she slid his bathers down, her nails dragging into his firm buttocks as the ocean claimed its second gift. She savoured the taste of the salt water on his skin as his shoulders enveloped her, one strong arm lifting her head above the water as his other hand wrestled with the flimsy straps of her bikini bottom.

His erection was stronger than the ocean as it pressed against her—his need, his want for her all-encompassing, as hers was for him.

The blissful stab as he entered her, swelling deep within, made her whole body arch into his. He rocked deep within her, defying the waves, each rush of water up her body a contrast as he pulled his gift back. Every time she attempted to catch her breath as the pounding waves receded he filled her further, refusing her even a second to regroup. Her calves locked behind him as Levander surged inside her, where he had lived in her restless, aching dreams every night since first they'd been together. With each deep thrust she welcomed him back, and as measured as the ocean an orgasm so intensely fierce she felt as if she was going under claimed her again.

When his first ever playtime was over, when they were too tired to be brittle, too happily exhausted to argue as blazing day faded into a long, long night he told her.

Some.

Drip-fed her his torture—about the lying-down rooms they'd been sent to, about the staff. Though most of them had cared, quite simply there hadn't been enough of anything to go around.

Not enough food, or clothes or nappies—the most basic necessities all lacking—and attention, affection, the most thinly stretched of them all.

Before he revealed anything though, he made it absolutely clear that he never wanted her sympathy or pity—but that if somehow, by knowing him, she could maybe understand him, maybe choose to stay, if that was what it took, then he would tell her.

'She was his cleaner.' Staring up at the sky as they lay together, wrapped in each other's arms, he told her, walked her slowly through his very private hell.

'When she fell pregnant...well, I am told my father said he would keep her as his mistress, that he would provide for her and the baby. But that was not enough for my mother. She wanted him to marry her, or at least be faithful... On both counts he refused. She was very proud, very headstrong....'

Millie smiled as he stated the obvious.

'What?'

'I like her already—you're clearly your mother's son.'

He frowned as if it had never entered his head—frowned and then smiled as he shrugged, as he accepted a little piece of his history. 'To her family's fury, she walked out on him.'

'Her family's fury?'

'Her family disowned her—and that was okay. For more than three years we were okay. Until...' He wasn't smiling now, took a moment to regroup, to continue. 'My father got married to Nina. She was pregnant with the twins, and my mother guessed that my father and Nina were planning to flee. He gave her a lot of money all of a sudden, and came round many nights in a row to play with me—but those are the sort of plans that can't be discussed. She had a cough then. I can remember that. But he didn't know how ill she was. All of a sudden my father wasn't there any more, and my mother was really ill. When she left me at the baby house to go to the hospital she said my father would come.'

'And they didn't trace him...'

He gave a wry laugh, but it wasn't mocking. 'They were not even married. She registered me with his surname, and in Russia you take you father's first name as your middle—Levander Ivanovich Kolovsky, which means Levander son of Ivan—but who was going to search? I was just one of many. Better than most, really.'

'How?'

'Because I had her for a little while... ' He closed his eyes and she didn't know if he was blocking it out or seeing it again. 'I had once seen normal—I knew how to behave, knew how to read, to write, because she had taught me. Without that I know I would have gone crazy.'

'Like the child you told me about—the one who screamed at bedtime?'

'Like him.' Levander nodded. 'But I am stronger because I had her. That is not me being sentimental—' he checked that she understood '—already I knew normal—we were poor, but we were happy.'

'You can really remember?'

'Very well.' He nodded again. 'I had a lot of time to look back. I remember her reading, I remember her singing, I remember I swore and she slapped me...' He actually laughed at the memory. 'Most of the children there don't even have that. They are abandoned there at birth—that is all they know. I did not scream or cry—I

believed my father was one day going to come and get
me, because that was the last thing she told me. I kept
to myself when I could, and learned to defend myself
when I couldn't—and I studied hard. I achieved the
Gold Medal at school, which goes to the best student.
I was accepted at Moscow University, and then my father found me.'

'He'd been looking?'

'Apparently he sent money every month—and let-
ters and cards, but I never saw them. I don't know if my
mother's family kept the money. I just don't know. Eventually he traced me. It caused a lot of problems when I
came to Australia. Iosef and Aleksi were furious with
my father. Furious that he had left me behind and that
they had never been told. They tried hard to get close
to me, but I just couldn't trust them. I was not easy to
live with. I was so angry with them—with the world.'

'And now?'

'Iosef left to study medicine as soon as he was old
enough. Aleksi is in London. We have never been close.
I never let them get close…' he finally admitted.

'What about Annika?'

'Annika…' He shook his head hopelessly. 'She just
wants everything to be fine.'

'Can it ever be?'

'I don't know. This is the first time I have ever spoken about it….' She thought about her own fears, her
own doubts, her own worries, and tried to fathom never
once voicing them.

'They are so ashamed of the past…but it is *my* past,

Millie. If they cannot accept that then they can never accept me. The finest tailor, the cars, the money—they only dress up the outside. That was my life, and they cannot face it. To this day my father and Nina live in fear that the secret will get out—that people will judge them...'

And it would be so easy to judge, Millie thought. So easy to loathe a man who could walk away from his own son.

'He says that he regrets—' His voice broke, just a tiny husk in that strong fluid voice, and it ripped through her. 'He regrets what I have suffered, and now he is trying to make it up to me.'

'Can he?'

'I don't know.'

She was crying as he answered, and trying so hard not to show it—scared to wipe the tears away in case he saw them. She could see now just how much Janey's words would have eaten at him—that his own child might have existed unknown on the other side of the world...

'All that time—all my life there—I wanted him to come and get me. I wanted him to see me and be proud— and in the end, yes, he did come and get me. I got my wish.'

But it was so very little, and so very late.

'Can you?' Millie rasped. 'Can you somehow forgive him?'

'That is something I need to decide.' Levander nodded at the insurmountable challenge. 'And given his health, I'd better make my decision soon.'

Levander's next question pierced the long silence

that followed. 'Would marriage be so bad? Do you see now how important it is to me?'

'It won't keep us together…' She swallowed hard, wondered how she could ask from him what she needed to hear. 'Levander, if you don't love me…a piece of paper isn't going to change anything.'

'It will change a lot for me.'

Which wasn't the answer she wanted. Even if he was trying to help, with each word he just hurt her more.

'I would look after you; I would never be unfaithful; I would always do the right thing by you. And if you still have doubts, then I tell you this—we don't have to love each other for this to work. We will love our child, and that will be enough.'

CHAPTER ELEVEN

'THE MALDIVES, PERHAPS...?' Katina suggested, handing Levander a thick brochure.

He gave it barely a glance, glancing down at his
watch and clearly itching to get back to work. 'Any
preference, Millie?'

'I don't know...' Millie mumbled, hating that they
were back. Her suntan was fading only marginally more
slowly than her hopes for the future she had been so
full of on the island—hopes that had convinced her to
say yes to the wedding.

Back in the real world—back where clocks ticked
and people demanded and schedules dictated—she
wasn't quite so sure they could make it. Wasn't quite
so sure that a baby, that sex, was going to be enough to
see them through.

'We'll have to go to London and see my family—
they'll want to meet you.'

'They will meet me at the wedding,' Levander answered easily. But, seeing her worried face, he gave a
little frown. 'There is no problem—I will pay for them
to come out, absolutely.'

'It's not the money,' Millie said, blushing as Katina coolly listened on. 'They won't be able to come to Australia even if they could afford it. Austin could never go on a plane—it would be too distressing for him. Mum and Dad have enough trouble getting him into a car—he hates anything like that.'

'Who's Austin?' Katina asked, pen poised.

'Millie's brother.'

'And he doesn't like to travel?'

God, she hated this—hated having to explain herself to strangers. Hated that they'd been back in Melbourne only a few days and they were already in their second meeting.

A meeting to arrange their wedding.

Somehow, the fact that he could never love her had made her decision easier.

No more pretending that in time love might grow. No more kidding herself that he wanted her for any other reason than the baby they had made.

And even if her heart said she was marrying for all the wrong reasons, on the flipside it told her she was marrying for the right ones.

She loved Levander—loved him enough to give him the security he craved for his child.

Loved their baby enough to give it one home.

'Would you prefer we marry in London?' Levander offered. Katina's lips pursed, but Millie shook her head, thinking of the pressure on her family, the nightmare of her mum attempting to socialise with the Kolovskys.

'I think here might be better.'

'Then we will marry here and go to London for the honeymoon,' Levander suggested. And even though it made perfect sense—even though he had offered her the choice—not for the first time she felt railroaded, as if the Kolovskys had got their way once again.

'I just don't see why it has to be so soon,' Millie attempted again.

'It is not so soon,' Levander said dismissively. 'In Russia, a marriage normally happens quickly—between one and three months after the engagement is announced. And given you are already five months pregnant…surely it is better we marry quickly? Get it over with…'

He made it sound like a trip to the dentist.

'The Kolovskys calendar is full for the next three months,' Katina explained, a little less patiently than she had the last ten times. 'And anyway, if we leave it much longer you're going to have rather a job getting into the dress.'

Another thing she hadn't thought about.

'Do you have any brochures? I don't know…' She gave a helpless shrug. 'So I can get an idea of what I want…'

'An idea of what you want?' Katina stared at her in bemusement.

'For my dress.'

'Millie—you're marrying Levander. Did you really think we'd be sending you down to the local bridal shop? Your dress is already taken care of. Nina herself is going to come and do the final fittings. Right.' Shuffling her notes, Katina stood up. 'Have a think about your honeymoon and let me know tomorrow…'

'Final fittings?' Millie turned on Levander the second they were alone. 'I wasn't wrong that night—I actually thought I was being ridiculous, but my dress *is* already chosen—already hanging there half made, waiting for a bride to step into it.'

'Of course.' Levander looked at her as if she were completely mad. 'There are probably fifty gowns there—and you will get the best one, naturally. Now, if that is all, then I should get back to work.'

Even though her mind was abuzz with wedding preparations, and her nights were filled with Levander, as the days slipped by more and more Millie realised her idea of a family and Levander's were poles apart.

The tenderness they had found on the island seemed to have evaporated as soon as they'd touched down on the mainland. The only trace of it to be found was in the nights, when he reached for her, but it only disintegrated again every morning.

And for Millie the disquiet grew.

The uneasy homesickness that washed in at times positively overwhelmed her each and every time she rang her family to update them on the rapidly approaching wedding day. Hearing her mother's genuine wonder and delight as she asked about the baby's progress was such a contrast to Nina's coldness that it was almost more than Millie could bear.

* * *

'I'm having the teeniest panic attack.' On the eve of her wedding, Anton was in his element when Millie dropped by, humming the 'Wedding March' as Millie paced on. 'And I want you to be completely honest with me. Would it be a terrible faux pas to wear Kolovsky to a Kolovsky wedding?'

She had to laugh. 'You're asking *me* for fashion advice?'

'I know.' He clapped his hands to his cheeks. 'Oooh, thank you, thank you, thank you, for asking me to give you away—it's going to be the happiest day of my life.'

At least it would be for one of them, Millie thought, bursting into tears for the forty-second time that day.

'It's nerves,' Anton assured her.

'It is,' Millie sniffed. She badly wanted to talk, to tell someone her tumble of thoughts, but after Janey it was just too big, too scary to indulge in something as simple as a much-needed talk between friends. But as she went to grab her bag, as she thought of going back to the hotel to have Nina sticking pins in her for the final check that her dress was perfect, Millie baulked. 'I don't know if I can do this, Anton.'

'It's definitely nerves, honey,' Anton insisted, pulling out a vast hanky and trying to make her smile as she wiped her eyes. 'You know you're the most hated woman in Australia at the moment!'

His weak attempt at humour didn't work.

'I want my mum!'

'Oh, you poor baby…'

He led her to the back of the gallery, where he made her a big mug of hot chocolate with marshmallows. It was the kindest thing anyone had done for her since she'd landed there—the kindest thing anyone had done for her without wanting something in return.

'I know it must kill you not to have your family here, but you do have friends. I was at the airport when you arrived back, you know...' He smiled at her shocked expression. 'You know I never sleep—I popped out to get the paper and there was that filth sprawled all over it. I figured you could use some moral support—not that I even got close... Talk to me, Millie.'

'I can't.'

'I know after Janey you're afraid to trust anyone,' he said gently, and as she opened her mouth to argue he spoke over her. 'But I *am* on your side. I'll come over tonight the second I lock up, and I won't leave your side till the wedding...' He gave a tiny wince. 'I've just got to pop to the hairdresser's at midday.'

'I'm sure there'll be one in my room you can use,' Millie said with a wry smile, but Anton shook his head.

'Luigi would never forgive me. I'm going to hold your hand every step of the way. Once the wedding's over, once everything's calmed down, things will be so much easier...'

'I hope so.'

'I guess the question is—do you love him?' He didn't follow it up with anything silly—just asked her the one thing in all this she could answer honestly.

'Of course.'

'Well, that's all right, then.'

'How is your mother?' Levander asked, sitting on the bedroom chair and smothering a yawn.

'Teary,' Millie admitted, standing in her dress as Nina and Sophia, the dressmaker, tugged none too gently. She hated how clinical it all was—hated that a silly little thing like him seeing her in her dress before the big day mattered to her so. 'Wishing she could be here.'

'You'll see her very soon.'

'I know.' Millie stared fixedly ahead wishing it was two o'clock tomorrow and it was all over with.

'I have to go soon…' Levander glanced at his watch

'Fine.'

'Iosef's plane is due in—I'd like to be there to meet him. We are going out for dinner with my father.'

'Of course.'

'Perfect.' Nina stood back and admired her top dressmaker's handiwork—as well she might. A sheath of thick ivory Kolovsky silk had been sculpted to Millie's body, every stitch, every nip, somehow turning her into the beautiful bride she had to be. 'Sophia will be over tomorrow to help with any last-minute alterations. Now, no eating from now till after the wedding.' Nina frowned, running a very unwelcome hand over Millie's slight bump. 'I can get you some of the special herbal tea the models use—to get a bit of fluid off.'

Millie didn't even deign to respond—just peeled off the dress and stood silent as Nina flounced out of the bedroom, carrying the dress as if it were some precious child.

'Ignore her,' Levander said.

'Oh, I assure you I try.'

'I know it is hard—to marry without your family. But it is not as if...' He didn't finish, so Millie did it for him.

'It's not as if it's a real wedding.'

'Of course it is real,' Levander countered, but Millie shook her head.

'You know, this should be like a dream come true—a fabulous wedding, A-list guests, a designer dress, a baby on the way, the man—' She stopped herself. How she wanted to tell him how she felt—that she loved him so much it hurt. Even if she understood that they were marrying for the sake of the child they had created it was killing her inside to know that was the only reason. That if it wasn't for their baby Levander Kolovsky would never have considered her as his bride. 'I guess it's true—we should be more careful what we wish for.'

'I don't understand.'

'It's a saying—be careful what you wish for, it might come true.'

As she delivered the saying the confusion that had been etched on his face disappeared. All expression did. Always pale, his skin was now as white as marble; even those beautiful lips were dusky in his grey features.

'That is how you feel?'

His voice seemed to be coming from far away, and his question confused her. Because she did know how she felt. Millie knew as she stood there before him that she loved him, and that was what was killing her. Being close to him and knowing she couldn't really have him—that this distant, remote, yet at times incredibly emotive man, couldn't give her the piece of him that she needed.

'You feel trapped?' Levander pushed.

And she nodded—because trapped *was* how she felt. Not by the situation, but by her feelings. She realised then that, as impressive as Levander's reasons were for a hasty marriage, if she didn't love him, didn't want him with every fibre of her being, she'd have walked away—would have made it on her own.

Would have managed just fine.

'Come!' Waltzing back into the bedroom and not even knocking, Nina called to Levander. 'We need to get to the airport, and Millie should get a good night's sleep.' Over her shoulder, unwittingly for once, Nina hurled another knife. 'Enjoy your last night of freedom!'

CHAPTER TWELVE

ANTON, FOR ALL that he wasn't family, made a very good mother of the bride—spoiling her rotten, policing everyone. And there were plenty to police. The hairdresser, the manicurist, the dressmaker, the make-up artists…

Artists!

Millie needed two, apparently. One for her face and the other to concentrate solely on her décolletage—to even out her fading tan and ensure her cleavage was spectacularly arranged.

Anton even made a fuss of Annika, Millie's very stunning bridesmaid and half-sister-in-law to be—who, given Millie was about to share her surname, actually opened up a touch as the room buzzed with the frenzy of getting her ready.

Finally, when Anton had shooed everyone out and it was just the three of them, he gave Millie the biggest of smiles, then promptly burst into tears. 'You look ravishing.'

'Thank you.'

'Now, I'm going to race over to Luigi's and get just

a smidgen of product put through my hair—and you, honey…'

'I know.' Millie shivered at the prospect of ringing her parents. 'Maybe I should ring them after the wedding…'

'No.' Anton was insistent. 'They'll want to wish you luck. You know you have to do this—by the time you're done I'll be back. Look after her, Annika,' Anton called, flying out of the door.

'Maybe it would be better to wait?' Annika gave a sympathetic smile and said absolutely the wrong thing. 'You might ruin your make-up.'

She didn't want this.

Tears were filling her exquisitely made-up eyes and she blinked them back, staring at her reflection and trying, for the thousandth time, to tell herself that everything was okay.

She was marrying the man she loved.

Marrying the father of her child.

Standing in her stunning wedding dress, with a packed church waiting to share in this most special moment.

So why did it feel as if she were walking to the gallows?

It was just homesickness, Millie told herself. If only her family could be here… But that didn't fit—because, as much as she missed them, it wasn't actually her family she needed today…

It was Levander…

Or rather his love.

Fiddling with the huge diamond on her ring finger, she recalled their lovemaking, tried to hone in on the magic they shared. But no matter how much she tried, how much she wanted to convince herself, at the end of the day it was the baby they were marrying for…

But was it enough?

'Your family must be very proud,' Annika attempted as Millie tried to hold down the single glass of water she'd managed that morning. 'Believe it or not, my father is proud too.'

'Believe it or not?' Millie frowned. 'Why wouldn't he be proud of Levander?'

'He is proud of Levander. I was talking about…well you two…' Annika was still going on, frowning at Millie's pale reflection and without invitation adding another dash of blusher. 'Even though you're not perhaps who we'd have first chosen it has all worked out well—Papa has got his wish and more.'

'His wish?'

'Last night it was made official,' she prattled on, less reserved without her mother around. 'My father always said that the Kolovsky empire would go to the first of his children who gave him a grandchild. And we all knew that he wanted that person to be Levander—the son he would give anything to make happy. Levander has been a driving force in the company and Papa is desperate for him to stay on. That night when you two met, when I was pleading with Levander to grant father his wish, he was so adamant the answer was no….'

She smiled down to Millie's stomach. 'Who knows how Levander's mind works?'

Not she. Millie's hands went to her stomach, held the tiny life that might not have been such an accident after all, and wondered if Levander, in his own dark way, had somehow decided to claim what he thought he deserved.

'Maybe he will get to see his grandchild too...' Annika said, her eyes following Millie's hands. 'You should have a scan.'

'I've had one.'

'Find out this time...' Annika stood back to admire her handiwork, to check that the bride they all so desperately wanted was passable enough—was good enough to take the family name. Millie felt like slapping her. 'Let's just hope we can tell Papa he is getting a grandson...'

Annika's mobile rang she turned her back. 'Hold on a moment... Levander—what does he want?'

To make his father happy.

The biggest, most difficult, most terrifying decision of her life was suddenly made incredibly simple.

She could almost have accepted him marrying her for the baby—marrying her out of duty—but the thought that he had engineered the situation in order to please his father, or worse to inherit the Kolovsky empire, filled her with horror.

Maybe she was an old-fashioned girl after all, Millie decided. Because the only thing she could marry for was love.

'I'll just be a moment...' Annika gave Millie a wor-

ried smile. "Everything is okay—you just keep on getting ready.'

As Annika fled to the bedroom Millie could hear her
shouting, hear yet another Kolovsky argument breaking
out, but she didn't even notice. The second the bedroom
door closed, Millie pulled off her headdress, yanked the
beastly dress down and pulled on her jeans, slipping on
some runners and grabbing her purse.

As Levander had said, it wasn't a prison... All she
had to do was open the doors and press the lift button,
then walk calmly out through the hotel foyer. Every
waiting camera was on the lookout for a blushing bride
in white, not a pale woman in jeans.

Walking along the tree-lined street, she didn't look
back—not once. She just willed herself to be calm,
to keep on walking, until she hit the main road—and
boarded a tram that clattered past, not knowing where
it was taking her and not really caring.

'End of the line, love.'

She hadn't even noticed the tram had come to a stop,
her mind lost in a whir of thoughts—trying and failing
to picture Levander's face when he found out his bride
wasn't coming, Anton's hysterics when he got back to
the hotel to find her gone, the shock of the guests, the
blitz of headlines, her parents' reaction...

Maybe she *should* have just gone through with it,
Millie begged of herself as she stepped off the tram
and stood shivering on the street. The bright winter sun
that had held so much promise this morning was now

shrouded in grey, and a bitter wind was skimming the Tasman and blowing across the bay.

St Kilda.

Where their rollercoaster ride had started—the last stop on their first date, on that magical tour of Melbourne. But somehow the world was a greyer, bleaker place without Levander beside her.

As she headed into the café, where they had sat and talked for hours, it was as if a curtain had lifted and the scenery had been changed. Happy families were at every table: children plunging long spoons into deep glasses of ice-cream, young, beautiful couples wading through the papers and idly watching the world go by, unaware of the seamier clientele that would frequent it later.

Sitting at a corner booth, Millie ordered coffee, clasped her hands around the vast mug and wondered if she'd ever be warm again—wondered how she could go back and face them all.

And she'd have to.

Her passport, her clothes…

Oh, God, what had she done? Maybe she should have just gone through with it. Certainly she should have spoken to Levander. But how—*how* could she…?

How could she tell him that the autonomous, principled man she'd fallen in love with didn't match up to a man who would make a baby to appease his father—however high the stakes?

'I am sorry.' His rich, deep voice broke into her racing thoughts, and her eyes darted up to where he stood over her. 'May I sit?'

She couldn't speak, so instead she nodded, bracing herself for a vitriolic outburst Levander style. She was bemused at the hesitancy in him, stunned when he took her mug of coffee from her and held her hands, before taking a deep breath and finally talking.

'I am sorry—sorry to shame you. But it is not your shame, it is mine—remember that. I will tell everyone.'

'Sorry?' Millie frowned. His apology was completely unexpected, and she was unable to look at him—just stared at his fingers entwined around hers, utterly perplexed by what he was saying and flailing for a response. 'It isn't about shame, Levander. It's… I just couldn't do it. Couldn't marry you knowing—'

'Pardon?' He interrupted her stumbling explanation—and for the first time she managed to look at him, saw the confusion in his eyes that mirrored her own.

'I didn't mean to run away—I wasn't planning it. I just…'

'You jilted me?' She winced at the phrase, but the question in his voice made no sense—and what made even less sense was the tiny flicker of a smile playing on the edge of his lips. '*You* jilted *me?*'

'Why do you think I'm here?' She glanced to the large clock on the wall, and then back to him. 'Why, when we should be walking out of the church arm in arm around now, am I sitting in a café in St Kilda, bawling my eyes out?'

'Because *I* jilted *you*.' His shocking words halted her.

'Because half an hour before you were due to leave for the church I rang Annika and told her I couldn't do it to you—couldn't force you to be my wife…'

'You jilted me?' It was so appalling, so embarrassing, she could barely get her head around it. 'I was left at the altar…?'

'Ah…' Levander shook his head. 'Apparently you were never going to make it to the altar…'

And she realised then why he'd given that strange smile when she'd made her stumbling explanation. The humiliation she'd thought she'd inflicted on him, the embarrassment, the shame she'd thought she'd wreaked on another human being, eradicated now. Millie actually managed a shocked giggle as she remembered Annika shouting on the phone as she'd sped out of the room.

'Can I ask why?' Her smile faded as he confronted her, the real issues bobbing back up to the dark surface. 'Why you chose not to marry me—why you think you and our child would be better off without me?'

'I don't,' Millie sobbed. 'I won't… It's just… Annika told me about your father—that she had begged you to have a child the night we met.'

'My whole family has begged me to procreate for years now.' Levander shrugged. 'Why does that shock you? You heard us talking that night…'

'I didn't hear *that*,' Millie gasped.

'Millie, I am loath to give him even a few more years' work from me—do you really think for one minute I would sign away my life for him?'

'I don't know,' Millie admitted. She was crying

now—crying in a way she only had since she'd met him. From the day she'd left his arms and headed back to England, from when the pregnancy test had proved positive, since he'd invaded her world and stripped her bare, inflamed her raw emotions till everything was in Technicolor—every thought, every feeling, more intense somehow. 'I don't know if I was just looking for an excuse not to marry you...'

'Would you believe that I am not trying to appease my father if I tell you that last night I spoke with him? We went out, and he offered me—'

'I know about that.' Millie shivered. 'I know that the first child to produce a Kolovsky heir gets the prize...'

'I declined. It is a ridiculous idea. How could I solely inherit when I have two brothers and a sister?' He took in her shocked reaction. 'I told him that I would continue to work for him—but only if I can do it from London.'

'London?' Millie blinked at him. 'You were prepared to move to London?'

'I still am.' He stated it as if it was obvious. 'I was hoping when I said it that we would be doing it together, as a proper family, but now I accept that is not possible. However, I still want to be the best father I can be—and I cannot do that from Australia. Even if we are not together, I know you will treat me fairly.' He looked at her stunned face and explained a touch further. 'I trust you, Millie.'

And for someone with his past, Millie realised that trust was almost better than love. Not that it helped right now—not that it helped when the man of your dreams was telling you the reason that he couldn't actually bring himself to marry you. But later it would. Millie knew that later, when she replayed this conversation, somehow the fact that after all he'd been through he actually trusted her might be just enough sustain her in the end.

'I woke up this morning and I realised I trust you—that marriage is not needed for the sake of our child. I know that you will put our baby's interests first—that I do not have to force myself into the picture to be there.'

'Because you *are* there.' Millie trembled. 'Whether we're married or not, friends or not, you will always be this child's father. Always.'

'I know that now. I know you would never keep me from my child. Not like—' He stopped himself then, and even though she was drowning in her own grief, choking on her own feelings, something in his voice reached her.

Her forehead creased into a frown. 'Levander—things were different then. It wasn't like now, when you can pop on a plane—they thought you were safe, they thought…' Her voice petered out as she looked beyond his effortless beauty, beyond those brooding eyes, and right into his very soul. She saw not pain, not bitterness or regret, but raw, unbridled agony.

The dawning suspicion, when it came to her, was so utterly devastating that her first reaction was to recoil, to close her eyes and block out what she could see written in his eyes.

'He knew, didn't he?'

'No.' Levander closed his eyes, pulled back his hand. But Millie wasn't about to let go, grabbing it back and holding tightly. 'He didn't know anything.'

'She did, though…' Millie whispered. 'Nina knew, didn't she?'

'Don't go there—it is not worth the pain.'

'Whose pain?' Millie asked angrily, protectively. 'What about *your* pain?'

'If my family were to know—if my father ever found out what she did… Annika, Iosef…' He dragged in a breath. 'They cannot know—it would finish him.'

'It won't finish me.' Somehow her voice was firm. 'You said you trust me.'

'I do.'

'So tell me.'

He swallowed so hard it was if he was choking. 'What I told you before—all of it is true except…' His eyes found hers then, his hands held hers, gripping them tightly as he told her the truth—the real truth this time. Not the Kolovsky version, but the truth of a little boy who had seen far, far too much. 'The day before I went to the baby house we went to my father's—Nina answered; she was pregnant. I remember that, and I remember my father wasn't home. My mother told Nina how sick she was. I remember because it was the first time I realised that my mother was actually dying—she was coughing and crying, and she told Nina her family could not afford to have me when she was gone…' He faltered for a moment, so Millie held his hand tighter.

She preferred the old version. Life had somehow been easier when she'd thought him bitter and jealous. The appalling truth was more than anyone should have to bear.

'Nina didn't care. I just remember them arguing. My mother was crying so hard she could barely breathe, and then Nina shooed us away as if we were gypsies come begging.'

Some agonies were just too big for tears. Life was so unbearable at times that to break down and merely cry would almost be an insult. Millie wanted to howl— wanted to scream at a world that had been so cruel. Rage was churning in her—a rage so strong it almost propelled her from her seat, to find Nina, to tell Ivan… But somehow she held it in check—she knew it couldn't possibly help him.

'Does *she* know…' She tried to keep the hatred from her voice. 'Does she know you can remember?'

'The day I found out you were pregnant I told Nina. Now she has to live with her fear. We all have to live with our mistakes. Last night you said you should be careful what you wish for…' A mirthless smile ghosted his lips, and his English was less than perfect as he struggled to tell her more about his past. 'When my mother took me to *dom rebyonka,* the baby house, she told me it would not be for long—that I was to be good and wait, and that my father would come and get me. I don't know if she went back to speak with him again. I don't really want to know. But every night I looked out of the window and I wished—I wished for him, for a family, and later as I got older I wished too for money, and I wished for beautiful women. I got every last wish. Compared to those poor bastards still there, I have nothing to complain about.'

'Oh, but you do.'

She got it then—as much as anyone who hadn't lived his life possibly could. Since she'd found out she was pregnant she'd wondered if she was up to being a mother—the mother she wanted to be—if she could provide for her child the happy, secure childhood her own parents had given her. But for Levander there were no happy memories, no foundations on which to build. Just a much too late glimpse of family was all he had known. A family fractured by his very presence. His arrival had split the family, caused his half-brothers' anger and blame, his father's guilt, his stepmother's fear.

'I wanted us to be married. I thought that maybe then I would have more rights—I knew that if the courts had to choose between us, if my past came out...'

'There'll be no court,' Millie whispered. 'I told you there was never going to be court—and anyway, Levander, no court would hold this against you. None of this is your fault.'

'I know that now.' Levander nodded, and with tears swimming in her eyes she tried to look at him as she attempted to say the bravest words of her life—to tell the man who had just jilted her, the man who had wanted marriage for all the wrong reasons, that no matter how others in his life had treated him, she loved him—loved him for everything he was.

'That night was the most rash, reckless thing I've ever done—but it wasn't an accident. I didn't fall into bed with you that night because of your looks or your money or...' Staring skywards for clarity was her worst mistake. Tears tumbled down her cheeks as she rewound a touch—aimed for total honesty. 'Okay, maybe your looks *did* play a part—but they weren't enough to hold me. It was *you,* Levander—you were the first person I'd trusted, the first person I gave myself to. And whatever the outcome—that night wasn't an accident. As dazzled as they were, my eyes were open. Did it never enter your head that all this time I've loved you?'

But how could it have? Millie realised as he frowned over at her. How could a man like Levander, who had never known it, believe in something as simple and as complicated as love?

'The *only* reason I couldn't go through with our marriage in the end was because I knew you'd never love me.'

'You *love* me?' He practically barked the question. 'Through-all-of-this-you-say-that-you-have-loved-me?'

'I'm afraid so.'

'How?' His question actually eked out a half-laugh. 'How could you love me when I was so horrible to you?'

'I just did...' Millie sobbed. 'I just do.'

'Tell me what this love is,' Levander asked. 'Tell me what love feels like.'

'Awful.' A new batch of tears was coming, and she covered her face with her hands, wishing he wouldn't torture her so. Surely knowing was enough?

'But it is good at times?'

'Lots of times.'

'So when you love someone, you think about them all the time?'

'All the time.' Millie nodded glumly.

'Like you think you are going crazy?' Levander checked.

'Completely crazy.'

'Would love make you worry that you are too bitter, too cynical? That somehow you might taint the other...?'

Peeking at his face from behind her fingers, Millie felt the world stop as Levander continued.

'And because of this love, do you want only what's best for the other person?'

'Always,' Millie breathed, and he took her hands down from her face and held them as he spoke on softly.

'This love would make you spend far too much on a picture because you *have* to have it—you have to have something...'

'Tangible?' Millie offered, only he didn't understand. 'Something you can feel and see and touch to know that it is real.'

'Tangible.' Levander nodded, as if he really liked the word. 'You buy an expensive picture because it is tangible.'

'Sort of.' She gulped, crying and laughing and loving him for faltering over a single world.

'So if you love someone—even though you want to spend every minute with them, even though all you want to do is be with them—still, if that is where you think they do not want to be, you would let them go? When you see her standing beautiful in her wedding dress, but her eyes are resigned...'

She wasn't laughing now. This was an insight he was giving her—insight into how lonely, how unsure of his own worth he was, of the terrible effects of growing up in a world utterly devoid of love.

Levander hadn't been able to tell her he loved her because he didn't even know what it was.

'Are you telling me you love me, Levander?' Millie whispered.

'I'm just checking with myself first,' he said.

From anyone else the pause that followed would have been an insult, but from Levander it was anything but—just a delicious, wondrous wait as he processed his thoughts, as he assimilated all the feelings he'd never till now experienced.

'I-love-you.' He said it like that, each word a firm statement, and even if they were the three little words she'd wanted so badly to hear, when he said them— when he looked at her and actually said them—nothing could have prepared her for the impact of him saying them.

If she lived past a hundred, Millie swore there and then that every time he graced her with those words she would relive this moment. Even though he hadn't even known what it meant to receive love, somehow he had found the courage to love her.

'I love you,' he said again, and hearing the honesty,

the wonder in his voice as he joined up the puzzle, knowing how alien it was to him, made the words all the more precious to her.

'Why are we sitting here, then?' Millie smiled through her tears. 'Why don't we go…?' She'd been about to say home, but Levander's hotel room had never been that, to either of them. But as her voice trailed off, Levander filled in for her.

'There's a church decorated and waiting, the priest is booked, and we've got a licence…'

'Everyone will have gone.'

'Perfect!'

'But I'm in jeans….' Millie gave a shocked laugh

'Even better.' Leaning over, he kissed her—one tiny kiss, but it was so laced with love, so utterly chaste and tender, it confirmed utterly what he'd just told her.

He loved her—*that* was enough—for anything.

'I will ring the church…' As Levander turned on his phone he rolled his eyes. 'Fifty missed calls—can you imagine Nina's face?' He winced as it rang loudly. 'It's Iosef. I won't take it. He will understand…'

'We need witnesses,' Millie said gently, as the ringing died away. 'Two, I believe. Why don't you ask your brothers?'

'My *half*…' Levander started but didn't finish. Love was flooding in now, and shining its light on so many dark places.

'Doesn't one have to be a female?' Mille asked, but Levander waved her away.

'Between the two of them—I'm sure they can rustle one up.'

And she watched, smiling, as he took the call—watched as he laughed with his brother as they shared their first secret, arranged for him and Aleksi to slip away from the drama unfolding back at the Kolovsky house and pick them up to take them to the church.

'What did he say?'

'That he would be proud to be there—and I hope you don't mind, but we have another guest...' As her face literally paled, Levander just laughed. 'Anton—he's distraught. They are on their way.' Standing up, he took her hand, led her out onto the street and into her new life. 'Now—may I suggest that we go and get married.'

EPILOGUE

THE ONLY ADVANTAGE to Levander's past was that he loved shopping.

And there was plenty to be done.

A vast, sprawling home on the outskirts of London had to be furnished and decorated and filled with memories and babies and love.

'I can see why she did it.'

They were lying on the grass—Sashar kicking on the rug between them. She watched the sky darken, feeling his hand on her soft stomach. They hadn't even made it indoors yet since Levander had come home from work. Still in his suit, he lay beside her, chatting, yawning, lazy and utterly relaxed, enjoying the evening with their baby.

Sashar Levander Kolovsky.

She'd loved looking through Russian names, and had been completely unable to make a decision. But a couple of days before he was born Millie had stumbled on the name Sashar.

'It means reward, I think,' Levander had told her. 'Or God remembers…'

Both meanings had seemed to fit, and now he was here, lying beside them—the absolute image of his father.

And his father's father.

Sometimes Millie felt a stab of guilt—guilt that they were on the other side of the world when his father was so sick, that maybe if they'd stayed somehow bridges could have been built.

But somehow by leaving they had been. Sashar had brought them the most surprising gift of all—forgiveness, where Millie had thought there could never be.

'I can see Nina felt she had no choice...'

Sometimes he spoke about it. Not often, but sometimes—just little snatches of stolen childhood—and she never cried on the outside. Just wept on the inside for all he'd seen and all that he'd never had.

'She had to think of her unborn children. If she had told my father—if he had insisted they take me to Australia too—well, they may never have got there.' He stared down at Sashar. 'I think I understand now.'

'And your father?' Millie gulped, wishing she could understand too—could be as big as Levander and somehow find it in her to forgive.

'He told me when I turned down his offer that I was like my mother—too strong willed and stubborn for my own good. But he was smiling when he said it. I guess he banked on how tough she was—convinced himself we would be okay. He couldn't have known that I was in an orphanage, waiting for him to come. You know, a family would come sometimes—dressed in beautiful clothes, smelling of rich perfume. They would bring chocolate, or gifts. I never got one—too old, too angry looking, too much trouble…'

'They didn't give you a gift?'

'The gift was for the child they would take—they were there to choose the child that would join their family. I wished that someone would choose me. Still, I got my wish in the end—you came back for me.'

He bent over and kissed her, and this time she did cry. Because, yes, he'd got his wish in the end, but it had been way, way too long in the coming. She cried not just for Levander but for all those little children who were too angry, too scared and too much trouble to be loved.

'We could go back…'

'Perhaps.' Levander nodded. 'Soon, I guess. For a holiday. I would like my father to see his grandson.'

'I'm not talking about Australia.' Millie smiled softly, and she felt his body still—so still even his heart seemed to stop for a beat or two.

'I never want to go back. Never again will I set foot in that place. No.' He shook his head, but she could feel his indecision—knew that this wasn't the first time he had considered it.

It wasn't the first time Millie had considered it either.

Seeing him hold his son—cherishing the little life they had created—she had caught the pensive look that dimmed his features now and then, seen the tightening of his jaw as he recalled all he had been through, and had known he was living it again, thinking about all the little ones who weren't as lucky or as loved as Sashar.

'Fine...' Millie nodded, but didn't quite leave it there. 'If you ever change your mind...if you ever want to talk about it—'

'It isn't like choosing a pet,' Levander insisted.

'It wouldn't be.'

'You don't understand, Millie—the damage that is done. These children are not cute, not easy to love, to live with—'

'I know that, Levander,' Millie broke in. 'My own brother isn't particularly cute or easy to live with. But he is very easy to love and, like my parents, I'd never turn my back on him.'

'No, you never would, would you?' It was a statement, not a question, and his voice faded. He stared down at her, seeing the infinite understanding in her eyes, and knew then that she didn't want easy, that she understood completely what she was saying—knew from her own brother that miracles didn't always happen, was fully aware of all she was prepared to take on.

Knew that he had her for ever.

'Could we do it?'

'One day,' Millie answered softly. 'When we're ready—whenever you're ready...'

And if love could travel, then it surely was travelling now—somewhere a piece of their hearts was already sold to the angriest, least loveable one. A child's wish, sent out to the universe, was in the process of being answered...

* * * * *

COMING NEXT MONTH from Harlequin Presents®
AVAILABLE MARCH 19, 2013

#3129 MASTER OF HER VIRTUE
Miranda Lee

Shy, cautious Violet has had enough of living life in the shadows. She resolves to experience all that life has to offer, starting with internationally renowned film director Leo Wolfe. But is Violet ready for where he wants to take her?

#3130 A TASTE OF THE FORBIDDEN
Buenos Aires Nights
Carole Mortimer

Argentinian tycoon Cesar Navarro has his sexy little chef, Grace Blake, right where he wants her—in his penthouse, at his command! She should be off-limits, but Grace has tantalized his jaded palette, and Cesar finds himself ordering something new from the menu!

#3131 THE MERCILESS TRAVIS WILDE
The Wilde Brothers
Sandra Marton

Travis Wilde would never turn down a willing woman in a king-size bed! Normally innocence like Jennie Cooper's would have the same effect as a cold shower, yet her determination and mouth-watering curves have him burning up all over!

#3132 A GAME WITH ONE WINNER
Scandal in the Spotlight
Lynn Raye Harris

Paparazzi darling Caroline Sullivan hides a secret behind her dazzling smile. Her ex-flame, Russian businessman Roman Kazarov, is back on the scene—is he seeking revenge for her humiliating rejection or wanting to take possession of her troubled business?

HPCNM0313RA

#3133 HEIR TO A DESERT LEGACY
Secret Heirs of Powerful Men
Maisey Yates

When recently and reluctantly crowned Sheikh Sayid discovers his country's true heir, he'll do anything to protect him—even marry the child's aunt. It may appease his kingdom, but will it release the blistering chemistry between them...?

#3134 THE COST OF HER INNOCENCE
Jacqueline Baird

Newly free Beth Lazenby has closed the door on her past, until she encounters lawyer Dante Cannavaro who is still convinced of her guilt. But when anger boils over into passion, will the consequences forever bind her to her enemy?

#3135 COUNT VALIERI'S PRISONER
Sara Craven

Kidnapped and held for ransom... His price? Her innocence! Things like this just don't happen to Maddie Lang, but held under lock and key, the only deal Count Valieri will strike is one with an *unconventional* method of payment!

#3136 THE SINFUL ART OF REVENGE
Maya Blake

Reiko has two things art dealer Damion Fortier wants; a priceless Fortier heirloom and her seriously off-limits body! And she has no intention of giving him access to either. So Damion turns up lethal charm to ensure he gets *exactly* he wants....

You can find more information on upcoming Harlequin® titles, free excerpts and more at www.Harlequin.com.

HPCNM0313RB

REQUEST YOUR FREE BOOKS!

2 FREE NOVELS PLUS
2 FREE GIFTS!

YES! Please send me 2 FREE Harlequin Presents® novels and my 2 FREE gifts (gifts are worth about $10). After receiving them, if I don't wish to receive any more books, I can return the shipping statement marked "cancel." If I don't cancel, I will receive 6 brand-new novels every month and be billed just $4.30 per book in the U.S. or $4.99 per book in Canada. That's a saving of at least 14% off the cover price! It's quite a bargain! Shipping and handling is just 50¢ per book in the U.S. and 75¢ per book in Canada.* I understand that accepting the 2 free books and gifts places me under no obligation to buy anything. I can always return a shipment and cancel at any time. Even if I never buy another book, the two free books and gifts are mine to keep forever.

106/306 HDN FVRK

Name		
	(PLEASE PRINT)	

Address		Apt. #

City	State/Prov.	Zip/Postal Code

Signature (if under 18, a parent or guardian must sign)

Mail to the **Harlequin® Reader Service:**
IN U.S.A.: P.O. Box 1867, Buffalo, NY 14240-1867
IN CANADA: P.O. Box 609, Fort Erie, Ontario L2A 5X3

**Are you a current subscriber to Harlequin Presents books
and want to receive the larger-print edition?
Call 1-800-873-8635 or visit www.ReaderService.com.**

* Terms and prices subject to change without notice. Prices do not include applicable taxes. Sales tax applicable in N.Y. Canadian residents will be charged applicable taxes. Offer not valid in Quebec. This offer is limited to one order per household. Not valid for current subscribers to Harlequin Presents books. All orders subject to credit approval. Credit or debit balances in a customer's account(s) may be offset by any other outstanding balance owed by or to the customer. Please allow 4 to 6 weeks for delivery. Offer available while quantities last.

Your Privacy—The Harlequin® Reader Service is committed to protecting your privacy. Our Privacy Policy is available online at www.ReaderService.com or upon request from the Harlequin Reader Service.

We make a portion of our mailing list available to reputable third parties that offer products we believe may interest you. If you prefer that we not exchange your name with third parties, or if you wish to clarify or modify your communication preferences, please visit us at www.ReaderService.com/consumerchoice or write to us at Harlequin Reader Service Preference Service, P.O. Box 9062, Buffalo, NY 14269. Include your complete name and address.

HPI3

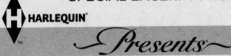
* * *

CHLOE stood up quickly, her chair tilting and knocking into the chair next to it, the sound loud in the cavernous room. "Sorry, sorry." She tried to straighten them, her cheeks burning, her heart pounding. "I have to go."

Sayid was faster than she was, his movements smoother. He crossed to her side of the table and caught her arm, drawing her to him, his expression dark. "Why are you running from me?" he asked, dipping his face lower, his expression fierce. "It's because you know, isn't it? You feel it?"

"Feel what?" she asked.

"This...need between us. How everything in me is demanding that I reach out and pull you hard against me. And how everything in you is begging me to."

"I don't know what you're talking about," she said.

"I think you do." He lowered his hand and traced her collarbone with his fingertip, sliding it slowly up the side of her neck, along her jawbone.

She shook her head, pulling away from him, from his touch. "No," she lied, "I don't."

She didn't understand what was happening with her body, why it was betraying her like this. She'd never felt this kind of wild, overpowering attraction for anyone in her life. But if she was going to, it would have been for a nice scientist who had a large collection of dry-erase pens and looked good in a lab coat.

It would not be for this rough, uncivilized man who believed he could move people around at his whim. This man who sought to control everything and everyone around him.

Unfortunately, her body hadn't asked her opinion on who she should find attractive. Because that was most definitely what this was. Scientific, irrefutable evidence of arousal.

* * *

Will Chloe give in to temptation? And will she ever be able to tame the wild warrior?

Find out in HEIR TO A DESERT LEGACY, available March 19, 2013.